THE OPPOSITE OF DROWNING

ERIN MCRAE AND RACHELINE MALTESE

AVIAN30
NEW YORK, NEW YORK
2019

Avian30
New York, New York
The Opposite of Drowning by Erin McRae and Racheline Maltese
Copyright 2019
ISBN: 978-1-946192-15-8

www.Avian30.com

First Avian30 Printing: August 2019
Printed in the USA

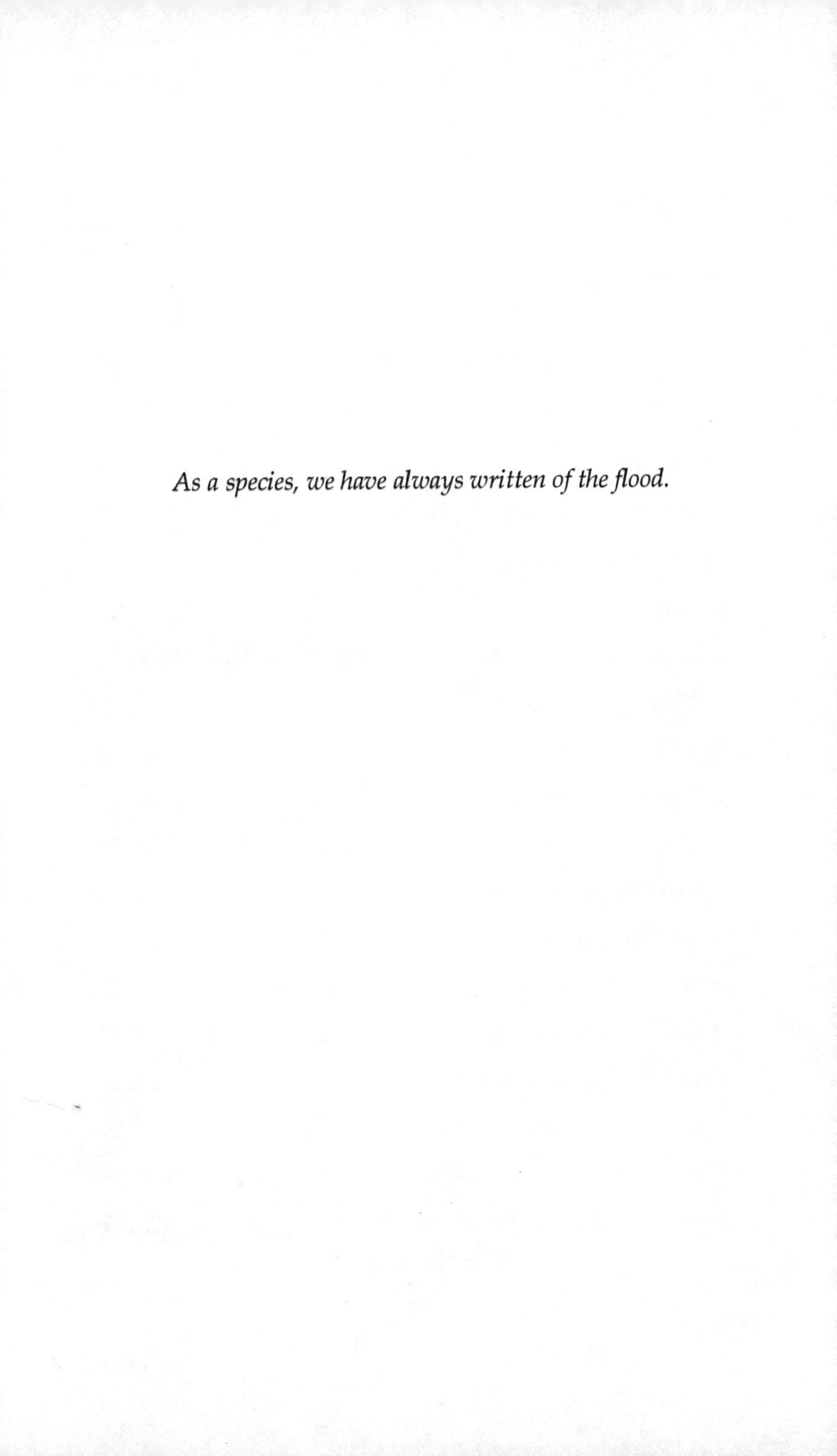

As a species, we have always written of the flood.

TABLE OF CONTENTS

1

♦

The Grace Kelly of Publishing

Harry

"I don't understand," Harry told the person on the phone. "The chapter was fine yesterday." He'd sent off what was supposed to be the final edit for proofreading before he'd gotten on a plane two days ago. The last thing he wanted to deal with was more changes on a project he'd been working on for over a year.

"Harry, you've got four ghost stories in a book that's supposed to be a memoir about food and travel in the folksy westernmost province of France," his agent, Anika, told him. Her tone was somewhere between weary and placating, which, as Harry knew from long experience, wasn't good. "Just because you write about them beautifully…. Look, you've already got a tone issue. Cutting one — just one! — of your tales about shades from the beyond will help balance it out a bit. If you want my suggestion, the one about the drowned city of Ys is particularly extraneous."

"The book is about the physical and emotional experience of a journey in Brittany. It's impossible to understand Brittany — not its food, not its architecture, not its people — without understanding its ghost stories,"

Harry protested, wishing he was in Brittany right now himself. Although, in truth, he would have taken just about anywhere that wasn't another anonymous hallway outside of a relentlessly organized conference on the second day of the five-hundred-and-somethingth annual Frankfurt Book Fair.

"Yes, and you have four of them, not including the one about the shipping container full of Garfield phones." Anika retorted. "None of them make the book accessible to your core reader demographic."

Harry was silent just long enough to convey his deep annoyance. Of which Anika was already well aware. "What are my options?" he finally asked. As if he still had any.

"You can make a case for keeping it, but then it's another week of back and forth with the powers that be. So why don't you just say 'yes, Anika,' and go back to your weekend of schnitzel and bookstalls."

"You make it sound so much more romantic than it is," Harry grumbled.

The Frankfurt Book Fair was a staple of the publishing industry calendar. He'd been coming here nearly every year since he'd started in the business. Now that he was about to turn fifty and was a managing editor at a respectable publishing house — as well as a vaguely successful writer of mid-list travel memoirs — he tended to regard the whole affair as a week-long slog. Who looked forward to endless meetings and too much drinking before returning home to deal with a disaster of an inbox?

"Also, I did get your draft of the Vienna book," Anika said. "Thanks for sending that along."

"Did you read it yet?" Harry perked up a little in hopes of praise.

"I got it yesterday, so no I did not." Anika laughed. "Now go enjoy your trip on the company dollar, I have people to talk to who are less annoying than you."

Harry said a relieved goodbye and turned his attention to his assistant, Jonathan, who had appeared in the hallway in front of him. As ever, he vibrated with an eager urgency.

"What is it, and is it a disaster?" Harry asked.

The corner of Jonathan's mouth quirked up. He was in his late twenties, far too pale, preppy, and dark-haired. A literary assistant straight out of central casting, Harry always thought. Together they made their way downstairs to the hotel lobby where, hopefully, Harry's next meeting would be more satisfying than the phone call with Anika.

"So the rep for that distributor you wanted to meet with keeps blowing me off," Jonathan told him. "And Hazleton cancelled the meeting for tomorrow, but Carla sent over the cover proposals for Sonia's new book, and Philippe called three times —"

"Philippe can wait." Harry flipped open his daybook to take note of the meeting cancellation.

"I'll save him for when you want to get out of something, then," Jonathan said placidly as they turned a corner.

Harry, more intent on being annoyed with this trip than where he was going, crashed into someone, while Jonathan dodged out of the way of the awkwardness.

Harry apologized automatically and took a step backward before even looking at the person he'd just collided with. When he finally did, he stared. She was beautiful, and he recognized her from somewhere, but he had no idea what her name was; Harry always remembered people's names. He frowned at her.

The tall woman with golden-brown hair who reminded him of no one so much as a brunette Grace Kelly stared back incredulously.

"I'm sorry," he said again, in case she hadn't heard his initial apology.

Her high heels put her gaze on a level with his, and her eyes were grey. Like the morning light on the ocean, if you went out to sail too early on the Connecticut River. Harry winced inwardly at the absurdity of his own New Englandness. Still, he definitely knew her from somewhere. But, alarmingly, the blank remained.

He cataloged the rest of her, hoping to jog his memory. She was young, probably under thirty, although Harry thought it unwise to dare greater precision. Her hair was twisted up off her neck in an elegant knot fastened with a pin. A pencil skirt and a smart jacket in soft blue wool, along with a pearl necklace — genuine, Harry's brain observed unhelpfully — nestled against her collarbones did nothing to diminish the retro look about her. Whoever she might be, this was a woman out of time. As Harry stared at her without saying anything, her blush-pink lips parted ever so slightly.

Shit. She wasn't walking away. Harry was now obliged to introduce himself. He held out a hand.

"I'm Harold Sargent. But please call me Harry."

She took his hand with firm amusement. Her mouth, which Harry was exerting a great deal of effort not to fixate on, curved in a faint smile. "I *know*. Elizabeth Ann Abgral."

Harry blinked. She knew him, and he didn't know her. Why was his brain betraying him like this? The last name rang a distant bell too; it meant that the woman in front of him hailed very much from the same brand of old New England society families Harry himself regretfully belonged to. But he still had no idea who she was.

"Really?" he couldn't help but ask, even if he knew it was rude.

"Yes, *really*," she said. "Your new consultant. For innovative digital solutions. To increase your publisher's profits and avoid layoffs."

"Oh!" Harry had known they were getting someone to come in for a year to whip them all into shape. And while he was all for improving job security, he had little interest in, or trust of, digital solutions and the wunderkinds advocating them. In all his grumbling about the decision to bring in a contractor, Harry had definitely not expected the result to be a young woman from a dream of the 1950s.

"So, Elizabeth Ann Abgral, does anyone call you anything for short?" he asked more sharply than was polite. Everything about this woman's existence — as a colleague and a human being — was throwing him.

She looked at him, arch and maybe just a tad put off. "No," she said firmly. "Not here."

♦

Although the work day theoretically ended with the conclusion of show hours, that evening Harry found himself at a poorly lit Mediterranean restaurant in Innenstadt with Jonathan, Malik Olowe from their company's London office, and the mysterious — and increasingly irritated with him — Elizabeth.

"Are you jetlagged?" Harry asked. He was trying to be considerate in lieu of grousing to her about the restaurant or the work day, but the question was still small talk of the most awkward sort.

Elizabeth clearly knew it, too. Her mouth twisted wryly. "Should I be?"

"It's a long flight. Some people never get used to it."

"Are you one of those?" Elizabeth asked, indicting him immediately for his uninvited expertise.

"I try not to be," he said sincerely.

She considered him a moment, her grey eyes flicking over his suit, now wrinkled from the day. "I didn't fly in from New York," she finally said.

"Oh?"

"I've been in Wales for the last month consulting on the digital presence for next year's Hay Festival. Since I was just wrapping that up, our boss asked if I could meet you all here."

"Our boss," Harry said automatically. "We'll be working together, then?" He hadn't imagined he and a consultant being on equal footing in the corporate org chart.

"Do you mind that? Us working together?" Elizabeth asked.

"No more than I mind everything else about my job."

"Are you always this sour?" she asked blandly.

Harry gave her a crooked smile. "It's part of my charm."

"If you say so."

"Only sometimes," he admitted. "But having you pop over from Wales…that seems both cruel and unusual. Most especially because there's nothing to do in that damned town." Hay-on-Wye was a small community that boasted over twenty bookshops, more tourists than locals, and was only otherwise of interest for being situated on the border of a notably haunted nature preserve. He'd once spent seventy-two hours there doing little more than trying to find a way to escape.

Elizabeth, however, clearly did not agree. In fact, she was staring at him in horror. "Are you an editor who hates bookshops?"

"No, I'm a writer who hates everything. Working in publishing just allows me to seem authoritative about it."

"Yes, well. I enjoyed Hay very much. Which I assumed you knew — that I was there, I mean — since we're working together." Elizabeth said with a decided lift of her well-groomed eyebrows.

When her phone rang, Harry was considering the possibility that not only was he wildly attracted to Elizabeth, but that he also hated her.

"Oh — I'm sorry. Will you excuse me," Elizabeth said before he could continue to dig himself into a deep hole defined by an utter lack of social grace.

She pulled her phone out of her purse and stepped a polite distance away from the table to take the call. She was not, however, far enough away for Harry to refrain from eavesdropping. He watched, not as surreptitiously as he should have, as Elizabeth spoke into the phone. In German. Until she switched to French.

After several minutes, she turned back to Harry. "Is tomorrow at five all right?" she asked.

Harry started both at the English and her renewed attention. "I'm sorry?"

Elizabeth blinked. "Five o'clock? In the evening? A meeting?" Her uptalk was nearly vicious.

"I don't know what you're talking about." Harry had zoned out somewhere in the middle of her multilingual high wire act.

"Really? You were listening hard enough."

"My German's not as good as yours," Harry offered. It was true, but not the only reason why he hadn't followed her half of the conversation.

"Well," Elizabeth said slowly, as if Harry might have trouble following her English as well. "A meeting tomorrow at five. With the Eastern European marketing people?"

"Have I met you before?" Harry blurted.

"Excuse me?" Now Elizabeth stared at Harry as if he were not just rude but as if he also had two heads.

"I'm just *sure* I know you from somewhere." Harry wondered desperately why Jonathan wasn't coming to his rescue, but a glance at his assistant answered that question. He was far too caught up in flirting with Malik to have any attention left over for Harry's woes.

"Well, if you do, I have no recollection of it," Elizabeth said. "Now - I have someone on the phone who might do marketing for you. A meeting?"

Harry made himself focus and mentally paged through his schedule. "Yes. Tomorrow should be fine."

"At five?"

"At five." Harry matched her half-mocking tone. Even though he deserved it. He hadn't been acting like a man who could keep track of his engagements. Let alone remember he had them at all. Which annoyed him deeply. He might have been wildly disorganized as a rule — hence his need for Jonathan — but he *always* remembered.

He also apparently couldn't stop talking. "Do you want to tell me about your French and your German?" he asked as Elizabeth slid back into her seat at the table.

"There's nothing to tell," she said patiently, as if she were humoring an old man. "Schoolroom French. University German."

"Yet your French is better?"

"I've been speaking it longer."

"Why French and not Spanish?" he asked. When he'd been growing up, everyone in his peer group learned French. But the gravity of the world and the people who thought they ran it had shifted and was shifting again. Someone Elizabeth's age he'd expect to have Spanish. Or Mandarin. He hoped she wasn't about to tell him she spoke those, too.

She looked at the ceiling for just a moment too long before returning her gaze to him. "I'm from the sort of family where girls learn French the way we once learned pianoforte."

"Of course you are," Harry said dryly. "Even with an MBA, you couldn't afford to be in publishing if you weren't."

That shocked a laugh out of her, a sharp cackle that contained nothing demure and that Harry loved instantly.

"I'm from Essex," he said, as if to explain his remark about her origins. "Connecticut. I grew up with girls like you."

♦

Back in his room at the hotel, Harry soaked for an hour in the bathtub. Which, miraculously, accommodated his six-foot-odd frame comfortably. When the water finally became tepid and he forced himself to climb out, he wrapped himself in his own bathrobe brought from home and settled in the armchair by the bed. He knew he was strange to pack such a thing, but years of conferences and research trips had taught him the value of making the road seem less alienating.

He should have gone right to sleep, lest his awkward remark to Elizabeth about jet lag become truth. But he needed to wind down. And he absolutely could not shake the idea that he'd met her somewhere before, whether she remembered the encounter or not. He grabbed his tablet off the nightstand and Googled her name.

She'd done her undergraduate work at Boston University, which wasn't necessarily impressive on its own, but the MFA/MBA graduate combo was daunting and spoke to family wealth that enabled her to afford such a thing. It was, of course, all information Harry could have discovered from her CV, had he known to expect her and bothered to look at it on the plane. But absolutely none of it told Harry where he'd seen her before.

Annoyed, he opened his email. Not his work account, but his personal one. Which immediately provided a new and much more acute sense of dismay in the form of dozens of emails from the Manuscript Miscreants, all sent within the last two hours.

The Manuscript Miscreants, which everyone agreed was an absolutely terrible name, had existed for longer than Harry wanted to acknowledge. Certainly they had existed for nearly as long as email and the commercial internet had existed. In the beginning it had been Harry and his three best friends: Meryl Kahan, Steven Stafford, and Dennis Chakraborty. It had never *really* been a book club — more an excuse to drink, talk, and complain about everyone they knew — but all of them had always read obsessively. It had worked as well for a catchall name for their clique as anything.

Over the years, the group had expanded as the four of them scattered for work and life and had brought new friends and sometimes lovers into the fold. Now the

Miscreants numbered about a dozen, and for the last decade and a half they'd spent the week of Christmas and New Year's together somewhere far from anywhere any of them called home.

The Miscreants were Harry's far-flung family of choice. Prone to disreputable acts, vicious gossip about anyone not in their circle, and inveterate appreciators of fine food and drink, this year they were renting a house in Trastevere. Formerly the worst, most dangerous part of Rome, where Harry, Steven, and Meryl had once stayed together when they were poor students touring through Europe the summer before their senior year at Yale, it was now the city's most fashionable district. And the Miscreants planned to terrorize it.

Harry expected today's emails to be the usual fare: twenty percent planning and eighty percent Meryl being funny about the horrors of her life as an economics professor at Florida State. What was actually there, however, was a flurry of emails back and forth with variations on the subject line of *Oh my God, Steven.*

Some were from members of the group at large, but most were in a backchannel thread limited to himself, Meryl, and Dennis. That Dennis was involved was unusual; he was generally too busy hosting his extra-late-night network TV talk show to bother replying to anything. Harry wondered what on earth Steven, who was usually the calmest, sweetest, and least drama-prone member of the group, had done to set off the firestorm.

And then he saw the original email, sent by Steven to the entire list. Harry opened it with trepidation.

Hello all,

I won't be coming to Christmas this year. Things seem to have progressed unfavorably, and the docs don't want me travelling. Sorry to miss it and hope to see you all next time around.

- S

Harry blew out a long, slow breath. Steven had been diagnosed with pancreatic cancer over a year ago. His prognosis had never been particularly favorable, but he'd stayed outwardly optimistic and Harry had stayed more or less in denial. Steven never talked about the future with anything but certainty that he'd be present for it. A message like this wasn't just a planning email for the sake of making everyone's holiday logistics easier. This was him, in his characteristically understated way, telling them things were very much worse.

The rest of the emails were, of course, all about Steven and his announcement and what the group could do for him and Mallory, his wife. They may have been a bunch of degenerates, but they took care of their own.

Harry opened an email window to send a reply just to Steven, and then stared at it for a long time. What could he say that wasn't trite, obvious, or blithe? How was anyone supposed to respond to a friend's email admission that he was dying? Especially with the history that lurked between them?

He considered, briefly, calling Meryl. It was late in Frankfurt but barely dinnertime in Florida. Whether she was dining or sleeping, Harry knew she would always pick up his calls. That was one of the rules of their friendship — sometimes intimate, always loyal, and never romantic. But Harry knew how to have a conversation about this even less than he knew how to write an email about it. Besides, he was sure there would be many nights in the coming months where he would call her at some terrible hour and need her to answer the phone far more than he did now. He didn't want to use up all her goodwill this early in the grim process ahead.

Harry pounded out an email, just to Steven, all in a rush, lest he overthink each word and phrase. Whatever was going to happen in the course of his friend's illness, it wasn't going to happen right now, and that included Harry's sentiments about it. He sent his regards from Frankfurt and then made what was likely an obviously reluctant offer to visit Steven in the wilds of Connecticut. Harry hated Connecticut and often went to pains to avoid his home state, as Steven well knew.

He stared at the shadows of the furniture in the dark room as he hit send. Harry wasn't a young man, and none of his friends were young either. But they had, until Steven's diagnosis, all been more or less healthy. They had even gotten used to Meryl's MS as simply a thing that was what it was. Now death was coming for one of them, and Harry felt so very, very old.

He felt, too, a fool for his peculiar fascination with Elizabeth, and shame threatened to drive him to bed without further communication. But the Miscreants deserved to hear from him as well; if he didn't whine about Frankfurt, people would note his silence and Steven would holler at all of them about going on with their lives as usual. So he opened a new email to the entire group and typed.

This is your annual "Does anyone want anything from Frankfurt, although God knows why you would" email. Also someone hired a twenty-something genius and she is perfect. Is this what a midlife crisis feels like? You've all been instructed to save me from myself.

He hit send with an inappropriate amount of gusto. The sheer absurdity of his confession would provoke the lot of them into being clever and give them all something other than Steven's situation to discuss publicly.

Too bad there was no more useful sacrifice, no bargain with the universe, he could make.

2

◆

An Odd Man on a Long Flight

Eliza

After doing business in three languages, enduring two fourteen-hour days at the book fair, and dealing with one completely ridiculous new colleague, Eliza finally, *finally* had a moment to herself. She was determined to take advantage of it by putting as much distance between herself and the hotel as possible with the intent to do some sightseeing. Everyone at her new gig swore that Frankfurt was boring, but Eliza relished finding small, private gems in unloved places. She also didn't trust the judgement of her new colleagues at all.

She was outside the Römer trying to appreciate German architecture and thinking that she should head back to her room to get some decent sleep when her phone rang. It was Cody, her fiancé.

"Hello," he said fondly when she answered. "Is this a good time?"

"Well, I'm wandering around Frankfurt trying to take in the sights. So it depends on what you want to talk about," she said and winced at herself. But Cody's calls lately had either been about his House of Representatives special election campaign or their wedding. And both of those topics were not only boring, they required her to take notes.

"Frankfurt has sights?" Cody asked.

"Yes, it does. Why does everyone hate Frankfurt? It seems perfectly nice!"

"I wouldn't know; I've only been to the airport," Cody said unhelpfully.

Still, Eliza was glad to hear his voice. She hadn't seen him in nearly five weeks, and she missed him. Curling up in her hotel room bed and chatting about little meaningless things seemed perfect, although she suspected this was not that sort of call. "What's going on?"

"I know this is the last thing you want to deal with this week," Cody said. "But my parents have started planning the engagement party, and I'm supposed to check in with you. If you're available."

"For the party or for a discussion about it right now?"

"Well, both. But for the moment, planning."

Eliza sighed. "Would your parents be very offended if I wasn't available to talk logistics?"

"Nah, I told them you're probably too busy. And the more details my mother gets to decide on her own the happier she is. As long as you're okay with that?"

Eliza was torn. While she couldn't have cared less about the details of her engagement party — or about having one at all — she knew it was an occasion that could not be avoided. There were things to be done, and because of who she and Cody were, they had to be done in a certain way. She could either grumble and take charge or let her future mother-in-law do so and just add the date to her calendar.

"I'm okay with that," she finally said. "Although, please, warn me if anything is going to be shocking about it."

She braced herself as Cody took a deep breath in response, but he remained silent.

"What?" she prodded.

"We're probably going to need to have press there."

Eliza felt herself physically recoil. "Ugh. Why?"

"I'm running for a congressional seat? I know, the whole thing will be weird. But all you have to do is smile and adore me, and you already do that anyway."

Cody wasn't wrong. And he was, at least, joking. But the only thing that worried Eliza more than being a society wife was being a political one. Conversations and considerations like this were very much why. She knew it wasn't kind of her, but she hoped he would lose.

♦

That night Eliza slept poorly and had dream after dream that she was running late. Late for flights, late for meetings, late even to her own wedding. She was relieved to wake up and realize it was five in the morning in Frankfurt and hours before she had to be anywhere. She had no planes to catch, her wedding was still more than a year away, and she had plenty of time to address anything needed before the work day began.

A quick glance at her inbox showed only a handful of emails, none of which were urgent. Going back to sleep would have been ideal, but Eliza was too keyed up from the nightmares. And the hotel had a pool.

She would never admit to anyone that, for as long as she could remember, she had always believed that the water called to her. Her affinity for it was not defined by skill or hobby so much as a need to be submerged in it that was as fundamental as her body's need for food. She'd realized young it was too peculiar to explain and had learned to swim laps to have the excuse.

She dug through her suitcase until she found her swimsuit. It took a little while; her clothes were tangled together messily. Not a useful state for them to be in, given how most of them needed to be perfectly neat and pressed. But if her clothes would need to be ironed anyway, she saw no reason not to let them get wrinkled in transit.

The pool, when she located it, was a dreary basement affair, long and narrow and split down the middle with a single rope marking it off into two lanes. It was, however, mercifully empty, and she shed the hotel bathrobe she'd used as a coverup and slid in. The water was too cold, so she did the only thing she could: dove under and began. Soon the world fell away — her bad dreams, her new job, the specter of her engagement party. There was only the strange muffled peace of the water around her ears, here under the earth. She counted as she swam, neither laps nor strokes, but a steady beat as if to music she could not quite remember.

Eventually, out of breath, Eliza stopped. She spread her toes against the tiled bottom of the pool and hauled herself up to sit on its side. Across from her, in the other lane, another swimmer — a man — slowed, then stopped as well. She'd been alone when she had arrived and hadn't heard or felt anyone enter the water. She wondered now if there was any way to grab her robe and flee to her room without looking like she was in a hurried panic to avoid human contact.

But when the man hauled himself out of the water, she realized it was Harry. She felt all the more impulse to flee. They hadn't even been colleagues for a day and now here they were in their swimsuits! Eliza took a deep breath. She'd been born a WASP for something, and if it wasn't to suppress all her emotions in this incredibly awkward moment, it wasn't for anything at all.

"Oh," he said, startled, when he finally looked up and saw her.

"Oh," she echoed. It only seemed natural. Their body postures mirrored each other across the water; why not their repressed horror too?

"Of course it's you." His voice wasn't mocking; he sounded and looked as dismayed as she was.

"Yes."

They sat in silence for a few moments, probably because standing up and revealing more of their bodies to each other would make the whole thing worse. Each of them absently kicked at the water which rippled between them, sending darts and flashes of light onto the ceiling.

"Good morning," she tried awkwardly.

"You're up early," Harry replied with only somewhat more aplomb. To Eliza's surprise he kept his eyes on her face. Not once did his gaze drop to her body, clad only in her blue swimsuit. With any other man she would have dived back into the water to cover herself with it; men could be so awful about their gaze. But now that they were here, she could feel no threat emanating from him. Only a resigned weariness.

"I couldn't sleep," she confessed. She tried to match Harry's courtesy and not look anywhere but his eyes, but she found it difficult. Not because of desire, although he was fit and handsome, all long limbs and strongly built. But because he was an infuriating and curious creature. She wanted to know things about him, even if the stories of men were often less written on their flesh than the stories of women.

"Neither could I," he admitted.

The conversation, stilted as it was, felt strangely intimate, even though they weren't really saying anything, just sharing space while they swirled their legs in the water and caught their breath from swimming. After their near-combativeness yesterday, Eliza didn't know what to make of it.

"Anything wrong? Other than jetlag?" she asked, mocking his remark to her at dinner in an attempt to get back on that footing.

Harry gave a surprisingly weary shrug. "One of my best friends is dying of cancer," he said. "Which was also true yesterday, but now he's doing it faster. And we're talking about it."

Eliza's training for any and all social eventualities continued to fail her. She did not immediately know how to respond. When she said nothing, Harry frowned — at her or at himself for being so honest, she didn't know — and began to hoist himself up from his seat at the edge of the pool.

"Well, fuck," she said, in lieu of anything else. She didn't want him to leave because of her silence.

He stopped and looked down at her. "That was rather my reaction, yes."

She hurried to scramble to her feet. Even on opposite sides of the pool she couldn't stand the idea of him towering over her any more than she could stand the idea of leaving him alone to his circumstances.

"I suppose the suggestion of *bier und brotzeit* would be inadequate?"

Curiosity sparked behind the sadness in Harry's eyes, and Eliza tried not to wince at herself. She'd effectively invited Harry out for a booze breakfast.

*

To Eliza's utter surprise, Harry accepted. And so, an hour later, she found herself sitting across from him in an excessively cheery bar decorated with beer steins a few blocks over from their hotel.

Having since, like herself, showered and changed, Harry was dressed for another day of meetings in a grey checked suit that had a flair to it that made Eliza think more of the flashy stock brokers of London's City than the dreary New York editor's life Harry presumably led. But even though he was starched and ironed to perfection, there was something about him that seemed rumpled, almost weary, nonetheless.

The news about his friend, perhaps. Or the exhaustion brought on by a demanding schedule. Or maybe it was that once she'd seen him undressed, dripping, and defenseless on the side of a hotel pool, the sharp lines of his clothes couldn't disguise his weaknesses so well anymore.

Eliza looked away from Harry and focused on the menu. He did the same.

"Do you need me to translate for you, Harold?" she asked as she stared down at the laminated paper. Better to tease than to dwell on thoughts of…whatever sort of thoughts she'd been dwelling on. Harry was a colleague, and Eliza had no business trying to figure out how he could look so put together and so at loose ends at the same time.

Harry gave her a sharp sideways look. "Please never call me that."

"I was testing it out."

"Well, don't. And no, thank you for the kind offer, but I am perfectly capable of understanding a menu."

"Not a fan of your name, then." She didn't mean to needle him like this, not really, but she didn't know how to do anything else.

"Harry is fine. Harold makes me sound…."

"Old?"

"Yes, something like that." He frowned and looked up from his menu at her. "What about yours?"

"What about mine?"

"Elizabeth Ann Abgral," Harry said slowly, rolling the sounds off his tongue. "That's a lot to contend with."

"I never met anyone who was so hell-bent on using all of it every time they address me." She wasn't sure what Harry was driving at.

"It's a New England patrician pain-in-the-ass of a name, and good luck trying to pass yourself off as anything but what your family has ever been."

Eliza was torn between offense and amusement. "You really did grow up with girls like me."

"Indeed."

"There's nothing wrong with my family," she said. He had, somehow, turned the tables on her, and Eliza felt defensive. There was, in truth, a lot wrong with her family.

"I didn't say there was. But New England names — and family legacies — are terrible. Rich and snotty and exploitative of someone. Did you have a governess as a child? Or just a live-in housekeeper?"

"My grandmother, actually," she said, although it absolved her of nothing. "And Abgral is Breton, technically."

Harry blinked twice. Hard. "Excuse me?"

"It's a Breton name. From Brittany? In France? It's not from New England."

He continued to gape at her in terrible, fish-like silence.

"Is something wrong?" She did not understand what was happening in this conversation.

"Are you sure we haven't met before?" Harry asked, with a frown of what might have been desperation.

This again. "If we have, I don't remember. Why do you keep asking that?"

"It's just…you seem so very familiar," he said.

"We're at an international book fair in Frankfurt," Elizabeth reminded him. "Everyone looks like someone you know from somewhere else."

Harry shook his head and tapped his fingers against the table. Eliza looked down at his hands, strong, elegant, and with a soft sheen to his blunt nails. A manicure.

"No. I can always place someone," he said.

"But not me?"

"No. I mean…." He deflated. "You're right. You must remind me of someone." Harry said, though he sounded less than convinced. "Where in Brittany? I mean, where in Brittany is your family from?"

"I don't know. My family's been in Boston since the Revolutionary War at least. I'm sure someone somewhere keeps track, but I try to ignore it. It's like having a pedigree. Like a dog. Or a horse." Eliza shrugged. "People get odd about it. As you probably know."

"Being Breton?"

Eliza squinted at him. Harry was peculiar and never seemed to say anything that made complete sense. "No. Being a Daughter of the American Revolution. Why are you so terrible? I grew up with a girl who was a Daughter of the Mayflower. She was also terrible and held that over me for years."

"You should look into that," Harry said.

"The Mayflower?"

"Your family history. You never know what you'll turn up," he said too casually. Clearly, whatever was on his mind, he wasn't going to share. "Have you ever been there?" Harry asked.

"Where?"

"Brittany."

Eliza shook her head. "We've always been a Paris sort of family." She was aware, as she said it, of how appalling she sounded. But she was a member of a family who still, in many ways, existed in the privileges of another time. Such an existence was beautiful and terrible, and she didn't always know what to make of it.

"It's an interesting place," Harry said as if their lives and the way in which they were conversing with each other were perfectly normal. "I've a book on it due out in some lifetime," he went on. "As a matter of fact, I've got to deal with my editor about some supposedly last points as soon as I get back home. I'm dreading every second of it."

"You're an editor who doesn't like being edited," Eliza said, charmed by the implied self-hatred.

He leaned forward as if to share a secret. "Terrible, isn't it?"

Suddenly, Eliza wanted to be generous with him, although she didn't know why. "I'll tell you what," she said. "I was going to hold out on you, but please, call me Eliza. And I'll try to remember not to call you Harold."

◆

After that strange, and oddly lovely, breakfast, Eliza didn't speak to Harry for the rest of the book fair except for the most cursory business. She would have suspected that they were avoiding each other after the odd intimacy of their swim and morning together, except that Harry was always there, lingering at her periphery.

She would see him out of the corner of her eye on the show floor, wearing one of his too-smart suits like armor as he made small talk. Or spot the back of his head three tables over at a big dinner to honor this or that publishing luminary. Each time she considered going over to say hello — his observations about the industry and their unsettling interaction would probably be more entertaining than the usual polite patter — but decided against it.

Harry's insistence that he knew her from somewhere disconcerted her. Eliza was not in the habit of believing men just because they were so very sure of something. But Harry's belief was so earnest, almost innocent, that Eliza struggled to dismiss him easily. Had they met before and had Eliza simply forgotten? Surely not. Harry was too well and eccentrically dressed, too peculiar a conversationalist, and too handsome for that. But he was so certain....

Eliza didn't know if she liked being someone else's mystery. She did know she was more annoyed than pleased that she and Harry were seated next to each other on the flight back to New York. To her relief, Harry left her alone with her thoughts as the plane sat at the gate and taxied toward the runway. Only once they were in the air and Eliza pulled a book out of the bag she'd stashed under the seat, did Harry speak.

He looked up from his own book, also clearly a book fair acquisition, despite how fretfully dog-eared it already was. "Oh! That one," he said. "I tried to get my hands on it but they were all gone by the time I got there."

"Mm. Me too," Eliza said absently as her eyes skimmed over the first few sentences.

"And yet...."

She looked up at him. "And yet, I went through all the effort to get this book and now you're interrupting my attempt to read it."

"Oh. My apologies."

Eliza went back to the pages, but she could feel Harry's gaze on her. He was restraining himself from asking how she'd gotten her hands on it. She could feel it.

She turned the page. "Being a pretty girl at a book fair means I can sometimes get things other people can't."

"Did you flirt with some poor sap until he surrendered it?" Harry asked.

Eliza was uncertain how he could take her terse words and focus on the page as an invitation to continue the discussion, but there it was. "No. I flirted until some poor sap was distracted enough that I could steal it."

She looked over the top of the book at Harry.

He looked like he was trying not to laugh. "You didn't."

"Oh yes I did." She smirked and held his gaze, but he didn't look away. Neither, then, would she. "If you want to read it when I'm done, you're welcome to borrow it."

"You'll hardly finish it before the flight ends."

"We work together. Presumably you will be able to find my office."

"Point," Harry conceded.

"Or I could read aloud to you." She was playing with him now in a manner she recognized was both slightly cruel and far more enticing than was appropriate. Because Harry looked tempted. She hoped he wasn't going to take her up on her offer. He was amusing, yes, but spending an extended period of time trying to speak over the dull background roar of the engines in the too-dry air seemed dreadful.

"Perhaps a raincheck," he said after a moment of consideration.

Eliza exhaled gratitude into the already stale cabin air.

♦

Once she'd finished several chapters, the activity of the last several days caught up to her and Eliza desperately wanted a nap. As she set her book in her lap, leaned back, and closed her eyes, she was suddenly aware of Harry. Not the sound of him shifting in his seat or the warmth of him so close to her. But rather the very idea of him existing in the world, as if, with her eyes closed, she could see him — and his strange amusement with her — better than she could with her eyes open.

Eventually, in hopes of convincing herself she was wrong, she opened her eyes and turned toward him. Harry was watching her, a little smile on his face.

"Do you want this?" she asked, holding up the book she had confessed to stealing. She was warm and drowsy and — so strange for being on a plane — comfortable. She couldn't have named the impulse that led her to offer Harry the book, but whatever it was, it felt natural and right.

"What?" Harry startled slightly as if he'd been somewhere very far away.

"You were staring. Do you want this book?" Eliza said, more slowly. Perhaps Harry was feeling the same odd comfort that she was. With other men — and Eliza had been hit on by plenty of men his age — his staring would have felt rude. Invasive. Proprietary. But as when they had met at the pool, he was simply looking with an abstract curiosity.

He held out a hand, and Eliza pressed the book into it. Then she leaned back and closed her eyes again. Within moments she was asleep, the sound of Harry turning pages soft in her ears.

She woke hours later to the announcement that the plane was beginning its descent into JFK. Groggily, she reached for the orange that had been left on her tray table during a food service she had apparently slept through. She dug her thumbs into the rind to split it open before gratefully popping sections of it into her mouth. She was so dehydrated. When she finished, she wiped her hands as daintily as she could and returned her seat into the upright position before a flight attendant came to nag.

"You'll want this," Harry said, startling her. He handed her the book she had given him earlier.

There was a piece of paper sticking out of the top of it, and Eliza's heart sank. Surely, this was Harry's way of slipping her his phone number. Except when she flipped to it, so she could express her displeasure at the implied proposition, the words died in her mouth. It was only a customs form, with Eliza's name and itinerary already filled out.

"I didn't know if you'd gone shopping or any of your other details, so I left those parts blank." Harry handed her a pen as well, as if filling out customs paperwork for colleagues was a completely ordinary thing to do. "Oh, and I didn't forge your signature."

The pen was warm from Harry's fingers. "You're an odd man," she said blearily, feeling relieved and, strangely, very grateful. "Thank you."

3

♦

The Curse of the Supermarket Sauce King

Harry

Twenty hours after landing in New York, Harry wished he was still enjoying the debatable pleasures of the Frankfurt Book Fair. He was on a conference call with his least favorite celebrity chef about his latest book that had already gone thirty minutes longer than scheduled, emails were piling up in his inbox, and he needed to finalize plans to visit Steven in Connecticut. The ever-faithful Jonathan was perched in a chair across from Harry's desk, notepad on his knee. Ostensibly he was there to take notes but really, as they both knew, he was providing moral support for Harry in this trying time.

And Philippe was always trying. Mainly because he knew the sales of his cookbooks kept the lights on, and he was so damn smug about it. Harry often wondered why Philippe didn't flee to a larger house, but suspected he — like all of them — enjoyed the pain of the familiar and being the biggest fish in a decidedly medium-sized pond. But that still didn't mean Harry was going to send him on a cross-country tour with a branded food truck.

"Look, Philippe, I appreciate where you're coming from. And I agree the food truck phenomenon is a great way to further expand the audience for traditional French cooking! But if you want to do that, you're going to need to drive the thing yourself because we are not dealing with a truck, supplies, permits, and business class airfare for you while I make my lovely assistant relive the very worst of his college days on a road trip from hell."

"At least I'm lovely," Jonathan muttered to himself.

Harry scowled at him. They were on speakerphone!

"But Harry…Harold — do you mind if I call you that?" Philippe asked in his cloying, and conspicuously fake, French accent. Making the H- in his name silent did not a native French speaker make.

"Yes!" Harry said. "Yes, I mind!" *Why does everyone want to call me Harold lately? What god have I angered?*

"But, Harry, I think this can expand an interest in my back list."

Harry sighed. "I don't think you're wrong, but it's still not happening. Talk to your sauce distributor. Talk to reality TV. If we can get some partnerships going we're happy to be on board and we'll revisit it."

After too many au revoirs, Harry ended the call with more enthusiasm than was strictly professional.

"Promise me you will not send me on that tour," Jonathan said sternly.

"It'll never happen," Harry assured him. "You know he's actually an Italian guy from Queens, right?"

Before Jonathan could answer there was a knock at the door. Harry looked at his assistant quizzically; was anyone expected? The younger man shook his head.

"Come in," Harry called. He was tempted to leave whoever it was in the hallway cooling their heels, but Jonathan tended not to approve of Harry exercising his petulance in such a way.

When the door opened, Harry had to choke back a noise of dismay. It was Eliza. Who Harry had watched sleep for an hour on a plane somewhere over the Atlantic Ocean until he, too, had given into the warm temptation of unconsciousness.

He *still* couldn't figure out where he knew her from.

Today she wore a dark blue sheath dress that placed her somewhere between a CEO's wife and a 1950s pinup. She'd traded her pearls for a fine gold chain that glinted softly in the light from Harry's desk lamp. There was a small pendant in the shape of a cresting wave dangling from it, and it hung slightly askew. Harry wanted desperately to reach up and set it to rights, but neither the gesture nor the thought was remotely appropriate. *What does her skin feel like, there at the hollow of her throat?*

Harry started, visibly he was sure, appalled at the thought and his own inability to shake off whatever it was about Eliza that captivated him so. Jonathan, still sitting across from him, gave a stern look that conveyed just how much Harry needed to pull himself together.

"Can I help you?" He had to say something, but his voice sounded strangled.

"I hope so. Do you mind if I sit down?"

"Not at all," Harry said, his manners kicking in so strongly he was tempted to stand and pull the chair out for her. He gripped the edge of his own seat to stop himself. He strongly suspected his life would be much simpler if Eliza turned around and walked out of his office forever.

"Thanks." Eliza sat down on the edge of the chair next to Jonathan's, her ankles neatly crossed and tucked under the seat. "So, I've been brought in to revamp your digital presence."

"Yes, we've covered that."

Eliza pursed her lips. "I'm going to all of the division heads, of which you are one, and asking each of them to give me an author to be a case study for digital innovation."

"Meaning?" Harry asked.

"Meaning I need data to work my magic, and I need to provide the powers that be data so they can help keep this company afloat. The easiest way to achieve that is you giving me a name. Preferably one with some clout." She tapped her finger impatiently on the screen of the tablet she carried.

"Philippe," Harry said without a second thought.

Jonathan looked alarmed. Harry didn't care. He was tired, Philippe needed attention, his own behavior with Eliza in Frankfurt had embarrassed him, and her mandate annoyed him.

"What's his last name?" Eliza asked, typing on her tablet.

"He doesn't use one professionally."

"Wait." Eliza frowned, a fine, barely discernible crease appearing between her eyebrows. *She's so young.* "Philippe, the supermarket sauce guy?"

Harry nodded.

"Really?" Eliza looked dubious.

Harry couldn't blame her. He forged ahead anyway. "Well, it's him or the author with the world's most successful line of do-it-yourself extreme dog grooming books."

"The world's most — you know what, never mind. All right." Eliza glanced down at her tablet. Harry wondered if she was regretting coming into his office. "You think he'll be game?"

Harry smiled with his teeth. "I'm sure he'll be delighted."

"Excellent, then. Thank you." Eliza stood again, the fabric of her dress — was it silk? It had the sheen of silk — rustling softly as she did. "I'll let you know how things go."

Once she had left, closing the office door gently behind her, Jonathan looked at Harry. Consternation was plain in every feature.

"What have you done?" His voice was barely above a whisper, his eyes wide.

"Given Elizabeth what she wanted. Given Philippe what he wanted."

"This will blow up," Jonathan said seriously, knitting his fingers together. "Probably in your face."

"You mean hopefully, don't you?" Harry teased.

"I might, yes! Until it all goes south and you panic and I have to clean it up." He uncrossed and re-crossed his legs, the fashionable lines of his slim-cut suit trousers showing off purple-and-red striped socks.

Harry tsked. "Jonathan. When it goes south at least we won't be left with a pack of angry poodles clipped, dyed, and styled to look like giraffes."

"How is this my life?" Jonathan lamented. "How is it yours, for that matter? You have books out. Money. Some of Manhattan's best real estate. And yet...."

"I ask myself this every day with what is, I assure you, an appropriate level of despair," Harry acknowledged. "But now everyone gets to feel useful and important. And I can fuck off to the wilds of Connecticut for the weekend."

"That's your way of asking me to look up the Metro North schedule again, isn't it?"

Harry nodded morosely, hoping he looked suitably pitiful. If he didn't now, he knew he would when he returned to the office on Monday, more travel-weary than ever and sad besides. All he wanted was to spend more than two nights in a row in his own bed in his own house. He might have generally slept alone, but his eighteen hundred thread count sheets couldn't be beat.

Eliza

Spending the night after her return from Frankfurt in a hotel and moving into her new apartment the evening after her first real day at the office was not Eliza's ideal plan. However, the horrors of conference scheduling and the vagaries of the New York rental market had given her extremely limited options. Which meant sending emails to all the authors the department heads had given her introducing herself and asking for meetings and then fleeing to her new neighborhood to get settled.

Her sister Marianne met her outside the building, her Lexus Crossover parked illegally and full of everything Eliza had thought she'd need for the next year. The apartment that came with her job was fully furnished, so at least she didn't have to worry about that. But she still needed clothes and makeup and books and bedding, not necessarily in that order.

"I could have had that stuff shipped," Eliza said as Marianne stepped out of the car to hug her.

Despite the fact that they shared the same parents, they didn't look much alike; Marianne, like Eliza, was tall, but where Eliza's hair was a rich chestnut Marianne's hair was golden blonde, her eyes honey-brown to Eliza's grey. Marianne's features — small, appropriate, and gentle, resembled their mother, but Eliza with her strong chin, certain nose, and broad forehead looked like one of their great-great-grandmothers who no one remembered except for photographs.

"And a hello to you too," Marianne said, giving Eliza one last squeeze before she stepped back on the sidewalk and looked her up and down. "How was Frankfurt? And Wales? Did you meet any dashing booksellers?"

"I'm engaged," Eliza said automatically and perhaps too quickly. Which was nonsense, as she had not met any dashing booksellers in Wales. Just an odd middle-aged editor and travel writer in Frankfurt. And she was very much engaged.

"Last I checked, that does not create a bubble around you that magically fends off attractive book people."

Eliza wished dearly her sister would shut up.

♦

"Why did you drive all the way down here to bring me a toaster and my clothes?" Eliza asked an hour later and a good deal sweatier. All the boxes from Marianne's car were now cluttering the tiny studio apartment. Eliza wondered if she'd brought too many dresses. As she'd been packing nearly two months ago in her parents' home in Boston, her clothes selection had barely seemed sufficient. Now she wondered how New Yorkers lived with so little closet space. "Not that I don't appreciate the help," she went on. "But that's a hike."

"You try living in Newton with a toddler and a house to keep up. You'd want to go on a road trip, too. If I have to plan one more cocktail party this month I'm going to lose my mind."

"You know, those are choices you've made," Eliza said quietly.

"Are they? Are they really? I can hardly be expected to do anything else."

That was both true and not, but Eliza thought the better of pointing it out. These miseries would be her own soon enough. "Trouble in paradise?" she asked with some trepidation.

"I wouldn't change it for the world." Marianne smiled with the obvious lie. "But I'd give a lot to live someone else's life for a day."

Eliza didn't believe that for a moment. Marianne had thrown herself so deeply into her society wife obligations, she hardly knew how to do anything else. Motherhood — her son had just turned two — had only further underscored an approach to life that was an odd mix of status and fear. Her monologues about organic food, unscientific concerns about vaccination, and whether three was too early to start violin lessons were more than Eliza could bear. If those were the rewards of a marriage well made, Eliza wasn't sure she wanted one. At least her inevitable role in Cody's political career would provide her with a somewhat different path.

And for now she had an apartment that was hers — and only hers — to arrange.

"Ugh, this kitchen," Marianne complained, looking over the tiny cupboards and the postage stamp's worth of counter space. "You're going to need a new microwave, I think this one's been around since the Soviet days. In fact," she poked the silver dial control dubiously. "I think this might have come *from* the Soviets."

"It's not that bad," Eliza protested, stacking cardigans on the armchair that had come with the place. She wouldn't be able to reach the dresser to put them away properly until they cleared out a few more boxes.

"You only think that because you've been living with awful European appliances for the last month," Marianne said. "You need a new one. But don't get anything too fancy, you'll get a nice one when you get married. Have you started your registry yet?"

Eliza made a noncommittal sound, and decided not to tell Marianne that she didn't need a microwave at all.

"You've got to register for the new KitchenAid mixer too, it's to die for."

"I hate cooking," Eliza said flatly.

"Well get it for your cook, then. She'll thank you."

"We don't have a cook," Eliza all but snapped.

"Yet!" Marianne sang. "Trust me, it's so worth it to have people helping out. Especially once you have kids."

Eliza stared at Marianne in horror. Did she not hear herself? Or did she not care that every word that came out of her mouth was laden with the ugly side of privilege and a heavy dose of assumption?

"I'm just trying to live my life right now," Eliza said quietly.

Marianne turned sharply, her curtain of hair flipping over her shoulder like the star of a shampoo commercial. "Oh God," she exclaimed. "Why?"

Eliza squinted and glanced side to side, as if the barren walls of her microscopic corporate apartment would hold the answer.

"Because it's amazing," she said at last with a certainty she hadn't known she felt. "I'm good at what I do. I get to travel all over the world. Last month I lived in Wales and this month I'm living in New York City...." She trailed off when Marianne didn't look convinced.

"One room," Marianne said, gesturing to the space. "High pressure obligations you don't need. A long-distance relationship."

Eliza sat down on the thinly padded window seat that hid a radiator. She pointed to herself. "Big life; small space."

Marianne smirked. "And me? Small life, big space? Is that what you're saying?"

"I don't know. Maybe. You only do things for other people. Maybe I think that's strange."

"And maybe I think you're selfish," her sister said.

Eliza smiled. "I know you do. You always have."

"You steal Halloween candy. And Easter baskets."

"I didn't say you were wrong." Eliza had stolen candy from her older sister through the whole of their shared childhood. "I admire you, you know. In so many ways. But I have this feeling," she said, looking out the window at the lights reflecting off the clouds rolling in from the ocean. "Something wonderful is going to happen here. Something impossible."

And it had to, because this cramped apartment was the last place Eliza would ever live alone. When she wasn't careful, she felt the future closing in on her, and it didn't feel kind.

Harry

Harry had been promising to visit Steven and his wife Mallory for as long as they'd been living in Bethel. Failing to ever follow through on that promise had been part of their ongoing cycle of ease and silence. Once Steven had gotten his diagnosis, it had been part of Harry's bargain with the universe. Steven couldn't die, not with so much left unsaid and so many promises left to keep.

He sent Steven an email from the train, apologizing. For not being in town when Steven got the news. For blowing off invitations to visit for years and always dragging him down to the supposed virtues of the city instead. And for vague, nebulous transgressions that seemed minor when they happened but felt huge now that there might be so little time to make up for them.

Steven responded within fifteen minutes with a message containing some of the most impressive profanity Harry had ever seen. Especially coming from Steven, who was usually calm and unflappable. Steven cursed Harry, his parentage, his manners, and his presumption that Steven was dwelling on his past or his illness.

Harry knew the screed was meant, at least in part, to make him feel better. It didn't quite work.

♦

Steven picking him up at the station made it worse.

"I was perfectly prepared to take a cab," Harry said by way of greeting. He spluttered with irritation as Steven grabbed his bag and tossed it into the backseat of the car.

"There's long list of things I'm happy to let you be angry about, but my not being bedridden isn't among them." Steven climbed into the driver's seat and pulled the door closed.

"Double negative," Harry muttered as he got in the car himself.

He darted glances sideways at Steven as they pulled away from the station. He was well aware that none of them looked the way they had when they were twenty, but Steven, it always seemed, had changed the least.

Both Harry and Dennis had grown rather soft. Meryl looked the best she had in her life. But even with the chemo that had left him with greying stubble under his knit ski cap Steven seemed to be a face out of time. His features were still strong, his skin only slightly lined. Some days that was comforting. Today, Harry felt spooked, as if Steven had stepped out of the stream long ago, leaving him to go on alone.

"Harry." Steven's voice snapped Harry out of his reverie.

"What?"

"I'm glad you're here. But this trip is not a pilgrimage. It won't be when I'm sicker either."

There were so many things Harry wanted to say, and all of them were horrible. How long? Why this town, so far from New York? But what came out was, "Did you really have to ruin Christmas?"

Steven made a derisive sound. "You don't even like Christmas."

"Fine, New Year's."

Steven gave him a lopsided smile. "You'll be fucking Meryl like you do every year. That won't change whether I'm there or not. Unless you can talk your new girlfriend into going?"

This was what Harry got for emailing his friends with updates on his angst over his new coworker. He'd well earned the teasing about Eliza. But he didn't know where to start with Steven's comment regarding Meryl. Steven had always been slightly judgmental about the two of them, and not without reason. Discussing — *defending* — Eliza was so much easier.

"She's not my girlfriend and no, I am not subjecting her to the Miscreants for anything."

Steven shrugged. "Suit yourself."

"You're being awfully passive aggressive."

"Did someone tell you death is enlightening? Because if they did, they were lying."

"I'm not used to you being sharp. I don't like it," Harry said. He felt so helpless. "And why do you even care what Meryl and I do?"

Steven took a deep breath. "Because once or twice it was me."

"That was a long time ago," Harry said. "And for all of a month on summer holidays." He hadn't expected the topic to come up so soon. Or even, for all his regrets and bargains, at all.

"It was."

"Are you jealous?" Harry didn't know why he said it. The question seemed cruel, unnecessary, and not one he wanted the answer to. But if quiet, even-tempered Steven, who was more often than not a balm against the world, was going to speak to wound so would he.

"No," Steven said. "But that doesn't mean a man can't acknowledge that the past never really goes away."

"Are we actually talking about this?" Harry turned his head to stare out the window.

"We don't have to. But we should, perhaps. Some day. Looking back on that year now seems different than it used to."

"It was decades ago. Of course it seems different," Harry snapped.

"I didn't behave as well as I could have."

"Well, neither did I. Neither did anyone! We were nineteen."

"Why did you never wind up with anyone, Harry?"

"Because I don't like people. Not because I was pining over you."

Steven shook his head and let out a long breath. "Look, next year, things may change."

"Is there any scenario where that's an improvement?" Harry asked bluntly.

"A few. I'm going to be fine for a while. The doctor said if we manage it right, I might even have four or five years left. Just, when it happens, it's going to happen fast, and there's no guarantee I'll get that long. And I don't want you idiots having to find me medical care in a city devoid of everyone but German tourists and our miserable book club of disreputable middle-aged drunkards."

"My German is very good," Harry volunteered.

"Your German is shit."

Harry was, inappropriately, put in mind of Eliza.

♦

Steven and Mallory's house was a new construction, a depressingly suburban colonial in a cul-de-sac. There was nothing to set the house apart from the other ones on the street, unless it was an even greater spareness and anonymity in the landscaping. In one of the neighbors' backyards a dog barked. The people next door had wrapped the railing of their front porch in fake, fall-colored leaves.

Mallory was in the kitchen, a dishtowel tossed over her shoulder as she stirred something at the stove. When Steven and Harry stepped into the room, she kissed Steven and said hello to Harry with a kiss to his cheek.

"Harry," she said.

"Mallory." They exchanged smiles, though Mallory's wasn't very enthusiastic. Harry could hardly blame her. She looked tired, though given the situation she was confronting, Harry knew *he* would look a good deal worse than tired. She had chin-length purplish-red hair and eye makeup that was several shades darker than what the rest of the women in their social circle considered tasteful. Not that Steven had ever chosen his lovers based on what others would think. The Miscreants had called her 'the child' when Steven had first met her going on five years ago now. The nickname hadn't been about her age — she was the same age as Steven — but about her fashion choices. That had felt unkind at the time. Now, knowing her current struggles and the grief that was in store, Harry knew it had been downright cruel.

"How was the train?" she asked him.

"Dreadful," Harry replied with a sigh. Harry liked Mallory, as he would have liked almost any person who found themselves drawn to and compatible with Steven. Plus, she had always shared his weariness and exasperation with the world in a way Steven, with all his gentleness and patience, never had. It was one of the reasons, he suspected, that she liked him better than she did the rest of the Miscreants. She was always freer with her tongue whenever she managed to separate Harry from the herd. Even if she had found out about her nickname when Meryl had accidentally included her in a group email about her.

"There's not much scenery to look at this time of year," Mallory said. "Especially with the weather we've been having."

"There's not much to look at any time of the year. Why on earth did you let Steven drag you all the way out here?" he asked.

"So I'd have to put up with all of you less. Coffee?"

Dinner was stilted, the conversation stiff and awkward. Harry thought that was rather less about him, and more about Mallory and Steven not knowing how to deal with the outside world interacting with their own private one. Harry couldn't help them with that and so strove to be as charming and normal a guest as possible, sharing stories from Frankfurt and his general dismay at Philippe's latest brainstorms.

Their conversation was interrupted by Harry's phone ringing. Apologizing, he moved to silence it, until he saw that it was from Anika.

"I really should take this," he said. He wondered if the publisher had decided to take one more last-minute issue with his Brittany book. Or maybe Anika had finished his Vienna book and had thoughts she wanted to share?

"Special someone?" Mallory asked.

"The specialest." He used his most cloying voice. "My agent."

Harry stepped out onto the back deck to take the call. It was dark now, and he gave an involuntary shiver in the chilly New England November evening.

"If this is about the Brittany book, the answer is no," he said.

"Actually, it's about your Vienna manuscript," Anika replied.

"And?" Harry asked, not without trepidation. He'd almost reached fifty, and he still had terror every time anyone gave him feedback about a new piece of work.

"What's going on with you?" Anika asked.

"What do you mean, what's going on with me?" Harry asked. She probably didn't want to know he was freezing his balls off in his dying friend's backyard in a particularly stultifying part of Connecticut.

"It's...workmanlike."

"Midlist author, midlist book," Harry offered, unenthused about being the butt of his own joke.

"You've always been better than your sales, Harry. And this isn't quite your best work."

"Not quite my best work, needs some revisions? Or not quite my best work...." Harry left it hanging.

"It's a piece of shit."

"Excuse you." Harry stood up straighter, laughing, even as a piece of him shriveled up, just a little, at the criticism. He trusted Anika, and she probably wasn't wrong.

"There's no hook, your themes are tenuous at best, and you somehow fell in love with the passive voice. What is up with that, by the way?"

"I was in Frankfurt?" Harry tried. As far as he was concerned, the German love for the passive voice was endemic.

"Yeah, for five days, after you sent this in. I mean, it's not hopeless, we can work with this, but you're going to want to do some thinking on what this book is about. Preferably before you blow by the due date. Which, it's my job to remind you, is coming up."

Harry dutifully agreed, and they set a time to talk more about the book once he returned to New York. After he hung up he stood on the porch, his arms folded on the railing, and stared into the quiet, uneventful, Connecticut evening.

That the Vienna manuscript wasn't his best work wasn't news to him. Harry had spent seven slightly miserable days there a year ago, battling a cold and trying to find something new and interesting to say about the city and all its terribly grown-up nightlife. He'd been suspecting he had failed, but had hoped that he was wrong on that point. Evidently not.

Vienna was perfect for him, in theory at least. A spectacular city for anyone over forty, Vienna in all its sophistication and East-West fusion was supposed to have been about enjoying his age. But now, one of his best friends was dying. His own body, though healthy, was creakier than it had been. And what did he have to show for any of it? Travel memoirs that sold decently enough to keep contracts coming in, but not enough to make any sort of name for himself? An unremarkable career minding other people's publication schedules? Who would want to read about that set against a fairly provincial outpost of a lost Europe?

Harry had more time left than Steven, but what was he actually going to do with those years except more of exactly the same?

No wonder his Vienna book wasn't about anything, he thought as he slid open the door and stepped back into the warmth of Steven and Mallory's kitchen. Beyond weariness, he didn't even know what his own life was about.

♦

Late that evening, after Steven and Mallory had gone to bed, Harry fled into the shower in the guest bathroom to stop himself from listening for their whispers amongst the sounds of the house. He was getting out when his phone, balanced on the edge of the sink, chirped with a text notification. Securing a towel around his waist, Harry unlocked it. This late he would normally ignore texts, but with the recent call from Anika, he didn't want to take his chances and miss anything that might be important.

To his very great surprise, the text wasn't from Anika or Meryl or Jonathan or anyone else Harry might have expected to hear from at this hour. It was from Eliza, and all it said was *WTF?*

Had she accidentally sent him a message meant for someone else? Something told him no. She was too precise for that. He jabbed at the screen to text her back. *If you mean what the fuck am I doing in Connecticut wondering why you're texting me on a weekend, I have no idea.*

Visiting family? came her reply.

Harry tugged his towel a little tighter around his waist and sat down on the edge of the tub. Texting one's colleague — no matter how temporary — while essentially naked in a bathroom probably violated all sorts of puritan workplace ethics considerations. But it was the twenty-first century, which was persistently terrible, and as long as he didn't actually inform her of the setting of their chat it was, he supposed, fine. At least for her.

Sort of, he texted Eliza. *What's going on? Assuming you didn't mean to message someone else.*

Philippe. What the fuck?

Harry smiled at the persistent profanity. He hadn't expected her to be foul-mouthed, and he was delighted by it. *While clarifying, please, clarify more,* he typed back.

I just got off the phone with him.

Hahahahahaha.

You're not helping, Harry.

I know. Sorry. Why were you talking to him outside of business hours? What did he do? And what do you need?

I wish I knew, her reply came.

He had expected a screed about the food truck issue, but this, in all its quiet, pulled him up short. "So do I," Harry muttered at his phone. "So do I."

Eliza

"Who are you texting?" Marianne asked. She was sitting with her tablet in the somewhat battered armchair, while Eliza sat cross-legged on her bed, her phone and laptop on the duvet in front of her. A bottle of wine and two glasses sat on the nightstand between them.

Eliza wished, not for the first time, that she was alone. *I should have considered the implications of inviting my sister to stay for the night with me in my studio apartment*, she thought.

"A coworker," she said.

"Wasn't that awful call enough? It's a Friday night. And you just started working there. Is this really necessary?"

"I'm keen," Eliza said drily.

"No, you're a book nerd with workaholic tendencies. Different issue."

"Okay, well, keen and annoyed. I asked Harry for an author to be a test case, he gave me Philippe, and I'm pretty sure I'm getting pranked."

"I take it Philippe's side of the conversation was worse."

"Considerably."

"What does he write?" Marianne asked.

"Cookbooks, duh!" Eliza said.

"Well, that would explain the food truck angle."

"But I am *not* getting him a food truck," Eliza stated.

"Can't he get his own food truck?"

"You'd think. He's Philippe!"

"Philippe who?" Marianne asked.

"Philippe Philippe. You know. The French guy with the jarred sauces and those ridiculous TV commercials."

"Oh *him!*" Marianne said. "I didn't know he worked with your publisher."

"They're not my publisher, they're my client. And yes, he does. I knew Harry was going to be a pain in my neck, but I didn't expect him to be quite so thorough about it."

"So you were texting…?"

"Harry," Eliza supplied.

"Mhmmm."

"What?" Eliza looked over at Marianne to see her faint smirk.

"Is this the same Harry you went out with for a beer breakfast in Frankfurt?"

When had Eliza told her that story? *Inviting her here was definitely a mistake.* "Yes," she admitted.

"Excellent!" Marianne bounced out of the armchair and onto the bed next to Eliza.

"Excellent *what*?"

"Not only have you met a dashing bookseller, you've met one you're going to see every day!"

"Which is good why?"

"Because he sounds lovely," Marianne gushed.

"I've hardly told you a thing about him, and he's really not." *But he is*, a part of her mind argued. *Infuriating and confusing and lovely.*

"Mm. Interesting, then. And you need an interesting man in your life."

"I have Cody," Eliza reminded her sister.

Marianne shook her head. "Cody isn't interesting. He's appropriate, and that's different. And where in the guide to making advantageous marriages does it say your fiancé has to be interesting? Nowhere."

"Cody's interesting."

"Mmph." Marianne clearly disagreed. "If he's talking about himself, then sure. Otherwise…." She let it hang there.

Eliza was torn between offense on Cody's behalf and a not-so-small amount of relief that someone else had voiced what she had so often thought. Even if it was her sister, who had terrible opinions about everything.

Eliza loved Cody, she did; he wasn't perfect, but then who was? No one else she had ever met, that was certain.

"You don't disagree," Marianne said to the silence.

"What's your goal?" Eliza asked. Agreeing with her sister about anything was unsettling. "Cody and I are getting married. That's not going to change because you think — what? That he's boring?"

"Oh, I'm not trying to break you two up," Marianne said breezily. "I think he's an absolute trophy for you, even if maybe you're having the wedding too soon. But he has his career to think of and everyone likes married politicians."

"The wedding's not 'til next summer!" Eliza protested. Weddings of the sort they were having took a while to plan, and they were far from rushing things.

"Yes, and you've been engaged since last year," Marianne said. "Cody certainly knew a good thing when he saw it, and made sure to lock it in. If I worry about anything, it's that you're not cut out for what he's offering."

"I'm not cut out for your life, if that's what you mean," Eliza said, somewhere between offended and angry at the world for setting out such expectations for the both of them. For all women, really.

"That's not what I mean," Marianne said.

"Are you sure? Because wife of a politician with a very bright future, and the ability and security to do whatever I want? I think I am cut out for that."

"Yes, but…. Eliza." Marianne looked at her seriously. "Like you said. This tiny little apartment excites you. And while I don't understand it, I do see it. So I wonder, a bit, about what you're doing."

Harry

"You're up early," Steven said the next morning, when he found Harry once again leaning on the railing on the back deck.

The sky was the violet of dawn before the sun came up, and mist flooded the space between the house and the woods fifty yards behind it. It was cold, beautiful, and miserable, and Harry wished he could stay here and stew in his thoughts forever. Maybe this was why Steven had chosen godforsaken Connecticut to live out the rest of his days.

"So are you," Harry said irritably.

Steven gave half a shrug and came to stand beside him. "'I'll sleep when I'm dead' sort of has new meaning this month."

Harry said nothing.

"That was supposed to be a joke."

"It wasn't very funny." He could hardly sulk, though. Steven had never been good at jokes. There was absolutely no reason to expect dying would make him funnier.

They stood in silence for a long time. Harry wondered if Steven was working up to something or if he was waiting for Harry to finally make useful words himself. But what was there to say? That he wished Steven weren't dying? That he could imagine a world where this house was theirs? That here, in the quiet morning damp, he knew Steven could imagine it too?

"How are you coping?" Harry eventually asked. "Actually."

"Sometimes there's a lot of crying. Sometimes I forget it's going on. It's like anything, really."

"That sounds tedious."

"It's all tedious. Like your job, Dennis's bad attitude, and the cagey way Meryl conducts her personal life such that I never know what I'm supposed to talk to her about other than people she dislikes."

"Which is a bit of a sore point, I'd imagine." By now the great Mallory Email Mishap was almost funny, but it wasn't yet, and probably was never going to be. When this was all over, Harry suspected Mallory would never speak to any of them again.

"Tell me about the girl," Steven said.

"Why? It was a thing I brought up to distract from your little announcement on the list."

"Well, now I'm bringing it up because we're abysmal at having this conversation, and I want to change the topic. I also don't believe you."

"She's business-dinner-fluent in French and German, she has a Breton last name, and I'm absolutely sure I've met her somewhere before," Harry spat out, suddenly as irritated with Eliza's existence as he was with Steven's dying.

His friend grinned. "Oh, this is so much better than a midlife crisis! You're being crazy again."

Harry gave an exasperated sigh. "Why does no one remember that it was Dennis who almost got trampled by the ghost horse? I'm just the guy who assigned linear narrative to all that batshittery."

"No," Steven said. "You're the guy who paid for all the booze on that trip. You're still absurd. The lot of you. It was a real horse and some fog. That's it. And now you're going to drag some twenty-something into it because of her last name and your bad memory."

"My memory is very good."

"*Was* very good. You're getting old. Nothing is more annoying to me than the fact that I am going to die, and then I will just be dead, and therefore unable to tell you that you're crazy and wrong about everything."

Harry, Meryl, Dennis, and Steven had all gone to Europe one summer while they were still in college. That had been thirty years ago now, but it had been the foundation for so much that had happened since. Meryl had broken up with Harry on that trip. And Harry and Steven had gone on to do…whatever it was that they'd done. Harry still didn't have a label for it, and for a man at ease with his own queerness that had always bothered him.

They'd been in Ducey, walking along the Sélune by the bridge, when they'd encountered the now-infamous ghost horse. The night had been both dark and foggy, and Harry had heard the beast before the rest of them. And he had heard it, he was sure of that. Fog could play tricks with sound, but that horse wasn't one of them.

He'd gotten out of the way, Dennis very nearly hadn't, and Steven and Meryl both swore neither of them had seen anything. Harry had, though: A tall, grey horse, trotting through the swirling mist, with neither saddle nor bridle. He'd reached out to touch its mane as it went past, and while the horse had turned its head and fixed Harry with its gaze his hand had passed right through it. There had been nothing physically there, except maybe a colder, damper, more solid patch of fog. Goosebumps still broke out up and down his arms whenever he thought of it.

That horse was the reason Harry had become so enamored with Brittany and its ghost stories, why Anika found repping him so frustrating, and why Eliza's Breton name had struck him so forcibly. Coincidence was a thing that happened — forty-nine years of life was more than enough experience to teach him that. But this was, he felt, something different.

What it was though, he didn't know. So he stood at the porch railing with Steven, watched the morning fog lift from the Connecticut woods, and was cold.

♦

The return from Steven and Mallory's was even grimmer than the journey out, and Harry felt heavy in body and spirit by the time he opened the gate to the mews which held his house. One of the last such alleys in the city, Harry normally enjoyed this moment of celebrating his long-ago victory over the horrors of New York City real estate. But tonight the clink of the metal behind him as he disappeared onto a street most of the city didn't even know existed felt lonely.

He made his way down the row to the brick carriage house second from the end. A light came on in the house across the way. His neighbor also lived alone but, unlike Harry, was constantly interested in everyone else's business. A house out of time that strangers couldn't pass without permission seemed an odd place for a busybody, but what did Harry know? No matter how well he understood places and words, people were confounding.

With a shake of his head he unlocked his front door and flicked on all the lights. The house was bright and airy during the day, but at night it sometimes felt too wild, the small yard behind it alive with something dark of the woods long vanished from Manhattan island. Tonight not all the 100-watt bulbs in the world could keep loneliness and ghosts, much less Steven's cancer, at bay.

He hooked his keys onto the dark wood peg that stood out against the salmon walls with white trim and set his overnight bag down in the entryway. He could deal with it tomorrow. Right now, he wanted to wallow. But like a paperback mystery purchased at an airport, he wasn't sure if the murder of his sorrow should be handled with a scotch on the rocks in the library or a rare joint while he sat in the bath.

Harry slipped off his shoes and walked past the stairs and down the hall to his kitchen where his answering machine blinked at him, indicating a message. It was archaic, yes, and he used his cell phone for most communication, true, but there was something to be said for calls made and received without the illusion of urgency. Because there was an intimacy to it, Harry gave out the number sparingly.

He pressed play.

"Harry. Darling." Meryl drawled sarcastically from the machine. "My ivory tower has seen fit to send me north. Call me back and tell me you want to have drinks on Tuesday." There was a kissing sound, also somehow sarcastic, before she hung up.

Harry frowned at the short notice and the timing. Neurotically, he wondered what she knew about Steven's condition that he didn't. After all, at Yale they had all referred to her as their witch.

4

♦

In This Company of Exiles

Eliza

Marianne left Sunday afternoon. Eliza ordered takeout from a Mexican restaurant down the street and ate it sitting in the recliner, her legs tucked under her and her e-reader balanced on the arm of the chair. As the sun set — later than it had in Wales or Germany, but still early; fall was definitely sliding into winter — Eliza lay down on the bed and stared out the window. She watched, enjoying nothing so much as the silence and isolation of this room so many stories up, as the sky faded from orange to deep blue.

She was squinting, trying to figure out if a faint light in the sky was a star or an airplane, when her phone rang. A quick glance at the screen showed that it was Cody. *Probably home after a weekend at some big campaign event and wanting to talk about his latest fundraising numbers.*

Eliza was about to pick up the call, her thumb hovering over the answer button, when she realized she didn't have to. She could call Cody back later and apologize for being asleep or busy with work or a hundred other excuses. He wouldn't mind, not really. And this night, so quiet and lonely, could keep being hers.

She muted the ringer and dropped the phone on her nightstand. Then she stood up, pulled her pajamas out of the dresser that was wedged tightly between the bed and the window, and shut herself in the bathroom. She was going to take a long, hot bath, and then she was going to sleep, and it was going to be glorious.

◆

As the workweek began Eliza was glad she'd taken some quiet time. Monday morning was a flurry of meetings and phone calls with people who either didn't take her seriously or expected her to be the company's savior. She wasn't sure which was worse. Then there was the weekly staff meeting, full of her new colleagues being self-important, having no sense of time management, and being wildly skeptical of everything Eliza was there to suggest. Which irked her no end, though she did her best to maintain a polite and professional demeanor. Yes, she knew that no one at the company had considered using digital games or apps or indeed any social media platform founded after 2010. That was why she was proposing those ideas now. If the limited digital marketing they were doing now was actually working, they wouldn't have hired her.

Through it all Harry was there, sitting across from her at the table. Though he turned to face whoever was speaking, his face was drawn as if he was tired or worried. When he spoke, there was a sharp edge of irritation to his words.

What's wrong? Eliza wondered. Being back in New York and jetlagged would be enough to ruin even the sunniest disposition, which Harry decidedly did not have. But after their strange morning encounter in the pool in Frankfurt, and their breakfast afterwards, she felt a concern towards him that went beyond what a few short days of acquaintance via business trip might usually inspire. She suspected that whatever was going on with him now it wasn't merely about the dreariness of a Monday at the office. She hoped he hadn't gotten any more bad news about his friend.

He was the first one out of the room when the meeting was over, so at least Eliza didn't have to decide whether to say anything to him. She returned to her desk, silenced her phone, and spent the rest of the afternoon lost in work.

♦

"Don't tell me Philippe has you burning the midnight oil. Again."

Eliza looked up from her desk, realizing two things as she did. One, it had grown fully dark since the last time she took a break from her work, and two, she should have closed her office door after her last foray out for tea. Harry was in the doorway, leaning against the jamb with his arms folded easily across his chest. He still wasn't ebullient, but whatever had been bothering him earlier seemed to have gone from his face.

"Not quite," she admitted, finishing a sentence without looking at the keyboard and hitting the period key with a particularly victorious tap.

Harry straightened up and put his hands in his pockets. "What are you working on then?" he asked.

"I do have other authors I work with. Most of whom are perfectly pleasant and obliging individuals who do not want food trucks and road trips and book tours."

"I think that's the first time anyone has ever used 'pleasant,' 'obliging,' and 'authors' in the same sentence," Harry said. "And if you're really here at eight in the evening doing actual work for this company, I'm going to doubt whether you're human."

"Maybe I'm not," Eliza said, falling into the same charged banter that had come so easily with him from the beginning.

"Maybe you're not, at that." Harry looked at her face square on, his eyes meeting hers and holding her gaze for far longer than was polite.

Eliza felt her cheeks go warm, not because she was embarrassed but because his face — his look — was just so *much*. There was an energy to him, a fire, that radiated beyond the confines of his body. He was an attractive man, that was undeniable, but whatever made Eliza feel that something in her soul was calling to something in his was beyond his looks.

She judged herself for the absurd thought. "I'm trying to write," she blurted, needing to break the silence and whatever force kept her eyes locked to Harry's.

"Ah." Harry also seemed to struggle to snap out of the strange trance that had ensnared them both. He shook himself like a man emerging from the water and resumed the tone of their earlier repartee. "Oh, God, don't do that. Hasn't publishing taught you anything?"

Eliza frowned. "I write, you know. I just do this too. I don't judge you, so don't judge me."

"You absolutely judge me." His laugh was warm, like chocolate, but without any sugar in it.

"Fair." She smiled and glanced down for a moment at her keyboard. "But am I wrong?"

"No, you're not. Fair indeed." Harry echoed.

Eliza sighed, but not really with annoyance. Maybe with relief? Her concentration had been broken anyway, and now that Harry was here she had to admit to herself she didn't mind his conversation. "If you're going to stay there bothering me, you might as well sit down," she said.

"No, you're working, I've taken up enough of your time. I can go —" Harry gestured over his shoulder.

He really would, Eliza thought. He, unlike so many people, really did seem to value her time as much as his own.

"It's fine," she said. "I could use a break."

Harry sat down in the chair across from her desk. "Why I came in here — I'm sorry I threw Philippe at you. He's the right choice for your project by all objective standards and as far as your job goes too. But still, I'm sorry."

"Thank you," Eliza said, surprised. She'd expected neither the apology nor the grace with which it was offered.

"If you want my advice about dealing with him…." His voice trailed off. "Do you want my advice?"

"If I said no would it stop you?"

Harry considered. "Yes," he said.

"Let's hear your wisdom then."

"Don't flatter him. It puffs him up too much. I know it seems the easiest way to get him to like you and be agreeable, but most people, I suspect, just want to be seen. Ask him how he is and then, no matter how much it pains you, listen to his answer. If he starts nattering about sauces and books and business, stop him until he gives you an answer that seems to reasonably belong to a person who isn't a C-list celebrity. It's kind enough. And he'll deflate a little."

"And is that successful? When you do it?"

"When I can manage it. But I'm not patient. Or —" he gestured to her.

"A woman?"

"Yes. I'm sorry. It's all horrible isn't it?"

Eliza shrugged. There was little point in discussing it. "This is hardly my first job, Harry."

"Yes. Of course. You said you could use a break." Harry crossed his legs. "What are you writing?"

Eliza hesitated. With many people — even, and maybe especially, with many people who worked in publishing — she wouldn't have answered. She got so much flak for writing what she did that it often wasn't worth it to let someone new in. But if she trusted anyone to be kind about this, it was, somehow, Harry.

"An essay," she admitted.

"Personal?"

Eliza nodded. "That dread domain of women."

Harry scoffed. "About what?"

"My family's beach house." She paused to give Harry one last chance to betray boredom or judgment. But he merely sat there, his head tilted ever so slightly to the side, his eyes fixed on her. Listening.

"I mean, not the house itself," she went on. "My grandparents owned it — my parents do now. We spent all our summers there when I was growing up. And it's just, it's the worst of everything I hate about New England. The money and the property and the performance of it all. Dinner parties my sister and I weren't allowed to attend until we weren't children anymore. Still in the school room.... It sounds silly, but sometimes my childhood feels like it happened in another century."

Harry chuckled, but it wasn't cruel. "Like *Pride and Prejudice* with different dresses?"

"Yes, yes! Exactly like that. But it was also...it *is* also...." Eliza glanced down at her laptop screen; it had gone black while she'd been talking and she absently tapped the trackpad to wake it back up. "It's very beautiful. And very beautiful things are dangerous. You can't trust them. It's where I learned to swim."

"It's on the Cape?" Harry guessed.

Eliza nodded.

"Beautiful and dangerous, indeed then. You must be a strong swimmer, if that's where you learned. The riptides are notorious."

He wasn't wrong, but Eliza shook her head. "The water is the only place I've ever been able to be something other than what's expected of me, and I've never known how to reconcile the wildness of that place — of that ocean — with the cloistered cruelty of the world that gave it to me."

"I know exactly what you mean," Harry said.

"Do you?"

"It was like that where I grew up too. Look, are you planning on staying much longer?"

"Why?" Eliza was flustered by his change in tack.

"Because I'm starved and was going to order Chinese. You want in?"

Harry

"Despair doesn't suit you, Harry," Meryl said.

The day after he and Eliza had eaten takeout together in his office, Harry and Meryl were sitting in Harry's living room, not entirely comfortably. They so rarely saw each other in their respective homes, and when they did Harry never felt like he even knew how to arrange his limbs.

He shifted irritably in his Eames chair and tried to figure out what to say. He hated sharing a house with anyone else, and a guest who could wind up in his bed was particularly awkward, no matter how close he and Meryl were and no matter how clear their understandings. Meryl was across from him, her cane resting against the arm of the settee on which she sat.

Harry was all for shared experience — food, travel, music. After all, that was how he, Meryl, Steven, and Dennis had bonded in college. But shared domesticity, even the threat of it, made his skin itch. There were too many expectations in it that he didn't have the interest to deliver on. Luckily for their friendship Meryl was much the same. But that did little to diminish this current awkwardness. Perhaps it was just Steven's circumstances, but Meryl's presence in his city was sudden enough that Harry was waiting for her to announce bad news of her own.

"I'm not in despair," Harry protested when he could no longer get away with staring at the framed mid-century prints that littered his walls. But his words were in vain, and he knew Meryl knew it.

She held out her empty glass. Harry took it, glad for the excuse to busy himself at his sideboard refreshing their drinks. "I have work to do," he continued as he poured her another two fingers of scotch over a single perfect ice cube. "Actual, productive work that doesn't involve my incessant navel-gazing. But I have to go back to Vienna if I'm to have any hope of fixing this book."

"So go to Vienna." Meryl was often a comfort to Harry, but she rarely had any time for his whining. Not that he had any intention of letting that stop him.

Harry handed Meryl her glass back, but didn't sit down again. He felt too restless. "I have finite vacation time, I don't want to go, and all I can think is that Steven will never travel outside the continent again," he said.

"Don't be morbid."

"I'm being truthful. And since when do you want me to be gentle?"

"I always, always want you to be gentle with me," Meryl teased. "I just think you should be a little less gentle with the world. You could do so much more."

"Yes, and everything I'm doing already irritates me. Why add to it?"

"I don't irritate you," Meryl said.

"No, you don't," he admitted. "Although I'm fairly sure you irritate nearly everyone else."

Meryl laughed. "Just because I accidentally complained about Mallory in an email *to* Mallory before I realized Steven was going to marry her is no reason to hold a grudge. If I had wanted to offend her, I would have done it much better. And I've been very nice since!"

"You're still proud of that." Harry needled her. Meryl was an imp.

"I can be proud of it, or I can confront the possibility I am too old to use email properly. I'll take the first, thanks."

"Why are you here?" Harry asked, thinking the better of it even as the words left his mouth. "I'm sorry. That was rude. You know I'm always glad to see you."

"No you're not. Not here, at least."

Harry finally sat down again. "Meryl."

"We're much better far from anywhere either of us call home," she said with a smile.

"That's true. You also broke up with me in Brittany."

"That was part of us being better."

"And that's *very* true." Oh, but Harry did love her. There was just no *in* about it. No matter how old they got, they would always be feral teenagers together.

"So," she said, suddenly studying her fingernails. "About that."

"Mmmm?" Harry said with some trepidation.

"How would you feel if home was the same place for both of us?"

Harry tried not to choke on his scotch. "Come again?"

"Columbia wants me."

Harry took a deep sip of his drink, but said nothing. He didn't know how he felt, and he didn't trust his voice.

"It means relocating here, Harry."

"Obviously," he said to stall for time. He sat up a little straighter, blinked, and then wondered if he was holding himself too still. Did he seem nervous? Worried?

"Is that going to be a problem?" she asked, slowly, as if she was already judging him for any number of things.

"Why would that be a problem?" Harry attempted casualness; Harry failed.

"Familiarity breeds contempt?"

"Meryl."

"Fine. Your frightened eyes."

"My life works very well the way it is," Harry said. But the truth was his life was changing, and right now it didn't seem to be working at all. Steven was leaving this world faster than anyone wanted. His literary career was, if not at a crossroads, at least at a slightly peculiar juncture. And his work life, never before a source of surprise, involved a woman he couldn't stop thinking about. "If you're closer, do we work better or worse?" Harry asked.

"We'll have to find a bar we like," Meryl said, as if to acknowledge the awkwardness of the evening without naming it.

"And Italy?" Harry asked. Every winter the Miscreants spent the holidays there. And Harry and Meryl spent every such holiday sleeping together. Their time together there — in bed and out of it — was oddly and desperately important to him. Not because of any wish for things to be different between them, but because of the ritual of it and the refuge, always waiting there for them in the dark end of the year.

Meryl waved a hand as if to say he was silly to worry. "I love you too, you insufferable idiot. There's a reason I only fuck you when we're both on holiday."

"Really, and what's that?"

"If I move here, you think the question is about the utility for you of my being closer. But I think, that if I move here, the question is about what the inherent nature of our interactions is. Regardless of where I'm based."

"The what's-it-all-for question," Harry said warily. Perhaps, just as he and Steven had needed to discuss awkward things, so too did he and Meryl.

He was saved by having to go through with any such act by his cell phone ringing. It was on an end table halfway across the room, and he muttered his thanks as Meryl reached for it and handed it to him.

He was nonplussed to see that it was Philippe. That he had Harry's personal cell phone number was a testament to his sales figures and persistence, but Harry still let the call go to voicemail. Meryl, who knew his habits of avoidance both professional and personal, raised an eyebrow at him over the rim of her glass.

"Business or pleasure?" she asked.

He let out an annoyed breath. "Certainly not the second."

Once the voicemail icon appeared on his phone he put it on speaker and played the message back so Meryl could share in his misery. It was more or less exactly what he'd expected: Confusion over various deadlines for his next three releases, misunderstandings of instructions, and several less-than flattering mentions of Eliza.

"He sounds lovely," Meryl observed.

Harry scooped up the phone and composed a text, not to Philippe, but to Eliza.

I've just had a call from your favorite test case. Is there something we need to talk about?

He didn't expect an answer right away, but his phone chimed almost immediately. He nearly fumbled it out of his hands in surprise.

I tried your advice. It didn't work.

Despite himself, Harry chuckled. Meryl watched him keenly. "The maligned Eliza?" she guessed. "Is that the girl you emailed us about from Frankfurt?

"Mm." Harry typed back, *What happened?*

There was a long pause as Eliza typed. Harry didn't dare look up at Meryl, but he was keenly aware of her gaze on him as he waited. Finally, the message appeared.

I proposed a food-truck-themed cooking game app. Philippe was not impressed. I pointed out that I've seen his royalty statements, we're not his only income stream, and that while I personally hadn't priced out food trucks, if he wants one so badly he can probably get one on his own. And now he's mad that no one priced out food trucks before we told him no.

How does he know no one priced out food trucks? Harry texted back.

Come now, Harry. Eliza's reply came almost immediately. *FOOD TRUCKS. I love them too, but really.*

Harry had to swallow back a bark of laughter. Eliza really was too wonderful. And Philippe was too terrible. Though someone — Harry, really — should probably have run the numbers on Philippe's proposed adventure, if only to cover this eventuality.

Meryl spoke as he considered his reply. "Should I infer anything from the fact you're texting her after hours when I know for a fact you avoid work like the plague any time you're not in the office?"

"You should also know that we ordered food in at the office last night and spent three hours sitting and talking. And eating too, I suppose." Harry looked up at his friend. "She's one of the very few people I've never wanted to avoid. I feel like I've known her forever, but that's simply not possible, and I can't stop thinking about her."

"And what on earth am I supposed to infer from *that*?" Meryl asked, sounding somewhere between shocked and amused. "Harry Sargent, sounding like a schoolboy with a crush."

"Whatever it is," Harry said without thinking, "it's not just a crush."

Eliza

Over the course of the next few days Eliza only saw Harry in passing, in the hallways or in the little kitchenette when they happened to be refueling on caffeine at the same time. Whenever they did run into each other, Harry nodded and smiled and asked politely how she was. There was a caution about him that hadn't been there before, as if he'd been as unsettled by the ease of their late-night dinner and conversation as she had been.

Eliza felt like she should be glad for that; Harry seemed to understand her too well for her own comfort. She didn't make friends easily, in large part because she struggled to find things she held in common with other people.

Except with Harry.

The next time she saw him for an extended period was in the next weekly staff meeting. He seemed to be in a better mood this time, making jokes and sarcastic asides which were received with varying degrees of amusement and exasperation by everyone else around the table. Which made her feel safe to open an email and send him a message while they were listening to Ioanna, their boss's executive assistant, give them updates on her behalf

This is the second week Ioanna's run this show. Does our boss even exist? And does she ever come to these meetings?

A few minutes passed before Harry noticed the email, but when he did Eliza saw the corner of his mouth quirk up before he tapped something out on his keyboard. A new message appeared in her inbox.

Oh, no. She never comes to anything at all. Most of the staff is convinced she doesn't actually exist.

Have you ever met her? Eliza replied.

Once. I think? It was a long time ago. I'm not convinced it was really her, perhaps she hired a body double.

Eliza glanced across the conference table at Harry. He was sitting with his hands folded in front of him, watching a department head drone on with a look of polite concentration and an air of extreme innocence. Eliza bit her lip to hide her smile.

*And her name is *Charley?**

Eliza ignored whoever was talking now in favor of watching Harry glance at his laptop screen, flex his fingers, and start typing.

It is. And if you're wondering if the whole situation is one big Charlie's Angels joke, be assured you're not alone.

Eliza had to fake a coughing fit to cover her laugh.

She then sorted through her inbox and only half-listened while someone else informed them of an industry cocktail hour in December that their collective presence was very strongly desired at. Another email from Harry appeared.

Oh goodness. A holiday cocktail party. Spare me.

Surely it can't be that bad, Eliza typed back, though personally she doubted it.

Surely it can, Harry replied.

Perhaps we should go together, then, Eliza offered.

And stand in the corner being as badly behaved as we are right now?

More or less.

When Eliza looked up from her laptop again, Harry caught her eye and shot her a smile that showed his teeth.

♦

The term 'holiday cocktail hour' was, of course, a misnomer; it would definitely last longer than an hour. And despite the twinkling lights, fake fir garlands and gold and silver baubles strung up around the bar — and the fact that Christmas was barely a week away — there was no additional holiday slant to the event. Eliza wasn't quite sure why she had to be here and was already regretting her choice of shoes. An evening in a hotel bar with the rest of New York publishing and annoyingly watery drinks was no one's idea of a good time.

Still, the evening wouldn't be a complete waste. Face time was always good, especially with her life as an itinerant consultant. She never knew where she might meet her next client or the person who would introduce her to them.

And Harry was there. They hadn't yet found a secluded corner in which to trade snark, but Eliza was sure that was a matter of time. For now she could make her own requisite small talk while watching Harry out of the corner of her eye.

Harry turned from conversation to conversation with polished ease. In itself, that was nothing remarkable. What was notable was the way Harry was going about it: A casual hand on someone's elbow. His head tilted to the side as he listened to someone talk. Or his head tilted down so that, even at his height, he could blink and look at someone through his eyelashes.

Harry was *flirting*. Not with any intent, as far as Eliza could tell. But here was a man doing what she had always done at this kind of event, for, she had to assume, the same reasons: To get what was wanted. In the cloistered, regulated environment of her girlhood — and now her adulthood — Eliza had despaired about her tactics being dictated by her gender. But here was Harry, calmly doing everything she had learned to do. The sight was a relief on a soul-deep level she hardly had words for. They were alike in ways she was still realizing.

He was wrapping up a conversation with a silver-haired man in a double-breasted suit that didn't quite fit the occasion. Eliza considered breaking off her own chat to go suggest they refill their drinks and find a quiet corner to retreat from everyone else. But before she could make a move, Harry lifted his eyes and met her gaze across the room. Eliza felt herself blush. She'd been staring, and now she'd been caught.

She stayed where she was, heedless of the conversation still happening at her elbow, while Harry made his way over to her. Eliza shifted her weight in preparation for turning to face him fully. She was trying to think of something to say when the heel of one of her hated shoes slipped and she gave an almighty wobble, complete with spilling her drink and nearly swinging her clutch into someone's face.

If she'd been blushing before, her cheeks were burning now. She apologized to all around her as gracefully as she could while also trying to get her shoe back on her foot and attend to the spill with inadequate cocktail napkins. Harry, the bastard, merely stood and watched, though if Eliza were honest with herself she would have hated him if he'd sprung to the rescue.

"How's your evening going?" he asked mildly when she had more or less collected herself.

"Fine, until you came over here," Eliza shot back.

"My apologies," Harry said, without the hint of a smirk on his face.

Eliza considered whether she might hate him anyway. "Have you had any successes tonight?" she asked.

"For myself, or for the company?"

"I would hope for yourself."

Harry did smile at that. "A few hints of interest. Some promises of future meetings. We'll see. You?"

Eliza shook her head. "The usual. Shaking hands. Making friends."

"I'm surprised you even came," Harry said. "It's not like you actually work for us. You wouldn't have incurred anyone's wrath if you hadn't gone. Or at the least left early."

"Meeting people today is good for having work next month. Or next year. Consulting being what it is."

"So this is what you do?" Harry asked, turning so that they faced the room together and his shoulder very nearly brushed hers. "Go from company to company, telling them to modernize and fuck tradition?"

That Harry cursed was no surprise to Eliza at this point, but hearing it was still a delight. Especially with him standing there looking so polished and mild-mannered. "More or less."

The reality, of course, was that with her impending marriage to Cody she couldn't tie herself to a long-term career in New York or most anywhere else. Contract work could move with her. A settled job…that would be harder.

"Sounds dreadful," Harry observed. "Having to start fresh every year or so."

"It's not my ideal," Eliza admitted. "Or at least, it's not supposed to be. Moving around so much, it's hard to feel like I belong anywhere. To a position or to a city. But maybe I don't. I get to travel so much, like to Wales. I have a lot of gratitude about those opportunities —"

Harry cut her off. "Fuck gratitude."

Eliza was taken aback. "Come again?"

"Fuck gratitude," Harry repeated. "What does it change? If you're grateful, keep doing what you're doing, and up your donations. Or do some damn activism, work for a non-profit. Telling me — telling anyone — you're grateful means nothing."

"What do you do?" Eliza was somewhere between offended and fascinated.

"How about we know each other a little bit better before I let you in to the charitable deductions portion of my tax return? My point is that expressing gratitude is not the same as demonstrating it."

"Do you think I don't know that?"

"No. But I think you were speaking from a script. You don't need to put on the performance of it with me. I'm not interested in it. I want to hear what you really think."

"All right, then," she said, feeling unbalanced and yet entirely at ease. "All that travel, all those experiences, but I never seem to put down roots. I'm the wrong sort of organism for that. I never feel like I'm *home*."

Harry nodded solemnly, glancing sideways at her. "I know what you mean."

"Do you?"

"I'm a grumpy middle-aged man who makes my livelihood from words. We're both from the same sort of place, and neither of us are at ease there. I know something about exile."

He said it like a joke, but Eliza knew he didn't really mean it as one, so she didn't laugh.

"Do you have plans for the rest of the night?" she asked.

"I was going to go home and stew over the mess of my Vienna manuscript. Why do you ask?"

"Do you want to go back to the office and order Chinese food again?" She hoped she didn't sound like she was asking him out on a date, although maybe she was. Mostly, she hoped he would say yes.

Harry smiled that small, feral smile that showed his teeth and that Eliza was learning meant that mischief was afoot. "I have a better idea."

◆

"How is going back to work a better idea when that's exactly what I suggested?" Eliza asked twenty minutes later as they stood on the sidewalk in front of their office building. The winter evening was cold and she tucked her gloved hands into the pockets of her coat as she looked up at the lit windows above them. Colored lights blinked in some of them, an attempt by their occupants to be festive.

"But this isn't what you suggested. Not exactly." Harry opened one of the big glass doors and held it for her. Then, instead of heading toward the bank of elevators, he led the way to the other side of the lobby and a flight of stairs running down to Eliza didn't even know where.

She soon found herself standing in a hallway she hadn't known existed. The corridor wasn't well lit and was punctuated here and there with doorways that looked like they might lead to store rooms. Or crime scenes. She knew if she had any sense at all, she'd be afraid.

"Are you going to tell me where we're going? Because this feels a little like a murder basement."

"You'll see in a minute." Harry strolled ahead of her down the hallway and stopped to peer through a little window set in one of the doors. "Good, we'll have it to ourselves. Here we are."

He paused to punch a code into a keypad on the door, and there was a soft mechanical whir as the door unlocked. Eliza followed Harry inside as he flipped on the lights. To her astonishment they were standing in a kitchen. Not a huge, industrial-sized one such that a restaurant or office cafeteria might use, but still big and gleaming and, as far as she could tell, well-stocked with equipment and food.

"What *is* this?"

"Secret test kitchen." Harry took off his coat and tossed it onto one of the stools that surrounded the central island. His suit jacket followed it.

Eliza had to tear her eyes away from watching him unfasten his cufflinks and roll up his shirt sleeves. "I don't know which of those words to ask about first."

"You can thank our beloved Philippe. Well, him and all our cookbook authors past and present. The powers that be need somewhere to make sure all those nice recipes work, and, of course, take photos of them. Hence...."

"Secret test kitchen," Eliza finished for him. "And so...we're going to cook? What, exactly?"

"If I'm not mistaken." Harry started opening cupboards. "We have a batch of Philippe's newest line of sauces in."

"You're joking," Eliza said.

"Only if you want me to be."

"I'm not great in the kitchen," Eliza confessed, watching as the small pile of implements and ingredients Harry laid out on the island grew.

"That's fine," he said easily. "Did you think I was going to bring you here and then make you work?"

I didn't know what to expect, Eliza thought. In manners and dress Harry was so like everyone she had ever lived around, and all of them would have expected a woman to cook. But he was so entirely different. His gentleness, laced as it was with alternating scorn and weariness, baffled her as much as it drew her in.

So she seated herself on one of the stools ringed around the central island. If Harry said he didn't expect her to help, she would sit right here and watch. She wasn't surprised, exactly, but she was impressed that he kept on working by himself. She'd been on many dates at many nice restaurants, but never had she had anyone make food for her like this: With their own hands, right in front of her, and evidently with a great degree of pleasure.

As he worked, Harry talked, narrating his actions as he diced vegetables and cracked eggs. The tone of his voice was instructive but mild; He wasn't trying to educate. He was just talking, as much to himself as to her. Eliza got the distinct impression that he talked this way when he was alone in his own kitchen.

Because Harry clearly did spend time in his own kitchen; his ease and skill made that evident. Watching his hands, Eliza felt like he was allowing her to see something very private, even intimate, about himself. *I've seen him shirtless in just his swim trunks, but even if I'd seen him naked it wouldn't be like this.* The thought made something at once pleasant and frightening shiver up her spine, and she felt her cheeks grow warm with embarrassment. It was hardly fair to think such things about a coworker who had escaped a stultifying event with her and was now making her dinner.

Actually, entirely fair, her traitorous mind informed her. *Not appropriate. But certainly fair.*

"Here, what do you think of this?" Harry plated an omelet, fluffy with farmer's cheese and herbs, and set the plate down in front of her with one hand and a knife and fork with the other. The utensils clinked softly together.

5

◆

Old News is a Terrible Way to Ring in the New Year

Harry

A few short days after the cocktail party — and after cooking for Eliza in the test kitchen — Harry paced his office. He was on hold with the airline: He was supposed to be flying to Italy tonight for Christmas, but unless he managed to change his flight the blizzard coming in was making it increasingly unlikely he was going anywhere. And he desperately wanted to get out of New York. Even if Steven wasn't going to be at the Manuscript Miscreants' annual holiday gathering and even if he still wasn't sure how he was supposed to feel about Meryl's relocation.

Harry felt a slight pang. If he succeeded in getting out of the city in time, it would be two weeks before he saw Eliza again. But she certainly had holiday commitments of her own. At least this way he wouldn't have to think about what he wasn't a part of.

What would it be like to go on holiday with her? that small, traitorous part of his mind, that had become much less small and much more traitorous in the past few weeks, asked. To not deal with the affable mayhem of his friends; to not stay in a large house that was still too small for all of them; to

71

spend the time instead, oh, he didn't know…in some little pensione somewhere. Outside of Florence, perhaps. Or south, towards Naples. Or the sun of Sicily. They could hike up to one of the old forts or go to one of the points where the seas met.

Harry was jolted out of his reverie by a ghostly shape drifting down the hallway toward his open office door. It was none other than the subject of his daydreams, wrapped in a misty grey sweater, looking unearthly in the morning light. *Like that damned ghost horse.*

"Hello," Harry greeted her. His phone, still playing hold music, was pressed to his ear.

She blinked at him. "I thought you were leaving today."

"I was. Am. Hopefully. Weather," Harry said with an explanatory gesture out the window where snow was already beginning to fall in thick, heavy flakes.

"Ah. Airline?" Eliza hovered in his doorway.

"Yes." Harry waved her into the office; if he was stuck waiting on hold forever, at least he could have some company. Assuming Eliza didn't have somewhere else she needed to be.

"Good luck, then," Eliza said, crossing the room to the armchair in the corner and settling down into it. She'd been sitting there much more often of late, whenever they ordered dinner in together and frequently during the day when she came in to grouse about Philippe or just bounce ideas off of Harry.

"What are you doing for the holidays?" Harry asked, perching himself on the edge of his desk.

"Back to Boston to visit my family. Of course." Eliza gave him a dry smile that didn't reach her eyes.

"Of course," he echoed. How well he remembered trekking back home over Christmas to see ageing relatives and attend stifling parties. He didn't imagine Eliza was looking forward to it any more than he had.

Eliza leaned her cheek on her hand. "My mother assures me that there will be an absolute whirl of social events and that there's no way I will have time to even think about being bored, so I shouldn't worry about packing as many books as I did last year." She gave an indelicate snort. "As though there's nothing better about the holidays than spending it schmoozing with people I don't know and share nothing in common with."

"Your father's business associates?" Harry hazarded a guess.

"Mhmm." Eliza looked like she was about to say something else, but changed her mind and looked out the window instead. "That snow is getting worse."

"Quite. You should —" he broke off his own sentence and stared at his feet, flustered and horrified. *You should come to Italy with me instead*, had been on the tip of his tongue. Which was the kind of thing he absolutely should not — must not — say.

Eliza glanced at him curiously. Harry wracked his brain for an idea.

"While I'm gone. *If* I'm gone," he amended gloomily. "There's a meeting tomorrow of reps for our mid-sized press association. You should go for me. Not to take notes or anything, Jonathan could do that if I needed. But you might make some useful friends. Or at least learn some useful things. And if you do, please, *please* send me snarky texts about it."

Eliza considered that for a moment. "I will," she said, finally. "On two conditions."

"What are those?"

"I get to call you to complain about Philippe, and next time you go to Rome, you invite me."

He stared at her. Had she read his mind? Been enjoying the same fantasies as he had been? *Hardly that*, Harry told himself stiffly. She was just being Eliza: Bright and sharp-edged and always with something funny and frank to say no matter the situation.

She'd fit in well with the Miscreants, Harry's oh-so-traitorous brain said.

He narrowed his eyes at her. "Deal."

♦

Twenty hours after he'd left his home, Harry finally trudged up the walk to the house in Trastevere. He hurt nearly everywhere, and he was in desperate need of a shower. So when his weary knock on the door was greeted with Dennis flinging an arm around his shoulders and dragging him inside, Harry had to take a deep breath not to snap at him. He let go of the handle of his roller bag and didn't even flinch when it clattered to the ground.

"I need a drink and a bath," he announced. "Preferably simultaneously."

Forty-five minutes later he was clean, dry, and much less grumpy. He also had a drink in hand because really, it was Christmas and why not.

All told, there were a dozen people in the house. Most were gathered in the living room, draped over sofas and each other with the ease of long familiarity. He could see a few of them in the kitchen, poking through cupboards and debating whether and when to make a supply run for groceries. Two more were kneeling together on the floor in front of the fireplace, surrounded by crumpled magazine pages and wood chips and arguing about the best way to build a fire.

Meryl rose elegantly from the sofa she had somehow staked out entirely for herself and embraced Harry warmly. She kissed him chastely on the mouth. "Welcome, weary traveler."

Harry let himself be pulled down next to her and put his head on her shoulder. As awkward as their last meeting had been, in Italy they always knew exactly what they were about. "What have I missed?"

"They've been arguing about who sleeps where," Meryl said, her tone half amused and half exasperated.

"Not enough bedrooms?" Harry surmised.

"You know them. There never are. But don't worry," Meryl said as she played absently with his hair. "You can come to bed with me tonight."

He twisted his head to look up at her, torn between contentment and a sudden uneasiness. He'd been looking forward to being with Meryl and enjoying their usual time together away from home — in bed and out of it. But now he was here, and faced with the usually delightful prospect, he couldn't help but be haunted by Eliza. He had no commitments to her, but he suspected he wouldn't be able to banish her from his mind.

◆

The next morning Harry sat at the kitchen table with a steaming cup of coffee at his elbow and his laptop open in front of him. In the quiet dawn hours before anyone else was awake, it should have been peaceful. Transcendent, even. But all Harry could think about was how wretchedly jetlagged he was, how the damp of the old house made his hands ache, and how Anika was right and his Vienna book absolutely, positively sucked.

He'd hoped that a re-read would restore his faith in it, or at least present him with a clear way forward. All he knew for sure, while he brewed another pot of coffee and tied his dressing gown more snugly, was that he was going to have to go back to Vienna. He wondered how he was going to swing that. His vacation time wasn't unlimited. Perhaps he could work remotely, as annoying as that would be. After all, no one at the publisher ever saw Charley in the office. Perhaps it was time for Harry to become an international person of mystery too.

He let his mind wander to Eliza; anything was better than dwelling on his clusterfuck of a manuscript. Her request and his promise to bring her here next time had only been a joke but perhaps a city was a city. Surely their joke — his wish — could accommodate Vienna as easily. He didn't know if she'd been there before, but decided to assume so. Otherwise she'd find yet another way to make a fool of him.

He leaned his chin on his hand and stared at the steam curling out of his fresh cup of coffee. He'd have to be particularly creative about the places he would show her. The Naschmarkt wouldn't be enough; he'd have to know the right stalls in the open-air market to bring her to. St. Stephen's and the daytime appeal of climbing its tower wouldn't impress her at all, but perhaps its strange late-night existence, when most of the sanctuary was bathed in purple light, would intrigue her. In the right season, Rathausplatz transformed into an ice rink would offer more than enough charm, but that was predicated on either of them knowing how to skate. Maybe Eliza could, but Harry had no such faith in himself.

He could see her now, sitting across from him at some restaurant, her fingers on the stem on a wine glass while they laughed about books they both hated. And then after dinner they would go back to their hotel, and Harry could thread his hands into her rich brown hair, and...

He growled at himself and took a gulp of the too-hot coffee. Maybe the heat would shock him back to his senses. Because apparently fantasizing about going on holiday with his publishing company's digital marketing consultant was something he did now, regardless of the fact that he'd never been on anything that could be considered a romantic holiday in his life.

But he wanted to be in her presence, whether that was at the office or in his home or wandering the streets of Vienna. In an effort to understand his own preoccupation, he paged through his memories. Eliza, curled up in the armchair in his office, her long fingers wrapped around a cup of tea and a teasing smile on her face. Eliza, cool and efficient in meetings. Eliza, on the plane back from Frankfurt, her eyes closed in sleep and her breathing soft. Eliza, the first time he'd met her, with her poise and her confidence and that strange familiarity that had unnerved him. No wonder he wanted her. His brain, his body... something in him was convinced he'd known her forever.

Maybe it's your soul a traitorous voice whispered from inside his own head.

"What on earth are you doing out here?"

Harry started. Meryl stood in the doorway to the kitchen, in silk pajamas and tousled hair. She'd been asleep when Harry slipped out of bed, and he'd tried not to wake her. But that had been hours ago. He waved blearily at his laptop and the cursor blinking maddeningly in the document that needed so much work.

She sighed with fond exasperation as she crossed the room and dropped a hand on the back of his neck. "Come back."

"I have to...." He trailed off as Meryl kneaded his skin, her fingernails scratching gently. He had so much to do and no idea how to achieve any of it. Steven was at home in Connecticut because he was dying, and here Harry sat having middle-aged angst and inappropriate dreams.

"Well, I'm going back to bed," Meryl said archly. "You do you, but that manuscript will wait."

Eliza

The storm that had almost delayed Harry's flight to Italy had ended, but another was pounding the East Coast as Eliza took the train from New York to Boston. *Thanks, climate change*, she thought as she watched the snow and wind scour the bare trees. At least Christmas would be white this year.

In Boston it was still snowing hard but the wind had calmed so that when she got off the train at South Station big, fluffy flakes settled in her hair and on her shoulders. Her phone buzzed in her pocket as she dragged her roller bag through the crowd of other passengers making their way off the platform and into the station. It was her sister, informing Eliza that she was waiting for her at the kiss & ride and to please hurry up before the weather worsened again.

Eliza found the car and climbed gratefully into its warmth. She didn't even manage to buckle her seatbelt before Marianne started rattling off the schedule for the week.

"So we're all having dinner with Cody's family tonight, the engagement party is Saturday —"

"I know that," Eliza protested. Their mother had been emailing them both for a week about all the upcoming events.

"— And Mom says to tell you the photographer is going to be at that too, but the actual posed shots for the newspaper announcement will be tomorrow and she's already made you an appointment for a bridal salon in February so you need to make sure you're in the country."

Eliza frowned. That, at least, was new data. "How are you?" she asked in lieu of responding. She hoped Marianne was as dismayed at being asked to relay all that information as Eliza felt to receive it.

"Terrible," her sister said.

"Why?" Eliza was genuinely concerned, but also hopeful that Marianne would let her into a life more internal than they usually discussed.

"Do you have any idea what it takes to get a child into the right preschool in the twenty-first century?"

That would be no, then. Eliza shook her head. "I didn't know there was any such thing as the right preschool. I mean, as long as it's safe…."

"Eliza!" Her sister was scandalized. "The right preschool is the right prep school is the right college. One wrong move and it's all for naught."

Eliza was pretty sure that wasn't true, and she swallowed down the urge to rattle off the studies linking childhood reading — not particular school facilities — to adult success. She didn't want to get into an argument, and she had something she wanted to confess to *someone*.

She took a calming breath and stared straight ahead. "I asked Harry to take me to Italy."

Marianne whipped her head around to look at her, briefly heedless of the road. "You can't do things like that until you've been married at least five years!"

"Are you joking?" Eliza asked, fairly certain she was not the least rational person in this car.

"When our kid is in school full-time, I am definitely having an affair," Marianne announced.

So much for my secrets.

♦

Eliza was met at the door by her mother, Catherine, who welcomed her with literal open arms and an air kiss. Her father came to the door, too, a gin and tonic already in his hand and a reluctant smile on his face. Catherine bustled Eliza into the living room, asking her about the train ride and if she was tired and whether she wanted a cup of tea. The moment gave Eliza the peculiar sense of being welcomed home, victorious, from a battle on some distant field.

Her father carried her bags upstairs for her, through neat rooms painted light grey with white baseboards and nickel-plated light fixtures that all matched aggressively. Eliza's own bedroom was decorated the same way, and when her father opened the door, she saw that her mother had even replaced the slate-blue duvet cover on her bed with a grey-and-white-striped one that better suited the season's style.

In Eliza's girlhood, the room had been full of her things and marked with her own sense of taste. But as the years had passed her mother had redecorated it, bit by bit, to serve as another guest room. The duvet cover had been the last remaining thing Eliza had picked herself. The loss wasn't surprising — the room wasn't really hers anymore anyway — but it still made her melancholy.

As she looked around the room her gaze fell on the only thing in it that didn't feel as impersonal as a hotel: Her grandmother's hope chest, set on the floor between the two windows with their deep window seats. Eliza had seen it thousands of times, but right now the sight of the box, sealed with an iron lock whose key had long ago gone missing, arrested her. She felt a chill down her spine, as if the box was designed to hold her body and not her trousseau. She worried suddenly that the long-lost key might somehow materialize at the engagement party and pass not into her own hands but Cody's.

Eliza shook off the horror as best she could and turned to take her bags from her father with thanks. If nothing else, the thought of chests and locks reminded her she needed to give Cody the spare key to her apartment.

She shooed her father out of the room so she could have a few minutes to gather herself before the madness of the holidays truly began. Then she pulled out her phone. But not to text Cody.

How's Italy? She messaged Harry as she sat down at her vanity to blot her makeup and retouch her hair. And when she opened her door and slipped out to face the rest of the world, she tucked her phone into her clutch. If she was going to survive the rest of the day, she definitely wanted a dose of Harry's snark and impatience in her pocket.

♦

The dinner with Cody's family and her own was less dire than Eliza feared. No one produced a key to the hope chest and no one who didn't understand publishing or the internet asked her too many questions about her job. Besides, everyone was much more interested in the latest polling numbers for Cody's campaign than about her latest career move. While Eliza cared about politics, she could have done without the constant prognostication. Winning an election wasn't a magic trick, but thanks to Cody she was surrounded by people who were sure that if the right offerings and utterances were made over and over again, the gods would reward them. Being around that was exhausting — even with occasional mental breaks provided by Harry's texts complaining about Italy being cold and his friends being irritating.

And being around that was what was expected of her. Constantly. Even with an entire life of her own in New York for at least the next year. People asked if she'd be campaigning for Cody on the weekends, if she'd be leading a Women for Cody Connor phone banking circle, and if she'd picked out her dress for election day yet.

Eliza didn't understand the question. "I haven't thought about it. I don't even know why I would think about it?" The pitch of her voice crept upward in something approaching panic.

Cody slipped an arm around her waist and pulled her close. "You know the media always films the candidate casting his vote."

"I do," she said, "but I'm not running for anything!"

"Well, you'll come up to vote, sure."

"It's a Tuesday. I have work. I requested an absentee ballot."

"A very responsible backup plan," Cody announced with a laugh, even though it was no such thing. "But I know you'll be asking for the day so you can pull that lever in person."

Eliza opened her mouth, made a vague squeaking sound, and closed it with a shrug. Around them, people commented on how adorable they were. Eliza wanted to scream.

◆

For as relatively pleasant and normal as dinner had been —
at least until the debacle about Eliza's vote — the next day's
photo session felt anything but. Of the many rituals
surrounding weddings, Eliza found engagement photos
perhaps the most baffling. It wasn't as if she and Cody had
just gotten engaged, and the photos for the wedding itself
would be much more elaborate. She especially didn't
understand a three-hour photo session with her mother, the
photographer, and the photographer's assistant in tow to
half-a-dozen of Boston's snow-blanketed spots of beauty or
historical significance.

"We look like a J. Crew ad," Eliza muttered as she
obligingly popped her knee to kiss Cody in front of the
white-capped Ether Monument. Because nothing said
romance like statuary celebrating the anesthetic properties
of a class of organic compounds.

By the time the shoot was over, Eliza was cold, her boots
had leaked and her feet were freezing. She wanted nothing
more than to go back to her parents' house and curl up in
her bedroom with a book. Or, better yet, her laptop. She
needed to do some writing of her own and recover from so
many hours of non-stop exposure to humans. But she
couldn't, because Cody was hosting a donor dinner and she,
as the doting fiancée, was expected to be present.

Harry

Steven's absence became truly felt by the group two days
before Christmas. Which didn't mean that they all didn't
miss him before then. There were whispers in corners and
quiet murmurs between conversation and bed partners
about him. Harry was fairly sure every person there was
carrying on their own private correspondence with Steven
via email, text, and phone. But no one said anything to the

group at large and no one sent anything to the mailing list, as if by keeping silent they could keep shadow at bay.

It was Harry who broke the silence, unintentionally, at dinner. He started telling a story about some past dissipation with Steven, only to realize the entire table had ceased their side conversations and gone silent to listen.

Dennis caught Harry's eye for a split second. Then he reached across the table for the wine bottle and announced, "Oh for fuck's sake, why the wailing and gnashing of teeth? He's not dead yet."

"Sensitively worded as always," Harry said. Really, he was relieved someone had spoken.

"Well, what do you want me to say?" Dennis demanded.

"It's a bit early to be having his wake," Meryl pointed out.

Dennis snorted. "Again, not dead yet. Get him on video chat, somebody. Let's tell embarrassing stories about him while he's still here to humiliate."

Late as it was in Italy, it was only early evening in Connecticut. Steven answered the video call with a blur of pixels that gradually coalesced into an expression of amusement and mild concern. Harry could hear the neighbor's dog barking.

"Miss me already?" Steven asked.

Harry, who had seen him barely a month ago, was shocked at the change in his appearance. He was thinner, with his cheekbones standing out above grey stubble on his cheeks. The line of his nose was sharper than usual. For years he'd worn T-shirts throughout the winter, complaining that Mallory kept the house too warm for his taste, but now he wore a turtleneck under a thick sweatshirt.

"We've been missing you for days," Dennis said. "But we're just all finally drunk enough to admit it."

"How are you?" Harry asked Steven.

Steven looked annoyed, though at them or the universe Harry wasn't sure. "It's December in Connecticut. I'm cold, damp, and irritated."

"It's about the same here," Harry offered unhelpfully.

"Oh, to be irritated in Rome. I'm so sorry for you," Steven shot back sharply.

Harry wasn't sure what to say; he wanted to bring the conversation back around to a kinder, or at least a lighter, place, but didn't know how. Incipient death made none of them funnier. Next to him, Dennis fidgeted with his fork, his shoulders hunched.

"All right," Meryl said, picking the tablet off the table and carrying it into the sitting room. "We'll give the boys a moment to cope with the fact that they're having feelings in public. Steven, is there anything you want me to bring you from Italy? And what about Mallory?"

♦

The conversation with Steven, though sobering to everyone in the house, did not seem to materially dampen anyone's eagerness for exploits. If anything, after they ended the call everyone seemed to get a bit more wild. Harry found he had less patience with people's shenanigans than usual.

Dennis tried to get him to talk about Eliza at two in the morning while they sat, shoulders pressed together, in the dark living room. Anything, Harry suspected, to avoid talking about Steven for a little longer. The embers of the fire, glowing dully in the grate, gave off not nearly enough heat. Harry snagged the bottle of amaretto off the floor and topped up both their glasses. Perhaps he could outdrink his friend, and Dennis would pass out before Harry could confess any of his woe.

Of course, that was not what happened.

"Forget this," Dennis said eventually, setting the bottle and both their glasses aside.

"Mm?"

"It's miserable in here. Go make us tea. I'm going to fix the fire."

Harry was grateful for straightforward instructions. He was equally grateful for the flames crackling merrily in the hearth when he came back into the room holding two empty mugs in one hand, the kettle in the other, and a package of loose tea in his teeth.

"All right," Dennis said, once they were settled back side-by-side on the couch, their steaming cups held on their knees. "Tell me more about her. And why you're not dating her."

"She works with me," Harry said, voicing one of his chief concerns. "I realize other men wouldn't care, but —"

"You'd hardly be the first person to carry on an affair in that office."

Dennis wasn't wrong; publishing was a hive of incestuous and ill-advised entanglements on the best of days. But Harry had a whole arsenal of reasons to squash this infatuation while there was still time. If there was still time. "She's so much younger than me."

"Harry. That's a feature not a bug."

"No it is not."

"Speak for yourself," Dennis said. As if *he* would ever date anyone so much younger.

Harry frowned. "Don't you understand I don't want to be that man? A woman half my age, who I work with. I'm about to turn fifty, and my best friend is dying. That should cause me to question my motives."

"I'm right here," Dennis said sharply.

"*One* of my best friends," Harry corrected, glad really for the reminder, however uncouth. He wouldn't be alone in the world without Steven; he'd just be without Steven.

"Better. Now finish confessing about the girl."

Harry sighed heavily. "What am I supposed to say? That she's like a third hand or an organ I didn't know I had? As if she's some trivial accessory to my stunted heart and disorganized life? Because it's not like that at all. I don't enjoy her company because she's young and beautiful. My life is filled with beauty, most of it far more appropriate."

"Fuck appropriate. What's this really about?" Dennis asked.

Harry blew out a heavy breath. "I can't stop thinking about Mallory."

"Oh God." Dennis sounded shocked, like he'd forgotten here in the early dawn what Steven's illness meant for his wife.

"Yes."

"Well, fuck." It was representative of how well Dennis knew Harry that he didn't say anything more. The moment wasn't about comfort, but shared irritation.

"My thoughts exactly."

"Please know," Dennis said, so softly that Harry almost had to strain to hear him, "that I'm only saying this because it's three in the morning in Rome and our lives are absurd."

"Yes?" Harry asked. He felt, for some inexplicable reason, afraid of whatever Dennis was going to say next.

"When events and circumstances intrude into our lives, it's important to respond to them. Don't make the mistake of thinking of those intrusions as only terrible things. Just because we're all getting older, that's no reason to think everything is cancer."

"Was that supposed to be uplifting?" Harry asked.

"Yes?"

"Try again when I'm sober?" Harry felt impossibly fond.

Dennis reached for him, insistent that he tuck his head down onto his shoulder. "Always."

Eliza

The engagement party on Saturday night was so aggressively New England in nature that it was held in the private room of a well-regarded seafood restaurant. Eliza had been to several of these things, for cousins and girlfriends of hers from college, and had never loved them. Evenings in hot, crowded, noisy rooms were unpleasant enough. Such rooms were even worse when she was the center of attention.

She had dressed carefully for the evening, in a jewel-toned A-line dress. But as she and Cody greeted guests she was aware that all anyone was looking at was the ring she was wearing for the first time on her left hand — and wondering what it had cost.

Cody, for his part, spent the evening being congratulated as though he'd made a particularly good political deal which, Eliza had to admit, he had. A wife who could host dinner parties and show up on his arm on the campaign trail and at fundraising events was a definite asset.

After the speeches, which were endless and boring and involved little more than her saying thank you after the men had gone on and on, Eliza fled to the bathroom. She needed to touch up her makeup and, more than that, she needed a moment to herself. She was reapplying her lipstick when her phone rang in her clutch. She fumbled to silence it, mortified that she'd forgotten to turn off the ringer before dinner, then saw who was calling.

"Harry, what the hell do you want?" she hissed into the phone, holding it carefully with one hand while she blotted off her excess lipstick on a bit of paper towel with the other.

"Oh, shit, hi. You're on the phone."

"It's still vaguely daytime hours on the East Coast, what were you expecting? Why are you awake?"

"What time is it there?" Harry asked, sounding baffled in the extreme. Eliza realized, with a jolt of mingled horror and delight, that Harry was almost certainly drunk.

"Nine. At night," she added, to be clear. Harry might need it. "What's going on?"

"Everyone was boring me, I went through my phone to distract myself, and you're the only one I want to talk to who isn't in this house already. Or dying. But let's not talk about that."

Eliza frowned at her own reflection in the mirror. "Thank you?" she said hesitantly. Then she asked, "Are you okay?"

"I'm old, drunk, and cold."

Before she could stop herself, Eliza started laughing. The woman next to her at the long mirror gave her a scandalized look. Eliza, still laughing, retreated to one of the low sofas along the wall of the powder room. Beside her was an end table bearing a box of tissues and expensive potpourri in a hideously rococo bowl. Maybe it was just his mention of death, but Eliza was unpleasantly reminded of a funeral home.

Once her giggles subsided, Harry gave a wounded-sounding huff.

"What did you expect?" Eliza demanded. "Your publisher doesn't pay me to be sympathetic."

"How are things with Philippe?" Harry asked, as if either of them cared.

"Very well, considering I'm on holiday and haven't talked to him or looked at my work email for a week."

"Your dedication astounds me," Harry teased.

"In case you hadn't noticed, it's Christmas, and no one has done any work in days. Including you." For some reason, their usual banter was grating on her and she wanted to yell or cry. This week had been too long already, and she still had to get through Christmas and New Year's before she could go back home.

Maybe the powder-room tissues were more necessary than she had given them credit for. She plucked one from the box and rolled it between her fingers, oily lint sloughing off and clinging to her skin.

"Are *you* all right?" Harry asked, his voice quiet and concerned.

She laughed again, although this time damply and not at all loudly. "Yes, thank you, why?"

"You sound miserable."

"Since when are you my therapist? I'm just tired."

"What have you been doing?" Harry asked, his voice warm and languid now. Eliza could picture him reclining lazily on a sofa in some ridiculous Italian villa, a wine glass in his hand and a smirk on his face.

"Party planning."

"For Christmas? I thought your mother would take care of that. Or her army of event planners, at least."

"No," Eliza said. She suddenly felt cold, nerves or guilt or adrenaline — or all three — spiking through her body. She still hadn't told Harry she was engaged. And until now she could have passed that off as — it had never come up, it wasn't official yet, they were work friends who didn't tell each other personal things. Except they clearly were if she was hiding in the bathroom at her own engagement party so they could talk.

"No," she said again. "An engagement party."

"Lovely. Who's getting married?"

"Me."

There was a sharp intake of breath that Eliza could hear over the phone all the way from Italy.

"Oh," he said. Then, "Best wishes to you both." Eliza couldn't read his tone. Or rather, there was nothing to read; it was pure charm and politeness, and the good breeding to know that in their circles one never offered congratulations on the occasion of a marriage.

"Thank you," she said.

"When?"

"Next summer. Not this coming one, the one after."

"Ah."

Suddenly, all their banter and ease was gone. Eliza let her head fall into her hand — the one with the tissue still balled up into it. She wanted to apologize. She wanted Harry to ask for an apology so she could yell at him for his possession and presumption. But neither of them said anything.

"I miss you," she said finally. "I have to go." Before Harry could say anything else, she hung up.

◆

On New Year's Eve, a postcard arrived from Harry. The postmark was from before Eliza had confessed her engagement to him, and the picture on the front was of the Italian coastline. She turned the card over with equal parts eagerness and dread, both wanting and not wanting something that would make Harry's actions or her own confused feelings make more sense. All that was scrawled there, though, in Harry's looping old-world script, was wishes for a merry Christmas and a happy new year.

Eliza slipped the postcard into the book of short stories she'd brought for bedtime reading, and went back to getting ready for the New Year's party she and Cody would be attending. Plenty of time to worry about Harry — and what to do about him — on the train back to New York.

6

♦

A Meal for Penitents

Harry

After ten days in Rome it was nearly a relief to be back in New York, with its familiar grey skies and ugly, icy streets. A new year and a chance for a new beginning, Harry told himself as he sat down at his office desk. An opportunity for a few half-hearted resolutions he already didn't plan to keep and an inbox overflowing with unread emails.

Many of the emails were from Eliza, but they were strictly about business matters. Since their conversation on the phone the night of her engagement party, they hadn't spoken at all. And judging by her brisk, businesslike tone, they were not going to talk about that call, or anything else personal, now that they were back at work.

Which was likely for the best. There was nothing more Harry could say about Eliza's engagement, even to himself. He had already convinced himself he wasn't going to pursue a relationship with her before that data had emerged. And Harry didn't do the sort of relationships that might end in marriage. There was, therefore, no reason to regret and every reason to rejoice that Eliza had already made a good match for herself. A match with someone presumably her own age, who could offer support and companionship far longer than he could.

So, at least, Harry told himself. And had to keep telling himself as he prepared to encounter Eliza in person for the first time since the holidays. Rather than dropping by his office, she sent him a meeting invitation through the company scheduling system. On one hand, the advance notice spared Harry the suspense of anticipation and surprise. But on the other, he already missed their casual ease with each other's time and space.

Eliza arrived at his office, laptop and notes in hand as though this were a meeting that would require actual discussion about digital prototypes. She looked lovely as always, and Harry hated that his first reaction upon seeing her was to flick his gaze down to her hand and the ring that now rested there.

It was quite the rock, surrounded with accent diamonds to boot. The glitter and bright gold of it didn't suit her at all, but Harry knew better than to say such a thing.

"Best wishes again," he said once Eliza had sat down in the chair opposite his desk and not her more usual perch in his armchair. "If I'd known, I'd have sent a gift for the party. Or at least a card." His tone was mild; he genuinely did not mean it as a reproof, just a statement of fact. Still, there was something brittle about the smile Eliza gave him in return.

"It's quite all right," she said. "We've been engaged for almost a year already, actually. The party was to make everything official. There was an announcement in the *Boston Globe*."

"Not *The New York Times*?" Harry asked, moving things around on the ever-present mess of his desk so she would have room for her laptop and steno pad.

"Oh, no. You can only have an engagement announcement or a wedding announcement in the same paper, so the wedding announcement is going in the *Times*, of course."

"Of course," Harry said after a beat. And then, in spite of all that was strained and odd between them, he laughed. "God, you really are from the same fucked-up place I am, aren't you?"

"Where was your engagement announcement placed?" Eliza asked, a grin dancing at the corner of her mouth.

Harry blinked at her. "What?"

"Your engagement announcement, when you...." She trailed off. "You were married? Or maybe still are?"

Eliza floundering was as startling as her assumption. Harry shook his head.

"No. No, I've never been married. Or engaged for that matter."

"Oh." Eliza was clearly taken aback. "I'm sorry. I shouldn't have assumed."

"Don't be. I'm hardly offended." He couldn't wait tell Meryl about this. She'd laugh forever.

"Why not?" Eliza asked, with the brashness that Harry loved but suspected often made her life awkward.

"Aside from a general desire to avoid the absurdity of such things as protocols for announcements in the paper?"

"Yes," she said firmly. "Aside from all that."

Harry paused, wanting to be careful of how he answered, lest it sound like a judgment on her own choices. Or an attempt to make it competitively clear he was hardly lacking for companionship opportunities in his own life. "I have a friend. Who is also unmarried. And she always says that in her case it's because she has no interest in doing the small ugly parts of life with the people she actually loves."

"And is that true for you, too?"

"Not entirely," Harry said. "But it's close enough."

Eliza propped her elbow on his desk and her chin on her hand. Harry wondered if she was mimicking his own gestures on purpose. In any case, he wished she would stop.

"Tell me more," she said.

"Like what?" If charging ahead and starving the elephant in the room to death was the way they were going to go, so be it, but Harry felt uneasy.

"Is there anyone you do actually love? This friend of yours, perhaps?"

"Meryl is essential to me. But I don't love her in any way that involves big shiny jewelry, no." Harry indicated Eliza's ring with a little jut of his chin.

Eliza frowned and wiggled her fingers.

"It's very impressive." Not only was Harry failing to starve the elephant, he'd just fallen down a pit with it. The only question was whether he was about to get trampled.

Eliza looked up at him, her eyes wide. "It's hideous, isn't it?"

Harry laughed, panicked. "I'm not going to answer that."

Eliza took a deep breath and sat up a little straighter. Primly, she fixed her gaze on him again. "Well, then, it seems we're agreed."

◆

She's engaged, Harry sent to the Miscreants. Ten minutes later Steven had dug up the *Globe* announcement and sent it to the entire list. Harry had the worst friends in the world.

Eliza

Eliza counted it as a personal victory when she was able to derail the weekly department head meeting by showing off the early prototypes of the apps an indie game developer had started work on. Harry jabbed enthusiastically at the tablet being passed around as he played the demo level of the game designed to promote Philippe's books.

"It's probably not the food truck he envisioned," Harry said wryly.

"No, but every level a player passes unlocks a recipe, we can do in-app purchases, and if Philippe wants to do digital sauce coupons in there, we can make that happen. It's a win all around; everybody gets to make money." Eliza was pleased to note the nods of approval, however reluctant, coming from the people who had been most opposed to the idea of phone games. "Also," she went on, clicking through her notes on her laptop. "I couldn't resist the gaming draw of extreme dog grooming — you know, design your own dog, that sort of thing. I actually think it could be one of those unexpected internet obsessions. We are going to have to talk more about the look and branding of the game for the true crime line, however, because...yikes."

There were some chuckles from around the table. Eliza took that as a win, too, although the problem of making a game about crime without it being too gory or violent was a real one.

"When can it be ready?" Ioanna asked.

"The developer for the food truck game will have an initial version we can go live with in eight weeks. Ten at most."

Ioanna nodded, flipping through her calendar. "That's perfect. You can debut it in Paris."

"I'm sorry?" Eliza tilted her head at the apparent non-sequitur.

Ioanna nodded down the table at Harry, who suddenly seemed to be focusing on the tablet in his hands with extraordinary interest, though his hands were no longer moving. "Harry will be going to the Paris Book Fair in March. So we'll already have a presence there, and a Paris event will be the perfect place to roll out a game to promote our French cooking books."

"Of course," Eliza said automatically, knowing it was her job to be agreeable to this plan after Ioanna had helped steamroll objections to the games in the first place. But Paris with Harry? That was everything and nothing she wanted all at the same time.

◆

Eliza was unable to focus on the rest of the meeting. She was tormented by the thought that the both of them going to Paris was Harry's doing. It was an unkind fear, and one that suggested that, had their situations been reversed she might have very well chosen to abuse her own power. But their situations were not reversed, and she deserved clarity if nothing else.

When they had finally all been dismissed, she grabbed her things and followed fast on Harry's heels as he left the room. With only a wary sidelong glance at her, Harry led the way to his office. As soon as the door was shut behind them Eliza demanded, "Did you plan this?"

Harry didn't seem quite able to meet her eyes. "No. No, I didn't."

"Are you sure?" Harry's lack of eye contact was not reassuring. But at her question, his gaze snapped to her face.

"Did I *plan* to have our boss send us both to Paris when we —" He cut himself short. "I learned you were going when you learned you were going. If I had known —" He stopped again. "I didn't know. I promise," he said, his voice lower, but his tone no less distressed.

When we what? Eliza wanted desperately to ask. Not because she didn't know. But because she wanted to hear him say it. But that was out of the question.

"Okay. Thanks. I just wanted to know. I — thanks," she said, nearly babbling. She knew she wasn't making much sense, and hoped Harry wouldn't ask her any questions. "I'll see you later," she said, and fled.

◆

"Work is sending me to Paris," Eliza told Cody later that night. Her phone, set to speaker, was on top of the tiny possibly Soviet-era microwave on her counter as she unpacked the groceries she'd picked up on the way home.

"That's nice," Cody said absently. "What for?"

"The Paris Book Fair. It's in March." She didn't tell him that Harry was going, too. There was, after all, no real need for him to know.

"All the way to Paris? For a book fair?" Cody asked. "That seems a little over the top."

"It's a very significant event for the publishing industry. And one of the biggest cultural events in Europe." Eliza smiled as she said it; that was part of the phone training she'd received growing up. A listener can always hear a smile, and it would help nothing for Cody to hear her teeth grind the way she wanted to.

"Oh, is it? I'm sorry. I can't keep track of all your events."

"It's fine," Eliza said, even though it wasn't. But Cody was in the middle of an election campaign. Of course he was distracted. Her mother would say she should be understanding of the pressure he was under.

"When is it?" he asked.

Eliza gave him credit where credit was due; at least he was asking her questions instead of changing the subject to himself. She told him the dates.

After a long pause, Cody said, "Uhhmmmm...."

"What's wrong?" Eliza asked. Still smiling.

"The election is that week."

"Oh. Yeah. I guess it is." Eliza didn't know how she could have forgotten, but frankly, she was glad she had. If she'd remembered, she would have had to decide before now whether she cared enough to try to do anything about it.

There was another long pause and Eliza filled it reflexively. "I guess I'll see if I can get out of it," she said into the silence. Too well, she remembered their argument at her parents' house. "But why does it matter?"

"Why does it matter?" Cody asked. Now she had his full attention — and the full heat of his indignation. "You work in marketing, I shouldn't have to tell you why it matters.

People aren't electing a name, they're electing their own political aspirations. Not to mention fantasies. If you're not there with me, it looks like you don't support me. It's an image disaster for the campaign."

I work in publishing, she thought fiercely. "I think you're overreacting."

"I'm not," Cody said in the stern tone that always raised Eliza's hackles instantly. How dare he speak to her like one of his office minions? For that matter, how dare he speak to his office minions like that?

Eliza felt too tired to argue and too angry to give him any more of her attention. "I'll ask about changing the work trip. All right?" She knew she sounded upset and reluctant, but that's exactly what she was.

"Thank you," Cody said shortly. "I hate to cut you off, but I have a dinner meeting with some people —"

"No worries. Talk to you later." Eliza couldn't wait for the conversation to be over.

"Love you!"

"You too."

Eliza ended the call with relief.

♦

The rest of the week passed unpleasantly. Cody didn't reach out to her again; Eliza knew he was waiting for her to call first. Doubtless he expected her to tell him she'd cancelled the Paris trip and would be appearing at his side on election day like the dutiful, image-conscious fiancée she was.

Eliza had no intention of doing any such thing. If Cody had been more understanding of her position, maybe. But she never wanted to be Cody's prop, on election day or any other day. The Paris trip was the perfect excuse to stay away, and if Cody wasn't interested in hearing her reasons she had no interest in spending any more time explaining them.

She waited a few days for the sake of optics, then sent Cody a regretful email that the publisher had turned down her request to skip the trip.

Eliza was self-aware enough to know that the Cody situation would have been easier to deal with if she hadn't also been dealing with the Harry situation. She felt guilty about her feelings regarding Harry and guiltier still about that guilt. There wasn't anything wrong with having a friend. Or a crush. Or a certain rapport with a colleague. There were all sorts of intimacies other than marriage, and she resented the world that made her suspicious of that truth. Which did not make her more inclined to do whatever work was required to repair things with Cody.

Meanwhile, her confession of her engagement — and her paranoia that Harry had arranged their assignment to the Paris trip — strained things with him as well. Not once during the whole week did Harry ask if she wanted to order in dinner together. He didn't even stop by to ask if she wanted to take a break and get coffee. She knew she should be relieved; having one less variable in her life to manage was a good thing. But she missed him. His company, the sound of his voice, and the way he seemed to have absolutely no expectations of her at all.

Harry

Harry spent the week in a moody misery. No amount of stern talking to himself could snap him out of it. Yes, Steven was gravely ill. Yes, he had a mess of a manuscript to fix — not to mention travel and leave plans to get approved. But all he could think about was Eliza, the fact that they were going to Paris together, and that Eliza had suspected him of arranging the trip.

Considering the circumstances Harry could hardly blame her. He was sure he hadn't done anything overt to betray his interest in her. But there had been so many little moments, some almost acknowledged between them. Which was exactly what he knew he should have avoided. Even if Eliza weren't engaged, she was too young and Harry was too old.

It wouldn't be fair. It wouldn't be kind. And it wouldn't be right.

But she was engaged and Harry's complicated feelings were all moot anyway. So why couldn't he forget about them and get his damn work done?

At the next department-wide staff meeting, Harry picked a seat at the far end of the table, hopefully away from anywhere Eliza would choose to sit. But Eliza was the last to arrive, and when she did the seat across from Harry was the only one still open. Without looking at him — for which he was grateful — she slid into the chair, opened her laptop, folded her hands delicately in front of the keyboard, and looked at Ioanna, apparently intent on the proceedings.

Harry tore his gaze from her and told himself not to wonder why she was late.

But no matter how hard he tried, he couldn't pay attention to the meeting. And he couldn't let his gaze wander to Eliza. If he did, every longing, messy, unfair feeling he had about her was going to be written all over his face. But even without looking at her, he was so aware of her, as if a thread of a thousand strands connected them.

Giving himself another internal scold to get it together, Harry tried to busy himself with his inbox under the guise of paying attention and taking notes. Which was how he clicked on an email from Steven without particularly thinking about it. He stopped cold.

Dear Harry,

Greetings from beyond the grave. Well, not really. But if you're getting this, I'm dead and Mallory has hit send. Sorry about that.

In the next days and weeks, you're going to hear all sorts of things about who I really was and how I really felt. Most of it will be vaguely accurate, but none of it will be as true as what you and I, divided by time and death, think of each other right now. I'm not even being poetic. This is a real thing. Discussion of our memories overwrites them.

When our friends say I was a scientist and insist that I have winked completely out of existence, consider the possibility that they are lying.

Sorry for the invite to the worst party ever, but please do help Mallory any way you can.

Keep an eye on your mailbox.

Cheers,
Steven

Harry pressed his fingers over his mouth and let a shuddering breath out through his nose. For a moment he allowed himself to cling to the hope that this was all a joke, even if it never had been Steven's way to be cruel. He'd known things had taken several turns of late, but a final one? He'd had no hint of it. Steven had spent a few days in the hospital but that was nearly routine for a man in his circumstances. No one, Steven and Mallory included, had seemed any more alarmed than they'd been for months.

Harry's email flashed with a new alert, and he glanced back at his inbox with dread, not yet ready to face the rest of the Miscreants' grief and confusion — they must have gotten emails as well. To his surprise, it was from Eliza.

What's wrong?

Harry took in another deep breath as he typed. *Dying friend has completed the task.*

Premature and unexpected despite circumstances? Eliza replied.

Rather.

I'm going to give you an opportunity in a moment. Take it.

Harry frowned at the cryptic email. He was in no mood for puzzles. Then another message arrived.

And whatever you do, don't pick up your laptop too soon...or too late.

As Harry looked up to see what on earth Eliza was about, she half stood to reach for the carafe of water in the center of the table. As her gaze met his with a deliberate intensity, she knocked it over, sending its contents everywhere.

Harry stared at her. She stood stock-still in apparent surprise at having caused such a flood. People pushed back from the table, and the water cascaded towards Harry's laptop.

He slammed it closed, cursed under his breath, and snatched it up. Eliza jerked her head towards the door as she began apologizing frantically for the chaos, including the possible ruination of Harry's laptop.

Go, she mouthed.

Harry did as he was told.

As soon as he was out of the room, he was glad that he had. The shock of the news about Steven, temporarily alleviated by Eliza and her insistence on a distraction, hit him full force.

Eliza found him, half an hour later, in a little-used fire staircase, perched at the top of the steps that ran between the floor his office was on and the floor the conference room was on. Without invitation, she sat down next to him and bumped their shoulders together.

Harry made himself sit up straighter which also had the effect of putting slightly more space between them. "Did I miss anything interesting?"

Eliza shook her head. "Are you all right?"

"I'll be fine, so long as you don't ask me questions like that."

"Okay," Eliza said and stood up again, this time holding out her hand.

Harry stared at her blankly. He was spending a lot of time doing that today.

"We're going to lunch," she said, opening and closing her hand insistently.

"You already caused a scene at the meeting, I don't need another distraction." Harry didn't care if he was being sullen. Steven was dead.

"And I don't need you in my life being a jackass," Eliza said. "But here I am. Let me take you to lunch and keep you company while the shock wears off, and then you can grieve on your own time."

Eliza must have sensed that Harry was in no state for lunch anywhere he would have to mind his manners. She bought them hot dogs at a cart down the street and then tucked her free hand into his elbow and led him off down the block again.

"What are you doing?" Harry asked when she led them up the steps at St. Patrick's Cathedral.

"Hide the hot dog and look natural," she said, which had to count as one of the top five most absurd things anyone had ever said to Harry in his life.

They wound up in a corner of the Cathedral, half hidden behind a column and a bit of construction. They sat side-by-side like two weekday supplicants, except for the occasional bite of food they snuck while reasonably sure no one at prayer — or any of the security staff — was looking.

"I suppose this means I really should get my plans in order about Vienna," Harry said, once they'd been sitting there a while in silence.

"Vienna?" Eliza asked. "I thought you were done with that book. Or at least in the editing stage."

Harry shook his head. "Turns out it needs more than edits. And I don't know how to fix it without going back there. With Steven ill and the holidays I'd been putting off dealing with it, but now...." He trailed off.

"You don't sound keen to get away," Eliza observed.

"Vienna is difficult. And at least as cold as it is here."

"Yes, but it's not here, is it?"

Harry tipped his head to the side to acknowledge that. "No. It's not. Which might be convenient under the circumstances. But being left alone with my words…it's not appealing right now."

"If you don't like the book, and your agent doesn't like the book, and you suddenly feel compelled to live your life before you drop dead, why are you going back to Vienna at all?"

Because if nothing else, I'll be able to escape from you, Harry thought.

7

♦

The Body Politic

Eliza

The day after she and Harry ate hot dogs at St. Patrick's, Eliza was at her desk trying to make sense of an email chain between herself, one of the developers working on Philippe's food truck game, and Charley. She had no idea how her invisible boss had gotten on the thread; she also couldn't figure out how to politely get her off of it again. Almost everyone else in the office had left for the day and Eliza was thinking longingly of being at home, in bed, with a book, when her thoughts were interrupted by Harry's voice.

"Do you have a moment?"

She glanced up to see him standing outside her office door, looking uncertain, as if he wasn't sure of his welcome now that Eliza wasn't helping him with an acute grief reaction.

"Of course. What is it?"

"Do you mind if I —?" He stepped into her office, then put his hand on the doorknob.

"Not at all." Eliza wondered what on earth he needed to talk to her about with the door closed.

He shut the door gently behind himself. "I wanted to thank you. For being so kind yesterday. And also to apologize for being, well, rude and difficult on several occasions."

Both the thanks and the apology caught Eliza off-guard. She had expected neither, either from Harry or anyone else in the same situation.

"You're welcome. And thank you. You have been, but you've been under a strain." She gave him a smile and was surprised to find that she felt the words much more sincerely than she had when she'd tried to excuse Cody for his inattentiveness. But then, Cody had never apologized for, or even acknowledged, his own bad behavior.

"Also, I'm sorry if I gave you any reason to think...." He stopped himself and started again. "I'm sorry you suspected anything about Paris."

Eliza shook her head. "No. That's...." *Don't you dare blame yourself for something he's equally a part of,* her mind whispered fiercely. "Life is complicated all over."

They were both quiet for a moment. Eliza wondered whether the mood was going to shift back into their old comfortable banter, or if they were going to stay in this new cautious awkwardness forever.

"Well," Harry said, tucking his hands into his pockets. "With that settled. Would you like to take a walk, maybe get some coffee? I've been trapped at my desk all afternoon pricing out flights to Vienna and desperately need a break."

♦

"What are your plans for when you're done here?" Harry asked as they walked down the street. The hour was already late, the sky having long since gone dark. Midtown had already emptied of its office workers and all the pricey coffee places had closed for the day. But there was a satisfaction in getting non-chain coffee from a bodega. And not just because it only cost a dollar.

"Imagine," Harry said, kindly glossing over the fact Eliza had not yet answered his question "there was an entire world before Starbucks."

Although tempted, Eliza didn't bristle at what could have easily been a comment about her age. She knew Harry well enough now to know that, rather, it was about his own. They walked back to the office slowly, steam rising from their cups in the chill January night. Eliza imagined that neither of them were particularly eager to go back to hunching over laptops and worrying about encroaching deadlines.

"I try not to think about it much," Eliza admitted while they waited at an intersection. "What happens after this."

"Really?" Harry sounded surprised. "It must have taken months to get this place to move on anything. Who knows how long it will take to get your next steps sorted out? I mean, I always assumed you were the sort of person who had everything planned out years in advance."

"I'm not saying I don't have plans," Eliza shot back. "I'm just saying I haven't been thinking about it much."

"Oh, do tell. Now I'm intrigued," Harry said.

Eliza sighed. "I suppose it wouldn't occur to you, but I seem to have stumbled into a part of life where everyone else makes plans for me."

"Your mother's driving you crazy," Harry said. It was barely a question.

"Among others."

"About the wedding."

"Of course."

"And you can't stand it."

"Not at all."

"So I should probably stop badgering you."

"Yes. No. I don't know. I never seem to mind talking to you, so…as you will I suppose."

"What do you want?" Harry asked. Something in his tone made it clear he didn't just mean whether or not he should keep asking her about her future.

Despite the cold, Eliza's steps slowed down. Harry matched her easily and without question, verbal or otherwise. Eliza found herself looking up at the buildings that towered around them. Lights were still on in offices here and there — empty rooms and cleaning crews mostly, but a few people working late, some due to passion, some due to obligation. She knew which description fit her and Harry, together or apart. She smiled. She'd never been in love with the myth of New York before, but here and now, she finally understood it. Perhaps because New York understood her.

Eliza turned her gaze back to Harry and his too-kind and slightly worn face, reddened now as surely as her own by the cold. "I don't want to be beholden to anyone." She took a sip of her coffee, grateful for the warmth as much as for something to hide behind.

Harry looked as though he was going to say something, but then he blinked and looked away. "I know the feeling," he finally said, as they reached the door of their office building.

◆

For the next two weeks Eliza went to work and got coffee and occasionally ordered takeout with Harry. Dutifully, she went through the motions of texting Cody and asking him how his day was and how his campaign was going as if they had never argued. He answered her in the same workmanlike fashion, and Eliza wondered if this was how the rest of her life was going to be: Arguments and playing nice and pretending to care and feel more than she did.

She was on her work line with Philippe doing the verbal equivalent of smiling and nodding while he fretted to her about whether his latest book would get the reception in Paris he hoped for, when her cell phone rang. She checked the caller ID.

Cody. She sighed. They hadn't spoken via phone since their disagreement, and Eliza was all right with that state of affairs. Now, an unplanned call from him in the middle of the day probably spelled a disaster he expected her to be invested in fixing. She wrapped up her call with Philippe, debating to herself all the while whether this was more likely to be an issue with his campaign or with the wedding planning.

Once she was finally able to say goodbye to Philippe and call Cody back, he greeted her cheerfully with, "Hi, sweetheart!"

"Hi, I'm on a deadline. Is this important?" Cody would think it was regardless, but there was no harm in making him consider the question.

"I'm coming to visit you!"

Eliza opened her calendar on her laptop, baffled by Cody's change of tone and attitude from their latest interactions. "Oh, all right. When? I'm free in a couple of weeks," she said. "I think —"

"No, I mean, I'm coming to visit you right now." Cody interrupted her. "My guy got me booked on one of the late afternoon shows on MSNBC…you know the one." Eliza didn't; she was a Rachel Maddow girl all the way, but there was no point in saying so. "About the special election, of course. So I'm coming to New York."

"Oh! That's nice. Where are you?" she asked, grateful when he took her nonplussed bafflement for enthusiasm.

"I'm about to get on a plane, you almost missed me. I'll be there in a couple of hours."

"Oh."

"I thought we could go out for dinner after the taping. Can I pick you up at the office?"

"I — yes, but your luggage…?"

"You gave me a key, remember? I'll leave it at your place."

"You've thought of everything," Eliza said, her heart sinking. She loved Cody, she did, but spending a surprise night with him while he was buzzing from a national TV appearance was the last thing she felt capable of dealing with right now. She had work to do and her own life here; why couldn't she be left to enjoy it on her own?

"I do my best," Cody said, a smile clear in his voice and her sarcasm entirely lost on him. "So. Dinner. I'll be there at seven I guess?"

At a quarter after six, Eliza was in her armchair in Harry's office, her hands around a cup of tea. She'd finished her work early and escaped here to savor the last few minutes before Cody arrived. Because when she thought about her life in New York and her desire to hoard every precious second of it, she thought of this — a warm mug, the quiet of a nearly empty office, this view, and Harry. However messy their interaction had been lately.

She leaned against the back of the chair and listened in a half doze as Harry rambled about his favorite theories about the meaning and origin of the Voynich manuscript. He had a lovely voice and a not quite newscaster-neutral accent that was a product of age and class and New England; Eliza knew her voice sounded much the same when she wasn't being careful to seem just like everybody else. But she had always been careful about everything around everyone. Except, increasingly, around Harry. He would smile slightly sometimes at the way she said certain words and that was always, somehow, worth the risk.

When there was a knock on the door, she was feeling too comfortable and lazy to even lift her head.

"Come in," Harry said, evidently annoyed his monologue had been interrupted.

"Harry?" It was Jonathan. "Is Eliza here?"

Harry nodded to Eliza's chair. Situated in the corner as it was, it wasn't immediately visible from the doorway.

Jonathan looked over at her and smiled. "Hey. I've got a visitor for you." And with that, Cody walked into the room.

Eliza sat bolt upright, spilling tea all over herself in the process.

"You have a habit of that," Harry said casually.

Eliza grimaced. "You're early," she told Cody, after a frantic glance at her watch to make sure she hadn't lost track of time. "Aren't you supposed to be on TV right now?" *And shouldn't I have been watching like a dutiful partner?*

"I was on TV thirty minutes ago. You weren't in your office, so they thought you might be here."

Jonathan discreetly exited the room and closed the door behind him.

"She often is," Harry said. Eliza could have killed him. Harry stood from behind his desk and walked around to greet Cody. "I'm Harry Sargent. I have the honor of working with Eliza. I'm glad to meet you."

Cody shook Harry's offered hand. Eliza could see the moment where he squeezed ever so slightly too hard, because Harry's eyebrows twitched up.

The whole charade was ridiculous. Cody was being obnoxious and Harry was being absurd in response, but Eliza was still grateful for the moment to compose herself. It wasn't quite spilling a pitcher of water on a conference table, but she appreciated it nonetheless. Except now she had to break up this little tempest of testosterone. She set aside her cup of tea, blotted herself with a napkin, unfolded herself from the chair, and went to Cody's side.

"I'm so sorry I missed you in my office, I wasn't expecting you 'til later," she purred, wrapping her hands around one of his arms and leaning in close. Harry turned his raised eyebrows on her. She turned even more pointedly to her fiancé. "I have to go back to my office and get my things, will you walk with me?"

They said polite goodbyes. Eliza turned and mouthed *I'm sorry* to Harry before she pulled the door closed behind them.

"What were you doing in there?" Cody asked as they walked down the hall together. To Eliza's annoyance, he put an arm around her waist. They were at her workplace, not on his campaign trail.

She fished for a reasonable excuse with which to answer Cody's question. "You saw the view," Eliza said. "It's like being in a library where I can spill tea on things."

"I don't understand that at all," he said.

"You don't have to."

"No need to be sharp."

"No need to worry about where I'm spending my time at work," Eliza countered. She hoped she sounded gentle to Cody. She certainly didn't to her own ears.

"Doesn't Harry mind?" Cody asked.

"No."

He seemed to ponder that for a moment and finally nodded. "I guess he likes to have someone listen to him talk."

"You'd know," Eliza said under her breath. She regretted it immediately.

"What's that supposed to mean?" Cody asked.

"You were just on TV!" she said, forcing herself to keep her tone light. She was growing more annoyed at Cody's presence by the second. "Getting the entire country to listen to you. What do you think it means?"

Cody did not seem particularly placated but shifting the subject to him was clearly helping. "Did you really not watch?"

Eliza knew she couldn't admit that doing so hadn't even occurred to her until he had appeared and caught her in Harry's office. "I figured we could watch it later, when it goes up online. I mean, I'm sure you have a commentary track. What was it like?"

"I should have had you in the studio with me," Cody said after some consideration.

Eliza was willing to do a lot of things, but taking the heat for not doing something that hadn't been asked of her wasn't one of them. "Then you should have asked."

◆

By the time they got back to her apartment, Eliza was already exhausted from the fight they weren't quite having. She felt like she was walking a tightrope between all the correct and supportive things she was supposed to say and the evening she actually wanted to have.

"I'm sorry we're both so out of sorts tonight," she said on reflex. "I get so used to my life here. It's easier not to miss you if I just focus on my quiet, solo existence. I didn't have enough time to change gears."

Cody flopped down onto her couch with his usual attractive ease. "Distance is never easy. And national TV! I might be a little out of sorts too."

Eliza smiled with relief. There was the gentle goodness that had gotten her into this mess in the first place. She sat down beside him.

"Plus," he added, turning to face her. "It's only for a little while. Once the election happens, we'll have to see how much of your contract you can fulfill remotely."

She blinked at him. "My contract's through the end of September. And it isn't remote."

"Yeah, but it's not like you actually need to put in face time and my offices will be in Boston and D.C."

"Yes, and New York is right in the middle, so that will work out just fine. My job is here."

"For now."

"Yes, for now. And for the foreseeable future."

"What are you going to do after I win and this contract is done? You can't expect me to be able to burn all that time on the train coming to see you."

"*If* you win the election," Eliza said. She crossed her fingers as if she were warning him about jinxing the outcome rather than scolding him for presumption. "Nobody said anything about you burning time on the train." *No one in his life has ever suggested he spend a moment of time on something other than himself and his career.* "But if you ever need me in D.C. — or Boston — the Acela can get me there in three hours. Which is no worse than a bad day on the subway here," she said with a laugh she didn't feel.

Cody, though, shook his head. "That's not going to work."

"Why isn't it going to work?" Tension crept into Eliza's body, and her voice, again.

"The logistics of it. We're going to be too busy as it is for you to have any job easily. Much less one in a completely different city from any one I have an office in. Plus, think of the press. Young, star congressman whose gorgeous wife doesn't even live with him?" Cody shook his head, smiling as though Eliza's career, Eliza's *life*, was just a scheduling issue.

"Are you listening to the words coming out of your mouth?" Eliza asked. She felt cold. How had she not seen this coming?

"Tell me why you're so upset about this," Cody said. He clearly thought she was the problem, and he was the one offering thoughtful solutions. "I didn't know you felt this way about New York."

"Because we never talked about it! Any time Boston came up, or New York came up, you said we'd talk about it later," Eliza said, her voice rising. "And now, apparently, it's later, except we're not talking about it at all because you've already decided! Without even asking me what I want!"

"What do you want?" Cody ask, his own face darkening. "To sit around and write essays about summers on the beach? You can do that as well in Boston as you can here."

"Yes, you're right," Eliza snapped. "I can sit around and play with my books, whenever I'm not planning dinner parties for your political associates or hanging onto your arm at official functions."

"You know I know you do more than that," Cody said. It was so placating, and so absurdly out of the worst part of the 1950s, that Eliza had absolutely no response. To engage would have been to dignify the argument and she was not about to argue her right to a career and professional fulfilment with anyone, much less her fiancé.

"Except you clearly don't, because you are sitting here in *my* apartment, which *my job* is providing me with, and telling me that I am not allowed to work once you're elected. At which point, might I add, we won't even be married yet. Though that clearly doesn't stop you from seeing me as yours to do with as you please."

♦

Eliza woke far too early the next morning, if indeed she'd ever fully fallen asleep. Cody was dead to the world in bed beside her. She knew she was supposed to feel contrition: For her role in the fight, for not being the passive peacekeeper and smoothing everything over, for not apologizing and capitulating until there was no disagreement — or any sense of her own self — left.

Instead, she made herself coffee, showered, dressed, and put on makeup. She did not try to be quiet at all, but Cody never stirred. She left a note on the counter before she left. *Gone in to work to check on some things. Will be back.*

As usual she walked to the office. She was glad for the opportunity to move, for the brisk sting of icy air on her cheeks, and for the satisfying crunch of salt and ice under her feet. Once inside the building she encountered no one on her route up to her office. Which, at ten on a Saturday morning, was hardly surprising. Except that when she reached her floor she found Harry's door open. Glancing back to take another look, she saw the man himself sitting at his desk.

He looked up when she appeared in the doorway, though he'd seemed absorbed in his work and Eliza was sure she hadn't made a sound. He was dressed more casually than she had seen him before. He had on a button-down shirt with no tie; his collar was open to show his throat, including a spot low on his neck where he must have nicked himself shaving. His cardigan, in a lovely dark steel-blue wool, looked so warm and soft Eliza could nearly feel the gentle scratch of it on her palms. Which was maybe a thought she shouldn't have, given that she was engaged to another man. But it was the twenty-first century, and Eliza wasn't going to apologize to anyone, even herself, for having male friends. Or for looking at them.

Wordlessly, Harry's eyes tracked over her, from boots to hat and back again. Eliza was well-dressed; her hair was done; her makeup was perfect. There was nothing, to a casual eye, to let slip the fact she'd had a sleepless night or the reasons therefore. But Harry, she knew, saw it all.

He met her eyes only briefly and went back to his laptop. "I'm not going to ask," he said.

"What if I want you to?" she said defiantly. Because she did. She wanted Harry to challenge all of her terrible choices until she had no option left but to save herself from a life she had been raised to want, but was now realizing with chilling, creeping certainty, that she didn't.

Harry's eyes snapped back up to hers. For a moment, they stared at each other.

"I'm not going to ask," he said, more firmly this time.

Eliza turned and left his office.

♦

By the early afternoon Eliza had worked off enough of her frustration to feel capable of facing Cody again. Perhaps he would be reasonable. Perhaps, since he wanted to be a politician, he would be willing to negotiate. Maybe she had been overreacting. Maybe everything would be fine.

To her pleasure and no small relief, Cody was sitting on her couch working on his laptop when she let herself in. As soon as she shut the door behind herself, he put the tablet aside, stood up, and pulled her in for a gentle kiss.

As an olive branch, Eliza allowed it. He also took her coat and hung it up for her, and asked how her time at the office had gone, as if it had been a typical work day.

"I want to talk about some of the things you said last night," Cody said, taking her hand and leading her to the little table that doubled as both dining space and desk.

"Me too," Eliza said. She hoped desperately he wasn't going to ask her for an apology.

"If I win this election, I have to live in Boston and DC. There's not going to be time in my schedule for another permanent home anywhere else. But I don't want to take you away from work you love. So I've put in a call to my office, so we can at least start strategizing about how we can both do the work we want to do without living apart full-time. I've also got a contact at a publishing house in Boston, for you to look at if you want. So maybe we can explore our options, in both directions, and have a lot more conversations about this going forward?"

Eliza nodded. "I can work with that," she said. Cody was saying the right things, which she appreciated. Even if all publishing in Boston was academic publishing and she wanted nothing to do with it. But he was showing a willingness to have a conversation which had, until this moment, not felt guaranteed. She could wrestle with her conflicted feelings and point out the inadequacy of his solutions at another time.

◆

Can I have five minutes of your time? Eliza texted Harry on Monday morning as she walked to work. Given the note they'd parted on the last time they'd spoken, she wasn't sure what Harry's response would be. Or whether he would respond at all. That moment had been so odd.

But he did reply as she was entering the lobby of the building. *Of course. Work-related or otherwise?*

Otherwise, she confessed.

Unfortunately I have meetings this morning. May I come to your office at one?

Always so polite. Those perfect manners that were a hallmark of his upbringing and yet, there seemed to be such real warmth to them. Such kindness. Harry could say he'd grown up with girls like Eliza, but she had never known a man quite like Harry.

Yes. Please, she replied.

Good. I'll see you then.

Eliza spent the rest of the morning in a meeting with Celia, author of the extreme dog-grooming books, as part of her ongoing campaign to get her on board with a phone game tied to said books. Celia feared a digital angle on her living dog art would result in widespread internet mockery, and Eliza struggled to explain how much the internet kindly and sincerely loved kitsch without using the word.

As exasperating as the session was she was grateful for it; any work kept her from dwelling too much on her upcoming talk with Harry. At twelve fifty-eight, finally off the phone with Celia, she looked up from her desk to see him lounging against the doorframe. He wore his winter coat, a heavy dark-blue wool affair, and a checked scarf looped around his neck.

"Can I take you to St. Pat's for hot dogs?" he asked with a grin Eliza might describe as boyish.

She laughed in both surprise and relief. "If you want." She matched his playful tone. "But that feels like tempting fate." If he was going to confront her about the mess with Cody — which she was still sure he knew about, though he'd let her tell him nothing — he wasn't going to do so now.

"Indeed. Luckily, I've something else in mind. If you will?" Harry said, nodding toward the hallway.

Eliza stood, closed her laptop, and reached for her coat, hanging from a hook by the door. Harry was there first, though. He held it to help her into it, every bit of the gesture that of a considerate gentleman. Never, in all the times someone had held a coat for her, had the hair on the back of her neck stood up in a pleasant frisson as it did now.

She felt a bolt of guilt. She was enjoying Harry's company in a way she didn't Cody's. Not right now, at least. Not with things so unsettled between them. But that was natural, she supposed. She and Cody were used to each other, and facing huge stressors — a wedding, the election, public life. There would be ups and downs. And she was working to fix things with Cody, yes. But that was currently a painful and a precarious situation that was going to need more from both of them before things were fully right again. There was no shame in feeling easier, and happier, with Harry. She needed something easy in her life right now.

Eliza pulled on her gloves and adjusted her scarf in the elevator on the way down. "All I wanted was to talk," she said. "We don't have to go anywhere."

"Perhaps," Harry said. "But I've been cooped up inside all day and need a break." He looked at her sidelong in the mirrored walls of the elevator. "And I'm going to guess that you could use a break, too."

From his tone Eliza couldn't tell if he meant a break from her relationship troubles or from the extreme-dog-grooming game. She didn't ask. In either case he was right.

"Where are we going?" Eliza asked when Harry took an unexpected turn down a street they hadn't taken before on their occasional outings for coffee or lunch.

He gave her a small smile. "You'll see."

They walked in silence until they reached one of midtown Manhattan's big glass buildings. Lunch crowds swarmed around them. There was little, as far as Eliza could tell, to recommend this place to anyone, much less anyone who needed a break from work and life.

Harry seemed to suspect what she was thinking. "Wait until you see it," he said and opened the door for her. Inside was a lobby, just like any other corporate building, but Harry led her past a bank of elevators, around a corner and, suddenly, out into a lush, warm, green space.

A wintergarden, and not one Eliza had known existed. Many stories above, through the glass ceiling, she could see blue sky and the pale winter sun. Down below, trees and plants ringed a pond — complete with a waterfall — that bubbled quietly to itself.

"I didn't even know this was here," Eliza said.

"Good. I was hoping you didn't." Harry led her along the little path to a bend where one bench was tucked out of sight of the others, but still in view of the little waterfall.

Eliza sat down next to him. She should ask, perhaps, why instead of going and getting a cup of coffee like two normal human beings on a break, Harry had brought her to one of the hidden gems of New York. But that would be treading too close to the danger that always lurked around the edges with them — but wasn't that what she wanted? The danger that came with the way she and Harry fell into each other and crashed against each other like waves?

"Why wouldn't you talk to me on Saturday?" she asked.

Harry shook his head. "You didn't want to talk."

"I did," she protested.

"You didn't. You wanted a solution. Which I was not in the position to offer. Did you two make up?"

Eliza looked at the trees growing indoors. Above them, clouds were moving in, and the bright sunlight faded. She thought about disputing Harry's statement. But she couldn't. She even knew the solution she'd wanted him to suggest. At least in the few fleeting moments she'd let it float up from deep in her subconscious where it bobbed at the corner of her eye, faint in her peripheral vision, like a ship far on the horizon that disappeared whenever looked at directly.

"I didn't tell you we fought," she said.

"It was rather obvious."

"I'm sorry," Eliza said.

"Whatever for?"

She sighed. "I don't know. Are we friends? Is anything we talk about anything we should be talking about?"

Harry looked unsettled. "We talk about books."

"Does that mean we're friends or that we aren't?" she pressed.

"We talk about books we don't like. That means we're friends."

Only friends? Eliza wondered. She wished she were brave enough to ask the question aloud. But then where would that leave her? She'd already put so much work into keeping things solid with Cody. There was no point in overturning that boat. No matter how pleasant the faint scent of Harry's cologne was, or how much she wanted to press her lips to the hollow of his throat.

"Cody and I did make up," Eliza said. "For now at least. Most of a woman's life is cajoling other people for her freedom, though."

Harry nodded solemnly. "It's a terrible business. And very much another reason I've never been married."

"Not wanting to be nagged?"

"No. Not wanting to be anyone's jailer." Harry paused and then looked at her keenly. Too keenly. Eliza wanted to look away, but his gaze kept her pinned in place. "You don't need me to tell you to advocate for your own desires," he went on. "But whoever tells you that you have to give up your freedom to be an adult — or a woman — is lying."

For a moment Eliza wondered if Harry was going to tell her she should break off her engagement. She wondered, too, if she wanted him to as she had for that moment on Saturday.

But Harry, unperturbed by Eliza's inability to say anything, offered a far simpler suggestion. "I believe we passed a coffee shop on the way here. May I get you something?"

It would have been easier, Eliza thought, as Harry left with a promise to return quickly, if he had come out and told her not to marry Cody. If he had made some proposition or offer instead. Then she could have yelled at him and stormed away. And there would be no reason to come back and make amends, to fold herself up again until she fit into the mold her mother and her husband-to-be had made for her. She could simply be quit of Harry.

There would be freedom in that, to be sure. She would be gone from this job next fall and none of it would matter at all.

But Harry had said nothing of the sort, just brought her somewhere lovely — and been lovely — and then left her alone in peace with her own thoughts.

Which made everything more complicated.

8

♦

In Countries of Exile

Harry

Steven's memorial service was in Connecticut in the first week of February, two days before Harry had to leave for Vienna to re-tackle his mess of a book. The Manuscript Miscreants spent the night before the service in a hotel bar drinking to Steven's memory and re-telling all the stories they had told at Christmas, when he had been alive and talk of his death had merely been a joke in bad taste. Harry was mostly silent; he felt too old and too tired. Besides, Dennis could tell most of the stories he could as well, if not better. He retreated to his hotel room early to be alone with his thoughts, but lay in bed in the dark for a long time, wondering if he should be using his time better. On his manuscript. Or on any work at all.

Certainly, not on continuing to think about Eliza, which he really needed to stop doing. As much as he would have enjoyed having her here, she had better things to do than the emotional labor of attending to an old, sad man.

The memorial the next morning itself was subdued, if not downright dismal. Once it was over Harry could remember nothing of it except the sight of Mallory in profile, her face too pale and her dark hair making the shadows under her eyes more evident. There was a luncheon after for family and friends, but the Manuscript Miscreants slipped away in twos and threes. Harry said the goodbyes he couldn't avoid and escaped back to his hotel room, this time with Meryl.

"Connecticut in February," he said as he sank down into one of the armchairs by the window, "is the most miserable place on earth."

Meryl sat down in the other armchair, leaning her cane against the side of it. She didn't dignify Harry's statement with a response, and he was well aware it didn't deserve one. They sat in silence for a long time, his eyes tracing over patterns in the wallpaper. As much as he wanted to be in his own home, he was glad he'd taken the room for tonight as well. The idea of having to get himself packed and to the train station today was utterly intolerable. Even if he was going to get home tomorrow afternoon and then have to leave for the airport, and Vienna, that same evening.

Gradually Harry shifted his gaze to Meryl. She was watching him now far more than she was looking out the window at the parking lot, thinly dusted with snow.

"How's your move coming?" Harry asked in a strained attempt to break the silence.

"Well enough." She shifted in her chair. "Finding an apartment in New York is a nightmare. Especially from afar."

"Stay at my place," Harry said impulsively.

Meryl raised an eyebrow.

"Not — while I'm there," he hastened to add. "I'm leaving tomorrow for Vienna, and I'll be gone for a week. If it works for your schedule, I'll give you a key now and you can use that as your base."

"I appreciate it," Meryl said. "Really, I do. But I've never intruded on your hospitality like that before, and I'm not going to start now."

Harry allowed that with a bow of his head. He was relieved they had both gone through the motions, but uncertain how he felt about the outcome.

"Now, I'm going to ask you something," Meryl said.

"What's that?"

"Why haven't we fucked?"

"Excuse me," Harry spluttered. "We don't always sleep together. Also, we're not on holiday."

"No, but we are at Steven's funeral. I have no expectations that have been disappointed, mind, but I am surprised. I thought you'd want some comfort. So my question is this, Harry. Have we not fucked because we're too close to New York and because my move makes everything too awkward, or have we not fucked because there's someone else?"

"There being someone else has never stopped me sleeping with you before," Harry deflected with something like panic. He was well aware of his own feelings for Eliza, but he didn't know how to discuss them with someone else. Even Meryl.

"Is it the girl you work with? Is she still engaged?"

"She is," Harry said, answering one question without answering the other. "I'm not sure for how long."

Meryl gasped. She turned towards him, eager. "What have you done?"

"Nothing. And I'm going to continue to do nothing" Harry said, "Sometimes, people's lives fall apart without outside help."

◆

Vienna, Harry mused forty-eight hours later as he took the CAT from the airport into the city, was either the very best place to have a midlife crisis, or the very worst. It was, on its surface, a quiet, serious city, with more opportunities to experience classical music than to get into any sort of decadent trouble. But the people who thought that didn't know much about classical music or the multi-course, multi-bottle, and multi-hour dinners that sprawled out across the city's restaurants.

When Harry had first come to Vienna, as a man less than half his current age, he had thought it a city keeping secrets. But over time he had learned to think of it merely as a city without shame, and that it had no need to flaunt the pleasures it so readily offered.

He'd chosen a B&B in Margareten, in part because ball season made hotel rooms somewhat difficult to come by on short notice, and also because he thought human contact beyond subdued and impersonal-by-design service might do him well. He could have rented an apartment, but on this trip he felt no interest in cooking for himself. Vienna's food culture, with its celebration of game meats and rich stews infused with the flavors of both east and west, was made for this time of year.

The streets, as he wandered them, were full of the debutantes and their escorts who had descended on the city. They came from the rest of Austria, from the broader German-speaking world, from the expanse of the European continent and beyond. They hustled through the city like thick patches of clouds, the young women in white dresses, the men in their tails, their rosy cheeks a testament to the weather as much as the embarrassment, no matter how coveted, of entering society. Harry wondered if Eliza had been a debutante and how significant her debut had been. Had it been a purely Bostonian affair, or had she made it to the International Debutante Ball hosted traditionally at the Waldorf? Harry was sure he could look it up, but he was also sure he didn't want to.

He'd attend a ball later in the week — it was something people who read travel books cared about — but right now he had no idea how he'd find something to say about that, or anything else, that wasn't about *her*.

◆

Late the next morning, after he'd spent hours typing and deleting useless words on his computer, Harry shoved himself back from his desk at the B&B and stared at his keyboard in consternation. He was supposed to be fixing his book, which was supposed to be about the glamor and enjoyableness of Vienna. He was not supposed to be obsessing over his word count and watching the minutes tick by on the clock. He needed to get out of his room.

He stopped at the Naschmarkt because there was no point to being in Vienna without indulging in very good snacks. Hopefully, an excess of sugar and carbs would combat the jetlag he was already feeling. It was one of his favorite places in Vienna, the perfect example of the blend of East and West, youth and age.

To his own dismay, as he perused dried sugar fruits and a thousand types of peppers stuffed with sweet, soft cheese, he kept looking over his shoulder as if he expected someone to be there. *Someone.* He mocked himself. He was looking for Eliza.

He couldn't shake the feeling as he cut through Resselpark, passing students and tourists enjoying a rare moment of winter sun on the broad, shallow steps of Karlskirche. It would have been so natural to sit there with her, sharing coffee and pastry from the market.

Harry cursed. It had been foolish enough, not to mention self-indulgent, to bring her to the wintergarden in New York. He didn't need to populate this place with his fantasies of her as well. So he pushed on.

He stood in Stephanzplatz looking up at the cathedral. Making a visit to a church that shared the name of his recently dead friend was possibly a mistake. Steven, if he were alive, would not have the slightest bit of patience for Harry's moroseness on that front.

He caught the last tour down to the catacombs, which was definitely a mistake. The last thing Harry needed, when he was feeling old and tired, was to be led through tunnels and caverns full of bones. Ordinarily it would have fascinated him, but today it felt gruesome.

When his group emerged from under the ground, they and the other tourists were being shooed out of the Cathedral in preparation for evening mass. Harry dodged the docents and found himself a seat in the last pew. Maybe the moment would make a good passage in his book. As he sat here, he thought of Eliza and the day Steven died when they'd sat in St. Patrick's Cathedral together, hiding their smuggled lunches.

Eliza

With Harry in Vienna, Eliza was left at loose ends. She had plenty of work to do, and a million things to deal with in her personal life, but the city was dreary without him. Even if the sun had finally come out within a day of his departure.

While his absence did not alleviate her workaholic tendencies, it did remove her desire to spend more than eight hours a day in the office. She caught herself looking up from her screen constantly, hoping to catch a glimpse of him in the hall, come to plague her with Philippe's latest complaint or another pronouncement from their perennially unseen boss.

Embarrassed, she'd slam her laptop shut and escape the office entirely. She went in search of cafés and public spaces to work in, like the hired gun she was. As soon as work hours were over she took long walks through the city by herself, soaking up the atmosphere of a place she loved. Like a woman who would be leaving New York far sooner than she wanted to be, whether Cody let her finish out her contract in the office or not.

Let. She couldn't believe herself. Or him. She could say the election and the TV appearances and all the rest of it were simply going to his head; she'd be right. But the far more important question, which neither of them could answer right now, was when that would pass.

She guessed she needed to have faith in Cody's goodness, just like she had always had faith in his fidelity all the years they'd been long distance and racing after their individually successful destinies. But it seemed like such a big ask, that a man seeking public power would be willing to let control go at home.

More than once while she was holed up in a coffee shop Jonathan called Eliza's cell phone to remind her to return for a meeting. After a few days, he took to leaving her suggestions of cafés closer to the office from which she could be easily recalled. Eliza felt horribly guilty about it — managing her schedule was not remotely part of Jonathan's job description — but he just shrugged and suggested his intervention was easier than the alternative for the both of them.

As the days of Harry's absence dragged on 'easier than the alternative' became a grim standard by which she evaluated her actions every time she faced a choice. Yes, there was value in letting Philippe's tirades pass over her like water and smiling and nodding through Cody's calls about his campaign. But what if the alternative and all her rage and brilliance was the better answer, not just occasionally, but always?

9

♦

A Girl and her Key

Harry

Walking into the ballroom at the Hoffburg a few days after his arrival in Vienna was like stepping back in time, into a version of New York society that had never quite existed. The city had its balls and its debutantes to be sure. But it could never hold them in actual castles, and Harry wasn't sure it could assemble this many ball-goers and nervous, poised young women under one roof once in the year, much less night after night and ball after ball as was done here.

Harry had questioned the wisdom of going to a ball alone. The Viennese did not attend these events with the expectation of socializing with people they did not already know. His chances of talking with anyone here were near zero, and his chances of dancing even lower.

But there was, for all its absurdity, something splendid and melancholy about standing alone by himself in this great room surrounded by beautiful women in ballgowns and beautiful men in formalwear. All he hoped for was one moment of serendipitous loveliness to make getting dressed up and coming out here worth it.

Harry drifted from the edge of the ballroom to a bar in an antechamber. Distracted by his thoughts, he ordered in

English. A girl nearby gave him a startled look before turning back to her group of friends. A moment later they approached him.

"Excuse me," the girl said. She was in her early twenties, with pink pale skin like she had spent a long time in a hot shower, and she wore a floor-length wine-colored gown "You're not from here, are you?"

Harry smiled politely, no more enthused about human contact that he'd been moments ago. "I'm from the States."

"Oh! That works!" From her accent, Harry guessed she was from London, or at least had spent a lot of time there. She glanced at her companions and then confided, "We thought this would be a lovely idea but everyone is here with people, and we feel a bit foolish. I hope you don't think we're rude to say hello, but we didn't mean to come all this way just to stand in a corner by ourselves."

"Not at all," Harry assured her. "As you can see, I'm companionless." In spite of himself, he was charmed by them, their attempt at manners mixed with sheer bravado. Their leader put him in mind of Eliza, although she lacked Eliza's poise and her emerging sense of scorn for this world. Too, she seemed so much younger. Harry sipped at his wine.

"You're really not here with anyone? We thought we'd just separated you from the herd," The girl looked surprised and looked around them as if to confirm that Harry was telling the truth.

"Alone, as you see me." Harry dipped his head. "Harry Sargent."

"I'm Rose," the girl introduced herself. Her companions introduced themselves as well.

"Do you dance?" another of the girls, Jane, asked a bit too eagerly.

"I do."

"Dance with us? Just — we practiced, a lot, before we left home, and now we're here and this isn't a place where we can dance with each other."

"Oh, I don't think that's true at all," Harry said. He'd seen a handful of same-gender couples since he'd arrived, and women dancing with each other due to awkward gender ratios was a tradition as old as war.

"None of us know how to lead," Rose confessed in a rushed hurry.

"Ahhhhhhh." Harry did so love to dance, and social dancing was not innately a sexual thing, but the American in him did feel a slight pause at having to share space so closely with any of this bevy of girls he had just met. Even so, he smiled. He'd come to Vienna for some sort of story, after all. Someone else's would certainly do far better than his own. He made a decision.

"I'd be honored," he said and held out his arm to whichever of them would take it.

"Is this all right?" Harry asked once he'd led Rose to the dance floor before they entered the dance embrace.

"I did ask you to dance," she reminded him.

"Yes. But one makes no assumptions."

She had a decent sense of the music, but her practice had not been adequate to so advanced a ballroom. The second time she accidentally stepped on his toes Harry winked at her. "Breathe and relax," he said. "You're thinking too much."

"I'm sorry," she apologized, flustered. "I thought I was better at this than I am. Clearly."

"No need to apologize," Harry said. "You can't hardly improve without practice. You feel my hand here?" He pressed against her back where his hand rested, careful not to touch her bare skin.

She nodded.

"Lean back into it and go where I put you. The problem isn't that you're stepping on my feet, but that you're touching the floor entirely too much. Let me do the work."

They started again, this time with Harry counting the rhythm softly to her until she relaxed enough to actually let him lead.

She smiled up at him. "This isn't so hard."

"No, indeed."

"Why are you here?" Rose asked. When Harry blinked, uncertain if she meant the city or the ball, she clarified. "Vienna, I mean."

"I'm writing a book," Harry confessed. He'd yet to find a way to say that he was a writer without sounding absurd and had given up trying years ago.

"Oh! Brilliant!"

Harry smiled at her gently. Saying he was a writer was unfortunate enough. Saying he was a struggling one tended to be absolutely deadly. "Hopefully it will be. Eventually. It's still very much a work in progress."

"What's it about?"

"I'm not sure yet. Which is part of my problem. Why are you here?"

"Hen party." She looked slightly sheepish. "Multi-day multi-country hen party."

"Ah. And who's getting married?" Harry hoped he didn't sound as awkward as he felt as he whirled her around the dance floor. After all, a random girl's marriage was of no particular concern to him beyond a vague hope that she found happiness in it. Eliza's, on the other hand…. It was best not to think about it.

Eliza

Eliza's doubts about the wisdom of flying up to Boston for a weekend to go wedding dress shopping were proved to be just within an hour of her arrival. While brunch was supposed to fortify her for the task ahead, her mother and sister were listing off who she should invite of her college classmates and childhood acquaintances.

Eliza didn't care enough about the question to get involved in the conversation, which only prompted her mother to try to engage her interest more. She had to swallow down several pointed remarks about the absurdity of inviting people she'd never liked and hadn't spoken with more than was socially required in years. Yes, this was a society wedding, but really.

"Oh, sweetheart, why didn't you get your nails done for today?" Eliza's mother asked once they had ordered. "Your hands look dreadful."

Catherine closed her fingers over Eliza's, who stared at her own nails. Sure, her manicure was chipped, but that wasn't anything new. Despite being trained to be compulsively well put together, getting her nails done ranked below both coffee and books on her priority list.

"Why?" she asked. "No one's going to be taking pictures today."

Her mother and Marianne looked instantly affronted.

"Close-up pictures, of my hands, that will be distributed in any official format," Eliza clarified.

"Well, still," Her mother protested. "There's no reason not to look your best and show off the ring."

Which was the most accurate indicator Eliza could possibly get as to how this day was going to go.

At the bridal salon they were introduced to their consultant, who smiled coolly and asked Eliza what sort of style she was interested in.

"Ball gowns," her mother answered before Eliza could open her mouth. "Youthful, but not too frivolous. Strapless is fine, but nothing plunging," she said, giving a pointed look to a nearby mannequin exhibiting a very large skirt and a very low bodice. "And understated, *please.*"

"Are you shy or is your mother overbearing?" her consultant asked as Eliza was whisked off to a fitting room after a cringeworthy discussion of how there wasn't a budget. The dress would cost what the dress would cost.

"I do like simple," Eliza said. Too many of the dresses were coated in sequins and crystals in a manner she found garish. "And I'm not totally opposed to a ballgown, but could you find a sheath for me to try too?"

The first dress brought out for her had so much fabric in it Eliza could hardly move. She was desperate to take a picture of herself and send it to Harry with the caption *I look like a cupcake*. But as much as he'd be on her side, the joke wasn't one she could make. Not with him.

The second was more promising: layers of sheer material that might have, but did not, resemble a Disney princess dress. As the consultant helped her with a veil, she caught her own eye in the mirror through the layer of tulle. She could make this work. Her mother, when she saw it, agreed, dabbing away tears.

The third dress was the sheath. As Eliza stepped into it and the consultant did up the back she was overcome by a sensation that she'd read about in bridal magazines but had been sure did not actually exist: The sense of *Yes, this dress, this is the one.*

The sensation only increased when she saw herself in the mirror. The clean, white lines of the dress as it flowed down her body, the fine illusion netting that formed the yoke and the sleeves, an acknowledgement of the flesh without putting it on display. This was a grown-up's wedding dress, and it suited her.

"You look beautiful, of course," her mother said with a frown as Eliza paraded herself, much more willingly this time, in front of the mirrors for inspection. "But it doesn't quite suit the tone of the event."

Eliza stopped cold, her arms still slightly outstretched, and stared at her reflection in horror. Her mother was exactly right. The ballgowns — the princess dresses — were right for the wedding her mother was planning and the marriage that she and Cody were supposed to have. This dress she was wearing right now, this grown-up gown, this was the perfect dress. But it had nothing to do with Cody, or the day of her wedding to him.

Eliza did the only reasonable thing: She burst into tears.

There was an instant commotion around her. Marianne cooed that they could surely come to some compromise with her mother, the consultant made generally soothing noises, and her mother both rejoiced at this level of emotional investment and tried to scold Eliza back into composure.

Eliza put one hand over her face to hide the fact that, despite her mother's entreaties, she had not worn waterproof mascara today. She held the other out to ward off her would-be consolers.

"Please," she finally managed to get out. "I need a moment. Can I have a moment, please?"

She needed much more than that. She needed Harry. But she needed space to breathe first.

Finally, the consultant managed to herd the two other women away from Eliza and got her back into the dressing room and onto a chair, where she pressed tissues and a glass of water into her hands.

"Take deep breaths now," she said, her hand a soothing warmth on Eliza's arm as she knelt in front of her chair. "Big emotions are completely normal. There now," she encouraged, when Eliza managed to get her breathing back under control.

"Is it normal to decide to call the wedding off while trying on dresses?" Eliza asked.

The woman patted her arm kindly. "It happens more often than you'd think. Are you thinking you'll elope, or do you want to break off the engagement entirely?"

Eliza stared at her and had to take several sips of water before she could overcome the urge to break into hysterical laughter. "You really do deal with everything here, don't you?"

The woman gave her a beatific smile.

"I can't do it," Eliza said. She smoothed her hands over the cool white fabric she still wore. "This is the right dress. But it's not...this wedding — It's not the right life at all."

Harry had been correct. A truly happy life was about freedom. Marriage, if it suited anyone, should be about stepping into a life of possibility, not a cage.

Harry

Harry had three principles he tried to adhere to when he was writing. The first was that writing was a job like any other, and he couldn't refrain from producing words simply because he wasn't in the mood. The second was that some days just left a man feeling unproductive at his occupation, and there were only so many hours it was useful to sit at desk willing oneself to make a word count that just wouldn't come. The third was that, as a writer, he was obligated to trust himself and follow his inspirations and obsessions.

If he couldn't find a way to make his Vienna manuscript both marketable and satisfying to himself, he could at least write about what was haunting him here: His age, mortality, the winter loneliness of this city, and Eliza and Eliza and Eliza. Once he got his melancholic moonings onto paper, maybe he could get them out of his brain and finally be able to focus on the work he needed to get done here.

Of course, once he gave himself permission to write about whatever he pleased, the words flowed easily. Twenty thousand words that first day. Another ten thousand the next. And then he kept going, writing and polishing until he had ninety perfect and complete pages with no purpose he could actually discern. It wasn't a memoir or a travel book. It was too long for magazines and too short for publishers. Anika was going to kill him. Eliza was going to kill him. Although she didn't need to know. He'd called her Betts in the manuscript anyway, as if saying her true name would conjure some sort of doom.

But the shame he expected to feel, about the state of his life and the state of his heart, was absent. Instead he'd written freely, even finding a way to work into this narrative the legend of Ys that had been so cruelly excised from his Brittany book.

Because Harry knew Eliza from somewhere. And he had met her in the water, in that ridiculous hotel pool in Frankfurt. They lived, each of them, trapped behind gates — she of her family expectations and impending marriage, and he of the iron that protected the mews which held his strange little house. Maybe, somehow, one or the other of them could find the keys that would set them both free.

And if that imagined and hoped-for act destroyed everything else? If Eliza had the same role as the woman in the story, Dahut, who unlocked the gates and let the sea flood the city? Harry didn't think he cared at all.

Eliza

After the scene at the bridal boutique, Eliza's family treated her as if she were the heroine of a Victorian novel: Suffering from the amorphous burden of being a woman and the overwhelming demands of her impending destiny as a wife. It was galling. But it was also convenient. Eliza took advantage of the situation to stay silent as her mother and sister hustled her into a taxi and cooed over her all the way back to the house. As long as she seemed too distraught or exhausted to speak, she wouldn't have to tell them about her decision. She wouldn't even have to tell Cody.

How am I going to tell Cody?

There was simply no good way. In her family's home was too awkward. On his territory, too perilous. In public, over a meal, too cruel. And then there was the matter of the campaign. He was busy. He didn't need distractions. And he was a face that, for the moment at least, the entire city knew.

A hundred times that afternoon, as she sat on the cushioned window seat in her old room, she thought about calling Harry. He would have an idea. He would have a way to make her laugh and a way to make her certain. But that wasn't his job, and she didn't want her choice to be his burden. She wasn't choosing him over Cody. She wasn't. She was choosing herself over the life a marriage with Cody would limit her to. And her friendship with Harry was a part of that.

She'd never really had friends before. But Harry, and Jonathan, and really anyone at the publisher who found out that she had to work with Philippe. Some of the women in marketing had even started inviting her out for drinks, although she hadn't figured out how to say yes yet.

Right now, though, she needed to figure out how to say no. And so she paced. But there were no answers in walking, and she flopped back down on the window seat with far more force than its limited padding truly supported.

"Ow!" Something oddly shaped pressed against her thigh, the muffled outline of it digging into her flesh. She bounced up again and lifted the cushion.

A key.

The key to the hope chest she hadn't been able to find and had irrationally feared would fall into Cody's hands. She snatched it up and, after a brief consideration, dug in the desk in the corner for twine, for thread, for anything. When she could find nothing that suited her uses, she went to the chest and unlocked it.

She piled the contents on the floor — good plates, silver, a set of mother-of-pearl caviar spoons, table cloths, wedding lingerie that likely wouldn't fit her, a white quilt, and two pillowcases with lace trim. She grabbed one and tugged at the decoration. It pulled away from the plainer fabric of the case, but didn't tear. She took her teeth to it until it ripped free.

Eliza placed everything back into the chest as quickly as she could, relocked it, threaded the key onto the lace and tucked the key down her shirt. This was her freedom. For now, a secret, though not for much longer. But as long as she had the key, she could believe she would be okay.

♦

She lasted a whole day before she had to speak with Cody. He called her, all quiet concern, on Sunday night. He apologized for not trying to contact her before, but Eliza hastened to assure him it was all right. After all, she'd been pretending to have a migraine — circumstances in which she wouldn't want to be on the phone with anyone anyway. Then he asked if he could see her off at the airport the next day.

Eliza said yes. Although it was the most public, awful scenario she could imagine. But they were WASPs, and maybe the audience of the whole thing would force their permanent parting into quiet.

♦

In the car to the airport Eliza sat silently while Cody, still speaking in hushed tones, suggested she stay in Boston to see a doctor, or at least find a decent specialist when she got to New York. It was only when they went inside the terminal that he noticed the key, strung on its ragged lace, around her neck.

He touched it casually, the way he often touched her hair or her face. As if he owned it, or as if she was a pet whose attention he wanted. It wasn't his fault — he was benevolent enough — but he didn't know any other way to be.

"What's this?" he asked.

Eliza swallowed down a sudden burst of adrenaline. "The key to my hope chest."

"You found it!" Cody sounded delighted and — ironically, given the circumstances — more interested in the minutiae of her life than he had in ages. "I thought you said it was missing."

"It was. It was under a cushion in my old room. Which is strange, but whatever." *Ask, dammit, ask already so I can do this.*

"Why are you wearing it?"

Eliza took a deep breath. "Because it's mine. Because I don't want anyone else to have it or have access to the things in that box."

"What's in the box?" Cody asked, glancing nervously from side to side. "There's not something dead in the box is there?"

Eliza gave a sharp laugh in spite of herself. Oh he was lovely, sometimes. But this Cody, who cared about where she found old trinkets and who could make her laugh, she never saw him enough. If she did, maybe…but she didn't. And now she was here.

"There's nothing dead in the box," she said. "But I hate it. The box, the parties, the photos. The wedding boutique was terrible." Her words picked up speed as she spoke, as if water was bursting through a dam. "I've known this for a while, but finding the key made it impossible for me to ignore. I don't want any of this. I'm sorry. I'm doing this in an airport, and I am so sorry." Eliza twisted her engagement ring around her finger. "I can't marry you."

Cody's eyebrows knit together in concern. "If you want to elope —"

"I don't!" she said with a force that surprised her. "I don't," she said a second time, more softly, but more forcefully too. "I can't marry you. Or anyone. It's not what I want, and it's not who I am —"

He reached for her, as if he were going to take her hand, and then drew back. "Eliza, we can talk about this."

"We can, but my answer is going to be the same. And if there's any hope of this ever being all right between us, I would like, very much, if you would take this ring off my hand." She held the left one out. *Set me free, set me free, set me free* she chanted in her head.

"I'm not going to do that," Cody said.

She pursed her lips and looked down for a moment at her hand and at the floor. They were so close the tips of their shoes were almost touching. The world would never look this way again. Then she looked up at the man who was about to be h er ex-fiancé and stared into his eyes. He'd be a great and powerful man one day soon, but in a way that would be as completely boring and useless as nearly every other great and powerful man.

"Then I've made the right choice," she said.

Eliza took off the ring and pressed it into Cody's hand. She turned, walked to the security line, and showed her boarding pass on her phone, the guard allowing her to pass where Cody could not follow.

10

♦

These Messages from the Dead

Harry

Harry dragged himself into the little mews and through the front door of his house wishing he'd spent another day, or perhaps several, in Vienna. Anything would be better than being home with nothing to distract him from grief and his own inappropriate desire for Eliza. About whom he'd written a secret book and who he would have to see at the office tomorrow.

He dropped his suitcase by the door and stooped to pick up the mail that had accumulated on the hall floor. Most of it was junk, but amongst the anonymous white envelopes was a package. It was small, about the size of a trade paperback, and addressed to Harry in Steven's handwriting.

Harry left the rest of the mail where it was and took the package into the kitchen. He slit the flaps of the box open, careful not to cut or mar the so-familiar hand spelling out his name and address.

Inside was, indeed, a small volume. The cover was plain brown leather, the pages heavy cream. All of them were covered in Steven's tidy script.

You fucking bastard, Harry thought. He snapped the book shut and set it on the counter. *You sent me your diary.*

♦

Harry returned to his office the next day with the diary tucked into his bag. In the current circumstances, focusing on the minutiae of other authors and their careers was difficult. Which was no more than Harry deserved, and yet he felt a chill, no matter how irrational, every time he saw the diary sitting innocuously on the corner of his desk. Maybe he should have left it at home, but he wanted the diary to be somewhere he could keep an eye on it.

After a huddle with Jonathan to triage the worst of the disasters that had occurred while he had been gone he spent the morning playing catch-up with his inbox and avoiding picking up the phone. If people wanted to talk to him, they could come and find him. But even without the distraction of the phone his attention kept straying: To the city he'd just left, to the manuscript he'd just finished, to the woman he'd written it about — and to Steven's diary.

At lunch Harry grabbed a sandwich from a place down the street and cloistered himself at his desk again. He needed to deal with the thing he'd written about Eliza, and he needed to deal with Steven's diary. If he didn't, he'd never be able to focus on any of the work he was paid to do.

He managed the first issue by sending the book to Anika. *I didn't entirely waste the trip to Vienna,* he wrote her in the email. *These aren't the words I was supposed to write, but I still made words!*

As soon as he hit send, he wished he hadn't. He felt acutely embarrassed by his own weakness, and whatever ego had made him think the book about Eliza was a problem Anika could solve.

But calling Anika and telling her to ignore the email was even worse a prospect, so he turned to Steven's diary. Harry handled the pages carefully so as not to get any of his lunch on them, pausing here and there to read passages without any order or plan.

It was, all things considered, a perfectly ordinary diary. Steven had started it soon after his diagnosis. The earliest entries were about mundane things. His concern about his health and the effect an extended illness would have on Mallory. Griping about the weather. Recounting a stag he'd seen on a walk in the woods. Noting with pleasure phone calls he'd gotten from Dennis, Meryl, and Harry himself.

Harry's cell phone ringing startled him out of his perusal. He glanced at the clock and realized with a jolt an entire hour had passed. He set the diary down gently and picked up his phone with trepidation. It was Anika.

"Harry, what the hell have you done?" she asked without further greeting.

"What do you mean, what have I done?" Harry asked. There were a lot of things she could reasonably fault him for. But he wanted to know on which of many perfectly fair grounds she was going to attack him.

"You've sent me a ninety-page memoir — I mean, I think it's a memoir? — that's absolutely brilliant and perfect and I didn't know you had it in you, but what the hell am I supposed to do with ninety pages? Also your Vienna book is still missing."

He knew the only words he had been able to write in Vienna were some of the best he'd ever produced. And now, to his utter glee, they were making someone who wasn't him completely miserable. "Copping to the second and relying on your wisdom and expertise on the first."

"You're the absolute worst." Anika sighed. "Also, as someone who would like to consider herself your friend, can I suggest you get your personal life straightened out? For the sake of your sanity."

At that moment, the subject of those ninety pages appeared in the doorway of Harry's office. After days of daydreaming and writing about her Eliza was standing right in front of him. She was pale and drawn but also looking at him with a certain level of judgment and curiosity that he had missed desperately. Harry wondered what was wrong. He also wondered how much of the conversation with Anika he was going to be able to have without giving away the fact that he was suddenly being confronted with the subject of his book.

In her left hand Eliza held her tablet, but that wasn't what Harry's eyes latched on to.

"Your hand," he muttered at Anika. And then, even more absurdly, he hung up on her.

He stared at his cell phone, startled and confused by his own actions, then blinked up at Eliza.

"Are you okay?" he asked. She wasn't wearing her engagement ring. And that, combined with her pallor and the dark circles under her eyes, made Harry wonder. *What happened with her fiancé?* Hope and dread warred in his chest, and he chastised himself for both. Whatever Eliza was dealing with, he needed to not make it any worse. In any way.

"I'm fine," she said shortly. Then she gave him a faint smile that didn't reach her eyes. "Do you need to call back whoever you just hung up on, or can we talk about the media proposals for Paris that I'm afraid to show to Philippe?"

Oh God. Paris! Harry could feel himself panicking.

"Um. It was my agent. I should probably email her. At some point," he managed.

Eliza stared at him. "All right. Sounds good. I just have to —" she said after a long moment, turned, and fled.

Harry stared after her and wondered, sincerely, what the hell was happening — with Eliza's ring, with her relationship, with his book — and what on earth he was supposed to do next.

Eliza

As she ran down the hallway to escape Harry's office and her own inner confusion she'd found there, Eliza collided with Jonathan, caught her heel on the carpet, and nearly fell.

"I need to stop doing that," she said, apologizing profusely.

Jonathan caught her by the elbows to steady her. "Are you all right?"

"No!" she blurted. Her nerves had been on edge ever since the dress fitting. She'd gone to Harry's office only because she needed to ask him about the media proposals; she'd had no plan or intention of confessing or explaining anything. But seeing him had jolted whatever thin veneer of calm she'd been able to scrape together for the last two days, and now she was a trembling wreck.

"All right, well, you don't look okay. Why don't you come sit down for a bit?" He took her gently by the hand and led her to his cubicle around the corner from Harry's office. The space was small, but there was an extra chair that Jonathan sat her down in. He flicked on an electric kettle on top of a filing cabinet before sitting down himself.

Eliza folded her hands in her lap and tried to take deep breaths. She felt as near to panic as she had at the bridal shop. She was so relieved for Jonathan's kind intervention, but in spite of that — or maybe because of it — she still felt on the verge of tears.

"Thank you," she said when she felt sure enough of her voice to attempt speaking.

"Don't mention it." Jonathan waved her gratitude away. The kettle began whistling, and he spun in his chair to pour boiling water into two paper cups. Dunking a tea bag into each, he handed her one of them and then leaned toward her, bracing his elbows on his knees.

"Now. I'm not going to ask you what's wrong because it's none of my business," he said, "but I know my boss, and if you need me to yell at him on your behalf that's a lot of what I get paid to do."

Eliza gave a watery laugh. The warmth from the cup bled comfortingly into her hands. "No. He hasn't done anything to deserve being yelled at. At least not recently. But —"

"But?" Jonathan asked.

Looking at his serious face, his eyebrows drawn together, Eliza marveled that Jonathan was probably younger than she was. Perhaps his air of self-possession was as much of an illusion as her own, but she didn't think so.

"But I was going to get married next summer. We'd been engaged for a while and it was a perfect match except it completely wasn't. I went up to Boston this past weekend for a dress fitting and couldn't go through with it. I broke up with him yesterday at the airport right before I flew back here. Before I had a plan — I didn't like the plan, but I had one — and now I don't have any plan at all, and I have to cancel all sorts of wedding services and find a job for next year, and I don't even know where to start!"

"That was a lot of information all at once." Jonathan blinked at her very seriously. Eliza wondered whether that was a habit he'd learned from Harry. "And if you want to sit and drink tea and pretend we never talked about any of this that's totally fine. But I also have a lot of experience with logistical damage control. If you want moral support while you make a list of stuff you have to do in the next week or month or whatever, I am super happy to do that."

What Eliza most needed a plan for — how to encounter Harry now that she was no longer engaged — Jonathan couldn't help her with. But everything else?

"Moral support," she said, swirling tea carefully in her cup as if she were going to read her future in the leaves. "Sounds pretty fucking awesome."

Harry

It took Harry the better part of an hour, but he finally managed to compose an email to Anika complete with an apology for hanging up on her and a plea that they meet in person to discuss his situation further. To his relief, she offered to see him that afternoon, if he could be bothered to trek the three blocks down to her office. He agreed eagerly.

Sitting down across from Anika in her office, Harry felt like a schoolboy about to be scolded. Never mind that she was his own age and wore her greying hair pulled back in a soft ponytail, more hippie than schoolmarm.

"Did you have a nice time in Vienna?" she asked. The question was pointed even if her voice was conversational.

"For a given value of 'nice time,'" Harry said.

"Mmm. Well. At least you wrote. But Harry...."

He ran a hand over his face. "I know. I know."

"Do you now?" Anika asked. "I think that's unlikely."

"That's true, but —"

"Lucky for you, I'm smart, and I'm patient, and God help me, I'm vaguely fond of you. I think you have a couple of options."

"You do?" Harry dropped his hand from his face and looked at Anika with sudden budding hope. He'd expected to be berated. He hadn't at all expected to be thrown a life raft.

"Yes. I do. You may make questionable decisions but I'm very good at my job. So. Option one, you can rework this untitled monstrosity to make it a full-length memoir."

Harry made a face. The work stood on its own, for better or for worse. Weighing it down with more navel-gazing about his unremarkable life was not going to improve it.

"Yeah, that's what I thought. Worse, I think you're not wrong. It's exquisite as it is. But the length. I can't sell that. Not from you."

"So it's not publishable," Harry said with a flicker of relief. If Anika couldn't find a publisher for it, he was sure no one could. And then he would never have to be faced with the professional or personal humiliation of having written a book about a woman half his age. A woman who he had thought he could never have but had now possibly just dumped her fiancé.

He sighed inwardly at the thought. His self-discipline couldn't wait to fail him.

"Not as it currently exists," Anika replied. "Which brings us to option number two. Which is not optional."

"Which is?" Harry asked with trepidation.

"Fix your Vienna book. Stop blowing off that deadline, and stop pissing editors off."

"Or?"

"Or, Harry, I am going to fire you as my client."

"You mean that." The statement wasn't a question.

"You know I do. I meant it when I said I was fond of you. But that doesn't mean I have to put up with this nonsense, and I won't."

Harry believed her, which didn't make the sinking sensation in his stomach any more pleasant. Anika wouldn't be wrong to stop working with him, either. Not after the book he'd failed to write either on topic or on time. He'd missed deadlines before, everybody did, but not like this.

"All right," Harry said. "I'll fix the Vienna book. For real this time. And drop the book about…I'll drop the short book." He barely stopped himself from saying *the Betts book* in time. It was a conjuring and he was afraid of it. He was also so, so, screwed.

♦

Harry returned to his employer dismayed, chagrined, and working hard to figure out his next steps. Now he had two crises on his hands, Anika and Eliza, and not enough time to deal with the first and not enough data to deal with the second.

When he pushed open the door to his office, he found Jonathan standing over his desk laying out manila folders. Harry groaned at whatever responsibilities they represented.

Jonathan straightened up and turned around. "Quarterly sales reports for you to take a look at." He pointed at one stack. "Cover proposals for your feedback." He pointed to another. "And a final stack of random stuff people have wanted me to get to you for the last week and that I want off my desk."

Harry nodded mutely. No one liked a random stack. Not that he knew how he was going to passably perform his job in his current state anyway.

"What's going on?" Jonathan asked, frowning.

"This miserable job." Harry muttered. He picked up one of the folders and flipped through it, doing a poor job of pretending to look interested in its contents.

Jonathan heaved the very deep sigh of the extremely long-suffering. "You can tell me now, or you can send me a panicked email about deadlines and schedules at two in the morning that I'll ignore. In one of those situations I'm going to be infinitely more helpful to you."

Harry leaned against his desk and tossed the folder down.

"Harry," Jonathan scolded.

Harry shot him an apologetic glance and straightened the folder so that it was in line with the others. "I didn't write the book I was supposed to write in Vienna. Instead I wrote a book about my mid-life crisis brought on by a woman half my age — who was engaged, except she's just come back from a trip where I know she was wedding dress shopping, and she's not wearing her engagement ring."

"Are you talking about Eliza?" Jonathan looked gleefully aghast.

Harry gave him a baleful look.

"Don't glare at me, you're the one who apparently wrote the book about her," Jonathan retorted. "Though, let me tell you, you were not subtle about her before that."

"Then why'd you ask if it was her?"

"I like knowing my snark is tuned correctly."

Harry sighed. "Yes, it's about her. Anika says she can't sell it, and I was fine with pining after Eliza from afar, but now she's perhaps ended her engagement. What am I supposed to *do?*"

Jonathan looked as wearied by Harry's mental state as Harry himself felt. "Problems have solutions," he said, giving the folders on the desk a last nudge with his fingertip. "As to Eliza, you can get a grip and find some appropriate boundaries or you can be a human resources nightmare and send her an email like the gentleman that you are. Then you two can talk like adults who clearly have some sort of non-professional something going on."

"What?!"

"She curls up in your office chair like she's portraying domestic bliss in a coffee commercial."

"Why do I ask for your opinions again?"

Jonathan drew himself up into his primmest, straightest posture. "Because I'm right about everything."

"I hate you," Harry said weakly, but he felt his shoulders loosen slightly. Having someone else tell him what to do right now was exactly what he needed. "I don't suppose you also have a brilliant common-sense solution for what to do with my mess of a book?" he asked, already knowing that was hopeless.

"Which book?"

"Either."

"Sit down, write the damn Vienna book and try to remember it's not about you."

"Fair. And the other?"

Jonathan smiled. "Have you ever considered self-publishing?"

♦

Do you still want to talk about those media proposals for Philippe and Paris? Harry emailed Eliza that evening. He hoped that she had gone for the day, but whatever was afoot, she was having a rough time of it. He didn't need to make it worse. He did need to help her get her work done, even if he'd be happy to avoid facing her until tomorrow.

When half an hour passed with no reply Harry began to relax. After forty-five minutes he'd still heard nothing from her and also realized that he was hungry. Ordering takeout would solve that problem, but not his restlessness. He needed a break from his desk.

The test kitchen was empty and dark when he arrived. He flipped on the lights and turned on the radio, spinning the dial until he found NPR. The cupboards were as well-stocked as usual, and in no time at all Harry was whisking eggs for an omelet and humming to himself.

Until something moved in the corner of his eye. He glanced up involuntarily and nearly jumped out of his skin. Eliza was standing in the doorway watching him.

"I thought you'd gone home," Harry said inanely.

"I didn't."

"I can see that."

Eliza stared at Harry silently, refusing to grant him an explanation of what she was doing sneaking around the office at this hour.

Harry shrugged his shoulders, trying to rid himself of a sudden, unnerving chill.

Eliza stepped all the way into the kitchen and surveyed his work. "Omelets, Harry? All alone? Really?"

"You're going to judge my cooking?" He barely restrained himself from blurting out a question about her engagement.

"Your cooking is fine. I'm judging the fact you're cooking and didn't invite me down."

"I thought you went home," Harry repeated. "I sent an email, you didn't reply," he added by way of explanation. "I didn't want to bother you."

"I closed my email, I was trying to get actual work done."

"Ah."

For split second, it was as though Harry's vision shifted. Instead of standing in the office test kitchen, they were standing in Harry's kitchen at home in a scene far more domestic, but as strangely tense as this one.

He blinked, hard.

Eliza frowned. "What's wrong?"

"I'm…." As a matter of fact, Harry wasn't at all sure he wasn't in an accelerating process of losing his mind. But he could hardly tell Eliza that he was having domestic fantasies about her so vivid that he had, briefly, lost the ability to speak.

He turned his back to her and turned on the stove. The flame snapped to life with a click and hiss.

"Did you break off your engagement?" he asked. The words that he'd been working so hard to suppress came out of his mouth as if without his knowledge or permission. He winced at himself. So much for being graceful

Eliza paused before she spoke. "How do you know I was the one who broke it off?"

"Because I know you." That wasn't graceful either, but it was true.

"You do, and I did."

There. One piece of information I needed. And so many questions still to answer.

"You didn't tell me." Harry wasn't accusatory, just confused. About so many things. To cover, he poured the beaten eggs into the pan and sprinkled on toppings without paying much attention to type or quantity.

"It didn't have anything to do with you," Eliza said. "And what did you want me to do, text you from the scene of the crime?"

Yes. Desperately. "May I ask where the scene of the crime was?"

"In the airport. By the security line."

Harry tried and failed to stifle a laugh.

"It's in the papers too," Eliza said. "I either just ruined Cody's political career or made it."

Harry thought he could hear a smile in her voice. "Depends on the sympathy vote?" he asked.

Eliza nodded. "Something like that."

"Something," Harry echoed.

"What about this?" Eliza asked, gesturing between them with a courage Harry didn't share.

"What about it? We're friends." Internally, he cursed himself for saying the responsible thing.

"Are we, Harry?"

"I sure don't know what else we are." He risked a glance at her. She stood, her arms clasped demurely in front of her, but her eyes were sharp. Angry or hurt? He didn't know, but he was instantly contrite. Yet he didn't know how to take the words back any more than he knew how to bridge the perilous space between them.

Eliza gave a heavy sigh. "Do you need help?"

"Stop doing that," Harry snapped.

"Stop doing *what?*"

"Turning the subject. Pretending there's nothing peculiar between us."

"I'm doing no such thing," Eliza said. "You're the one insisting we're friends, all simple and neat. I'm the one asking you if you need help before you burn your food."

"There you go again!"

"Do you want to start a fire, Harry?"

Harry cursed and turned back to his smoldering omelet.

"I'm sorry," he said as he plated the thing, not that it was edible. "It's been a long day. Week. Month. Year."

"I *know.*" Eliza's voice was weary, her face strained. "For both of us." She perched herself on one of the bar stools arrayed around the central island and arranged her skirt carefully, giving them both time to recover themselves. Which should have dispelled the tension but electricity still crackled in the air around them.

"I'm going to have to start again," Harry said. "Do you want one?"

"If it's not any trouble."

"None at all."

Harry grabbed more eggs from the refrigerator and started on a pair of omelets while Eliza spent a solid five minutes poking at the complex coffee machine trying to get it to work. Harry churned through a mess of thoughts in his mind, doing his best to organize them into anything useful. Eliza was now single. They were going to Paris together. After all the time Harry had spent fantasizing about going on holiday with her, now he had to face the near-reality of it.

"Harry?" Eliza said eventually.

Harry realized he'd been quiet for far too long. "Yes?" He only barely restrained himself from adding an endearment.

"Where did you go?"

"Nowhere. I was just enjoying being here with you." *Well now I've done it.*

But any hopes he might have had for a reaction that would help him decide what to do next were for naught. Eliza simply smiled at him as if he'd said the most natural thing in the world. Which, of course, he had.

She put down her coffee cup, and her hand rested naked on the countertop. Harry desperately wanted to take it up in his own. It would have been so easy. But he couldn't, not here at work, not without her permission, and not so soon after a breakup he still knew nothing about.

And even if none of those things had been true, she was still too young, and he was still too old.

Eliza

The first few weeks of March were not that different, at least weather-wise, from February. While less cold and damp than Boston, the season was still a grind that Eliza and the whole of New York was ready to see end.

But the dreary weather was no reason to remain locked in her house. Not when she had effectively blown up the life she was supposed to have to stay in this city. The second a weekend morning featured a temperature above freezing, she was out to explore.

As she walked towards Union Square the key to her hope chest, tucked under her scarf, bounced against her breast. She'd have to figure out what to do with the thing eventually. The contents of the chest could go to someone else, but the key…. She couldn't give it away or set it down on a shelf or even fling it into a river. As long as it existed, she felt like she ran the risk of being made subject to someone else again. She could only fend that off by making sure it was in her possession all the time.

Perhaps she needed a therapist, if she was afraid of such a small piece of metal. Or, perhaps, she was the only rational one left in the whole damn world. Her mother, now that she was speaking to her, was making all sorts of dire predictions about the loneliness, regret, and general unhappiness that would be sure to attend Eliza's newly single status. As if she was going to be doomed to the sort of existence a cemetery ghost might have. Which struck Eliza as far more unhinged that her superstitions about her key.

Marianne was not much better, but her reactions were far more interesting. While she was as aghast as their mother, and convinced Eliza was having an affair — or should, immediately! — she was also quietly impressed. And, Eliza suspected, grief stricken, that her sister had done something Marianne had wished to and never found a way to accomplish.

Cody, meanwhile, hadn't contacted her at all. She supposed that was for the best. After all, she had nothing else to say. But she did hope he was all right. And might have wished for some care from him for her absence. *What a completely unfair time for him to finally respect that I know my own mind.*

Perhaps Eliza felt a tug of regret as she arrived at the farmer's market, a vague sense that this might be a pleasurable experience to share with someone else. But Cody, had he been here, would have tried to hurry her along. For him food was for sustenance or status. Not browsing and consideration and joy. He never would have understood her need to join the crowd jostling for cheese and bread and vegetables and unusual flavors of jam.

But Harry would. Harry did.

11

♦

In This City of Lights

Harry

In the weeks leading up to the Paris trip Eliza was as present around the office as always, but she held herself apart from him. There were no dinners eaten together at the same desk, and while she did drop by occasionally to vent about Philippe's ongoing campaign for a food truck, the after-hours text messages ceased.

After their strange evening together in the test kitchen, Harry tried to be grateful. He had made his resolution, and Eliza's distance should have made it easier for him to avoid having regrets. But it didn't. His life was simply less enjoyable without her enmeshed in the little details of it.

In an effort to stave off the grey that descended in the face of her reasonable choices, he spent time trying to make his own, making significant headway on the Vienna book and finally getting a workable version of it to Anika. If it was impossible to keep his mind off of Eliza, whether he was in meetings or at his desk, he tried to breathe through it and accept that his obsession wasn't about her at all, but his own wounded self.

Eventually, their departure date and additional cruel realities arrived. As Harry sat in the terminal at JFK waiting for their flight to board Jonathan sat next to him, his feet propped up on his carry-on. Eliza, to Harry's dismay, was already in line to get on the plane. Apparently she was a frequent flier mile whiz and had upgraded her seat to economy plus while he and Jonathan were stuck in economy. At least Harry could still visit her, assuming such a visit would be welcome. If she had upgraded all the way to business class, putting that impenetrable curtain between them, he would have been positively forlorn.

◆

Dawn in a plane was always impressive, even when it came at one in the morning according to Harry's body clock. Jonathan kept his head down on his tray table and tried to sleep, but Harry knew rest for himself was impossible until he got to a real bed. He and Eliza wound up watching the sunrise together in the little space between the galley and the bathrooms where they'd both gone to stretch their legs. While they sipped at tiny bottles of water that didn't do nearly enough against the dehydrating effects of air travel, brilliant light spilled across the sea of clouds beneath them.

But then the plane descended through those clouds. Below them was Paris, at seven a.m. local time, and it was raining. Harry wanted to do nothing but sleep forever, but first he had to deal with the circus of immigration, baggage claim, and customs, and then he had to put in a full day of work.

His colleagues were mostly quiet — Harry assumed they were in the same jet lag-induced brain fog he was — as they got themselves from the airport to the hotel and then from the hotel to the venue. Once there, Eliza vanished to go to a meeting with an e-publishing contact, and Harry and Jonathan were left to themselves to set up their table in the cavernous, fluorescent-lit event space.

"What did I do to deserve you?" Harry said when Jonathan produced cups of fresh hot coffee out of seemingly nowhere.

Jonathan tapped the lip of his cup off of Harry's. "Something very good in a former life a very long time ago."

♦

The three of them did nothing that night except eat crepes from a stand across the street from the hotel, then pass out in their separate rooms before it was even fully dark. The next day was a bustle of activity through which Harry wandered in a jetlagged daze. He didn't feel like he was coming back to himself until it was time to prepare for dinner that night. Thankfully the meal wasn't going to be an elaborate affair. The only people present were himself, Eliza, Jonathan, and Malik, the representative from their publisher's London branch who had been at Frankfurt as well. Jonathan in particular had seemed delighted to know Malik would be present.

By arrangement, Harry, Jonathan, and Eliza met in the hotel lobby to go to the restaurant together. Jonathan was there already when Harry got downstairs, engrossed in his phone as he made sure nothing fell apart, and Eliza….

Harry paused as he rounded the corner from the elevator bank to have another half a moment to observe her and get his bearings.

She wasn't doing anything in particular, just standing with an air of faint concentration as she observed the conversations and interactions around her. Her face, in profile against the bank of windows behind her, was absolutely lovely. She had changed from what she'd worn to the conference, and was a summer dawn in a salmon-colored sheath dress. The hair at the nape of her neck was slightly damp, and around her shoulders was a delicate silk scarf in a thousand shades of purple.

Suddenly Eliza looked around sharply, as if someone had called her name though Harry hadn't heard anything. Her gaze landed on him immediately. For a long moment they stared at each other.

Harry cursed whatever twist of fate had brought Eliza on this trip with him and indeed had brought her into his life in the first place. Whatever they were together, or to each other, it seemed fruitless to keep denying or ignoring it. Not when he could attribute the ruins of one book and the beginnings of another to his reaction to her; not when Eliza's engagement had, perhaps, fallen apart thanks to her reaction to him.

The two of them were like gravity, pulling closer and closer together. Collision was inevitable. And, staring across the room into Eliza's eyes, Harry knew they both knew it.

He was so very, *very* fucked.

♦

Over dinner all Harry had a mind for was to stare at Eliza across the table tucked against a window in the restaurant. Eliza, in the middle of her own conversation with Jonathan and Malik, caught Harry's eye far too often. Each time their gazes met she gave him a smile, too soft to be a smirk and too aware to be gentle, from behind her wine glass.

Halfway through the third course, Eliza slid her hand toward Harry's on the table. For a wild moment Harry thought she was going to take it, and his heart nearly leapt out of his chest in response. But all she did was tap a finger on his cell phone, sitting face down on the table.

He cocked an eyebrow at her. She looked insistently at his phone. So Harry picked it up and checked his notifications.

There they go again, read a text from her, sent ten minutes prior with no further explanation. Harry raised his eyes from it to her. She nodded, with an air of amused insistence, at Jonathan and Malik.

Harry tried to look at them without being obvious about it, but suspected any subtlety was unnecessary. The two young men were by now thoroughly engrossed with one another, leaning into each other's space and paying absolutely no mind to himself or Eliza.

Already an item, or about to be an item? Harry texted Eliza back. That Jonathan had been into Malik in Frankfurt — and that the attention was neither unwelcome nor unreciprocated — had been obvious. But he didn't know what, if anything, had happened in the meantime.

Your guess is as good as mine, Eliza replied. *About all sorts of things.*

Jonathan's intrigues aside, Harry suspected he had been caught.

◆

"Do you want another?" Harry asked what seemed like hours later, when Eliza finished her coffee. Jonathan and Malik still weren't paying them any mind, for which Harry was grateful. It felt indecent to have witnesses for what was happening with him and Eliza, even if they'd done nothing more than sit and talk.

Eliza shook her head slowly. "No."

"I thought I might walk back to the hotel, get some air, see Paris with fewer tourists. Care to join?" Harry tried to keep his voice light, as though this were just one more companionable excursion between colleagues. He didn't manage it. Eliza's gaze on his was knowing and heavy.

"I'd love to," she said.

Harry helped her on with her coat the way he had in her office so many weeks ago. He could feel the heat radiating off of her skin, at least before she shrugged on the heavy wool and buttoned it up over her scarf.

The rain that had been pelting down since the day before had stopped sometime during dinner. The streets were damp and shone in the lamplight as they stepped from the restaurant into the sounds of a Paris evening.

Eliza hesitated, looking around them. "Which way?"

Harry shrugged, not particularly caring. "I don't have a preference. What do you want to see?"

"No. I mean, I'm turned around, and I don't know where the hotel is."

"Oh. This way." Harry nodded his head in the proper direction and tried not to be surprised. To him, Eliza had a sense of direction about everything — her life, the publishing industry, how to tackle Philippe. It was strange to him that the streets of Paris might somehow be what foiled her.

They walked slowly, enjoying the luxury of not having to rush or even talk. Harry was grateful for the silence. Except for dinner, he'd been switching back and forth between English and French since they'd landed, and his mind was as exhausted as his body. He suspected that Eliza, having done much the same, felt similarly.

Paris wasn't the European city Harry most disliked, but it was the one he found the most overrated. But after eleven on a weekday night, most of the tourists had gone to bed, and anyone out after dark was going about the business of their ordinary lives. Harry watched as Eliza looked up at their surroundings, her eyes taking in the beaux-arts buildings reflecting the ambient light of the city. Perhaps his problem with Paris was simply that he'd never had the right company for it.

Next to him, Eliza drew in a soft breath. Harry turned to look at her. Her attention, however, was riveted by the view, her eyes bright and her lips parted softly as she took it in. He knew it wasn't her first time here, but that didn't seem to lessen her wonder.

"Short way or the long way?" Harry asked as they reached a branch in the road.

Eliza didn't answer, at least not in words. She slipped her arm through Harry's. When he turned his head to look at her, part in surprise and part in fearful, wonderful disbelief, she looked back at him steadily.

"Long way, then," he said. It wasn't a question.

"Long way," she confirmed.

◆

When they finally came within view of the hotel, Harry felt his steps slow. He had early meetings, but he didn't want this evening to end. With Eliza, time didn't seem to matter. He looked at her out of the corner of his eye as they walked and found she was looking at him, too. Time slowed further.

What to do next? was the only question left. The answer seemed obvious: Invite Eliza to his room and continue the conversation they always seemed to be having, in every possible way. While Eliza was looking at him like that — her features soft, her eyes shining — Harry could hardly remember why he'd ever decided that taking her to bed, not to mention pursuing a relationship with her, was a bad idea.

But he had come to that conclusion and with good reason. He couldn't decide to ignore it because he wanted Eliza, acutely and intensely, in every way possible.

Eliza met his eyes again as the elevator ascended. This decision wasn't his to make alone. Perhaps she would say something. They'd been dancing around this thing together for months, and tonight especially — but she made no further move. If anything, she seemed to be reminding herself of her own resolutions to avoid whatever this was between them. She broke eye contact and pulled out her phone. Probably to scroll through the messages she'd received while they'd been out.

Wiser than I am, Harry thought, with disappointment.

As the elevator doors opened Eliza reached out, and for a wild moment he thought she was going to invite him to go with her after all. But all she did was touch his hand before she vanished down the hall toward her own room.

At least, Harry thought, as he watched her go, *we still have a few days left.*

Eliza

The next morning, as Eliza got ready for the day, her thoughts kept drifting back to Harry and the evening they'd spent together.

They'd spent a lot of evenings together over the last five months, but none like last night. And now, more than ever, she couldn't get him out of her mind. She obsessed over the pleasant languor of dinner, the frisson between them as they'd walked the streets of Paris. And while last night hadn't been a date — certainly not with Jonathan and Malik there at the restaurant — she'd never felt so distracted by any evening she'd ever spent with Cody. Up to and including the night he'd proposed. She never should have said yes to him.

But Cody was no longer her problem and, just as importantly, not in Paris. Harry was a whole new world of challenge.

Her phone chirped with a meeting reminder, and she had to shove thoughts of Harry aside as well as she could to deal with the more prosaic aspects of her life. Namely, her job. And Philippe.

Her main meeting of the day was with a French digital branding company she was trying to partner with for Philippe's books and sauces. Five minutes in, Eliza knew the discussion would go nowhere, and she was sure everyone else in the room knew it too. But still they had to suffer through hours of polite — and sometimes less than polite — wrangling over a nonexistent deal that was never going to happen.

This was all, she reminded herself multiple times, Harry's fault.

Still, when she finally arrived back at the hotel, she couldn't help but keep an eye out for him as she crossed the lobby. She didn't know his schedule for the day and had no real reason to expect him to be there — but he was. Tucked into a corner seat, almost out of view behind the bar, he had his laptop on his knees and three paper cups on his armrest.

"Aren't you rather overdoing it on the caffeine?" Eliza asked, pointing to the cups as she sat down in the armchair across from him.

Harry glanced up at her. "If I'm going to be in Paris on this horrendous schedule, I'm going to drink all the precisely rendered coffee I can."

"Fair enough."

"How was your meeting?" Harry asked.

Eliza considered giving him an answer involving details, and even words, but instead she covered her face with her hands and groaned.

"That bad?"

"Worse. I'd rather drive a food truck for Philippe than sit through another meeting like that."

"Bad indeed." Harry looked like he was on the verge of laughing at her.

Eliza couldn't even be mad at him; the meeting had gone so poorly there was little left she could do but find the whole thing funny.

"For someone who works in publishing," Harry said, closing his laptop and setting it aside, "you're never working on books. Have you noticed that?

Eliza had to restrain the instinct, honed by so many years with Cody, of instantly defending her career choices. But Harry wasn't taking a dig at her; he was asking if she was happy.

"I do strategy," she replied carefully. "And, for a long time, that strategy has involved keeping my career options flexible."

They'd talked about that months ago, at that dreadful work cocktail party. But they hadn't talked about the real reasons behind her choices.

But apparently that time was done now. The next thing Harry said was, "Because you had to. Because of Cody and the commitments you made to his career."

"Well, yes."

"And now you don't have to worry about that any more. So what do you think is going to be next for you?"

He was looking at her so intently. What answer he might be hoping to find, she had no idea.

"I think I'm going to explore my options," she said. She desperately hoped Harry was one of them.

Harry

After Harry and Eliza discussed her disastrous meeting, they spent the rest of the work day on the exhibition floor, and then ate sarrasin crepes filled with ham and egg and gruyere while walking back to the hotel. As the evening wore on, Harry felt something between them shift.

No, that wasn't right. What was between them wasn't changing. What was changing — in sidelong glances, pauses that lasted too long, the brush of fingertips against a sleeve — was that they were acknowledging what had been between them so long. Without hesitation, without doubt, and without shame.

In the elevator Eliza made no move to hit the button for her floor.

"Are you sure?" Harry asked, hand hovering over the button for his own floor.

"Harry," Eliza said, exasperated.

"I just wanted to be certain." Eliza had spent so much of her life struggling with other people's unspoken expectations of her. Harry was determined not to add any of his own.

"I am," she said firmly.

As they walked down the hallway toward Harry's room, he took the liberty of putting his arm around her waist. He'd thought about this — and tried not to think about this — for so long that the warmth of her by his side shouldn't have lived up to his guilty fantasies. And perhaps, in some way, it didn't. For nothing about this felt illicit; it just felt obvious. And right. And easy.

It felt even better when Eliza leaned into him as he fumbled one-handed for his room key. With a soft laugh, she took it from him and slipped it into the door lock before he could drop it.

"Thank you," he said when she handed it back with a raised eyebrow.

Inside, the door closed between them and the brightness of the hallway. The room was dark, and the drapes were pushed back to show the sparkle of Paris at night.

He and Eliza regarded each other solemnly. Then Eliza stepped deliberately out of her heels. He looked down as she curled her stockinged feet in the plush of the carpet, then up when he felt her stare. Although she was tall, without her shoes her eye line was finally, slightly below his. She tipped her chin up to meet his gaze.

"You should kiss me now," she said. It was almost a dare, as if she didn't think he had the nerve to follow through.

Harry couldn't blame her. He'd been so cautious of her youth and her circumstances and her utter competence. But now that they were here, it would have been awfully unfair to make her do all the work.

He raised his hand to cup her cheek. Her skin was warm, flushed maybe, and smooth, youth unavoidable. When she gave him that faint half-smile he had become so impossibly fond of, he ran his thumb gently along her lower lip. His own breath caught in his throat as her lips parted slightly.

Harry dipped his head and pressed his mouth to hers. It didn't feel like a first kiss. Which was absurd, because Harry had spent nearly half a year knowing Eliza without touching her. But as he slid his hand from her jaw into her hair, his thumb pressed heavily just behind her ear with all the certainty of instinct and familiarity combined. Like every other time he was sure he had known her forever, he was also sure he knew everywhere she liked to be touched.

The moment felt drawn out, dangerous, the kiss gentle but shot through with tension. Eliza smelled like roses and amber, a heavier, sweeter scent than the perfume she'd worn in Frankfurt, and not something she ever wore at the office. Harry's five o'clock shadow scraped against her skin and she gasped, the sound half caught in her throat.

Harry struggled to keep his touches gentle. He had never wanted anyone the way he wanted Eliza, and now that he had her, warm and willing and responsive in his arms, his desire almost frightened him. But then Eliza sighed into Harry's mouth and wrapped her arms around his neck and fear, along with any reason to keep this slow or controlled, vanished.

Harry shifted his weight and shoved her against the wall by the door for a deep, searching kiss. When he felt her smile against his mouth, any cogent thoughts fled. There was only Eliza, the warmth of her, the eagerness with which she wrapped a leg around Harry's own and tried to pull him closer, even though they were already as close as two people could be.

Well. Not entirely. Not yet.

Harry undid the fastenings of Eliza's coat and pushed it off her shoulders. The logical thing, the romantic thing to do at this point, would have been to lead Eliza to bed, undress her slowly, and show her with his hands and his mouth and his body everything he felt for her.

But Harry was done waiting. He was clumsy and frantic as he tried to unfasten her blouse, the grey silk skin-warm. As he pushed the fabric from her shoulders, there was a ripping sound as a button tore free and fell to the floor. But then there was nothing between Eliza's skin and his hands…and a string of lace, from which dangled an antique-looking key.

He put his fingertips on the bit of metal. It was warm from the heat of Eliza's body. "What's this?" he asked. For a thrilled, horrified moment he remembered what he'd written about Eliza, and Ys, in the book he hadn't been supposed to write in Vienna. About the key that opened the gate to the city and let the waters flood in.

Eliza blinked at him, her lips parted, her cheeks flushed. She took his fingers and made him let go of the strange necklace. "A key."

Harry knew there was a story there — beyond the myth of Ys — but if Eliza didn't want to volunteer it, he was not going to press. He slid his hands under her skirt, shoving the fabric up. His hands encountered the soft scratch of lace, satin, and, when he slid his hands further down Eliza's legs, silk.

"Of course you wear stockings," Harry mumbled against her skin as he worked a finger under one of her garter straps.

"Of course," she agreed, as if she weren't as much of a panting mess as him. "Do you like them?"

"Yes," he said as he thumbed ineffectually at the catch. He cursed.

"Too challenging?" she asked.

"Not really." Harry gave up on trying to divest her of any more clothing and spun Eliza around to face the wall instead. He pressed against her, before pulling back only enough to push her skirt out of the way and over her hips. He yanked her panties down roughly to where the garters trapped them. Still, it was far enough, and she certainly understood what he was about, tilting the perfect rosy cream of her ass up against him.

He ran a finger along her slit, nearly coming apart as she whimpered. He cupped her then, velvet, damp, and rough, a knuckle pressed up against her clit. She rocked into his hand. Harry pulled back far enough to unfasten his trousers, but stopped abruptly with his hands on his own belt.

"What?" Eliza asked, twisting to look at him over her shoulder.

"I don't have anything."

Eliza blinked at him questioningly.

"Condoms," he clarified.

"Oh. Why didn't you say?"

Harry rolled his eyes then kissed the skin of Eliza's shoulder in apology. "I most certainly did say."

Eliza brushed her hair back from her face. "Whatever. I have an IUD."

"How modern. And solves only half our problems."

"Do you have anything I should be truly worried about?"

Harry shook his head. "No. I'm careful usually. I'm just trying to be responsible." *And it's so difficult, with you right here in my arms.*

"I'll risk it if you'll risk it," she offered. As if all they were up to was far more mundane mischief back at the office.

Harry cleared his throat delicately. "Just so long as you're aware.... I'm a bit of a slut sometimes. Though I haven't, in a while."

Eliza laughed harder than Harry found flattering under the circumstances.

"What? It's true!"

"I'm sure it is," she said. "I'm also sure I don't care. I trust you. I trust us. And I certainly trust modern medicine. Now can we please stop with all the talking?"

Harry didn't need to be told twice.

He took a breath to steady himself and then undid his trousers. He shoved them down and kicked them away, and then with his shirt and even his damn jacket still on, pressed one hand below Eliza's navel to maneuver her the way he needed her. With his other hand he steadied her legs as she spread them for him.

His first thrust into Eliza was like coming home. She whimpered in pleasure and fumbled for his hand, still pressed against her stomach. Harry let her have it, and groaned when she brought it to her mouth and sucked two of his fingers in. Then she pressed his hand down to her entrance again, against her clit and where they were joined together so intimately.

Neither of them were going to last long, Harry felt sure. And indeed, it was only a matter of moments. Eliza's breathing hitched and became unsteady. Her body clenched and spasmed around him. Harry's own orgasm left him gasping for breath.

Both of them were still trembling when Harry turned her back around to face him. They needed to get cleaned up, and he could not wait to sleep with Eliza's head finally on the pillow next to his. But first, he drew her forward, and pressed the gentlest of kisses against her mouth.

12

♦

The Bells and the Flood

Eliza

That night in Harry's arms Eliza dreamt of a shimmering blue ocean and a golden beach. The air was Mediterranean-warm, nothing like the cold Atlantic she'd lived so near for her entire life, and she was utterly alone. There was only water and sand and the evening sun painting the cliffs above her amber and ochre and seeming to set the water afire.

She walked at the tideline, shoes in one hand, the sand cool and soft beneath her feet. She didn't know how long she'd been walking when she realized there was another pair of footprints before her own.

Rather than dismay, to find herself not alone in all this calm and beautiful expanse, Eliza felt a relief such that she'd never known. She followed the footprints as they led away from the water and across the soft, dry sand.

There was a figure seated on the beach, an elbow resting on his knee and his eyes nearly closed against the low-hanging sun. When he saw her coming, he raised his hand to shield his face against the light.

"Well," Harry said. His collar was unbuttoned, his trousers were rolled above his ankles to keep the sand and water off, and his hair was wild in the sea wind. His smile was the most beautiful thing Eliza had ever seen. "It took you long enough."

♦

Eliza jolted awake in a bed that was not hers to find the room dark, the sheets tangled around her legs, and Harry's arm draped warm and heavy across her side. For a moment she wasn't sure what had woken her, but then she heard it: Heavily tolling bells, distant but clear, in the otherwise quiet Paris night. She grumbled at the intrusion and tried to pull a pillow over her head, but managed to hit Harry in the face with it instead.

"Mmm. What is it?" he asked sleepily, and for a moment Eliza could only hold her breath and stare at him, her whole being alight with the awareness of his body and his proximity.

The bells tolled again.

"Stupid Paris and its stupid churches," Eliza mumbled.

"What?"

"The bells, they've been going all night."

Harry frowned. "They don't ring the quarters in Paris. In Rennes yes, but not here."

Eliza considered remarking on his penchant for trivia, which, at the moment, made no sense to her. They weren't in Rennes — the capital of Brittany — but in Paris, and it hadn't been the quarters; it had been constant. Why it was stopped now, she didn't know. But she was tired, and he was close and warm.

♦

The next time Eliza woke it was to the electronic chirp of her cell phone alarm, muffled somewhat in the pocket of her coat, still on the floor where it had fallen last night.

Muttering apologies to Harry, she stumbled naked out of bed to find it and turn it off. Once she did, she realized he wasn't there and that the shower was running. She considered leaving him to it, giving them both a few moments alone for whatever processing they needed to do after last night, but swiftly discarded the idea. She wanted to be where he was.

"Do you mind if I join you?" Eliza knocked on the bathroom door, then slipped inside.

Harry, who had been standing with his head tipped back under the pathetic European excuse for water pressure, looked at her in surprise. "No, not at all." Always the gentleman, he stepped aside so she could get in.

It was as comfortable to share the shower and then the bathroom counter with Harry as it had been to share books and office space with him. Wrapped in a towel that was far too short, she borrowed Harry's comb and untangled the knots in her damp hair while he shaved. Over and over again they caught each other's eyes in the mirror. Each time it happened, one of them smiled before they exchanged pleased slightly self-conscious looks of shared delight.

"I have to go back to my room for clothes," Eliza said eventually, once she had pulled her blouse and skirt from last night back on. She didn't bother with her stockings.

"Or we could stay here all day," Harry suggested.

Their eyes met again. He was serious. For a moment, Eliza wavered. She wanted nothing more than to stay. But Harry — and his offer, she was sure — would still be here tonight. In the meantime, she had a job to do. And so did he. Meetings and presentations and networking that couldn't be put on hold. She shook her head.

"I'll see you in a few," she said, and leaned in to kiss the corner of his mouth before she left the room.

◆

Eliza changed her clothes quickly. She barely had time to dry her hair and kept glancing at her phone while she did her makeup. She smudged her mascara for her trouble and was running three minutes late when she finally pulled the door of her hotel room closed behind her and made a dash for the elevator.

She willed it to move faster, painfully aware of how late she already was. Despite Jonathan and Malik's shameless flirting, she had no intention of letting them — or anyone else — know what was going on with her and Harry. With that in mind, the only thing she could do was operate with efficiency and perfection as she always had. And not look at Harry. As long as she didn't have to look at him, she would be fine.

That, of course, was impossible to achieve. As soon as the elevator doors opened and she stepped into the lobby she saw him. He was standing by a window, a paper coffee cup in his hand and his head bent to talk to Jonathan. The morning sun, pouring through the windows, highlighted the lovely line of his back. Malik stood beside them, scrolling through something on his phone.

Eliza was well-practiced at putting on a game face and getting through social situations by dint of manners and willpower. But when it came to this she was at a loss. They'd never had to exist together in public, and Eliza was belatedly realizing she had no idea how.

She drew herself up, took a deep breath, and crossed the lobby to where her lover and her coworkers stood.

Harry turned round before he could have possibly heard her approach. "Good morning," he said with a smile no more and no less friendly than ever.

Thank goodness one of us knows how to do this. "Good morning, Harry."

If either Jonathan or Malik suspected them, they gave no sign.

After the brief walk to the convention center she didn't see Harry for hours, which was probably for the best. There were panels and workshops to attend, notes to take, and hands to shake.

But there were still moments, sitting in the back of a panel audience with a notebook on her lap and her attention drifting, when she couldn't help but think of him. Harry's hands on her hips, digging into her skin to hold her close, his lips on her neck and his voice in her ear. She flushed, and her hands clenched involuntarily with the memory of pleasure. Harry had been perfect. And she had been perfect with him.

The panel on innovation and social media that afternoon, on which Eliza was a speaker, started late. When she finally did take her seat at the table she was discomfited to see Harry in the audience. What was he doing here?

Her discomfiture only increased as the session went on. Harry never took his eyes off of her. Had he come to his senses after last night so quickly? Had he decided to come watch, and judge, and find fault with her? It was the kind of thing Cody would have done, offering condescending criticism in the guise of helping her improve her performance. Harry wasn't Cody, but if things between them had changed last night, maybe they'd changed for the worst.

After the panel was over she lingered in the room to chat with a few attendees who had more questions. Eventually she realized Harry was still there. Out of the range of conversation, but definitely standing close enough to be hovering.

"Do you need something?" Eliza asked, once the rest of the gaggle had dispersed. She tried to keep the question even but wasn't sure she succeeded. Harry looked concerned, perhaps confused, and shook his head. *Infuriating man.*

"I have a meeting in —" Eliza glanced at her watch. "Eight minutes. Walk with me?"

"With pleasure," Harry said.

Eliza looked at him in surprise, but he seemed to mean it. He certainly fell into step beside her eagerly enough. "So all of a sudden you're interested in social media?"

Harry nodded.

"Really? Because you've never cared much for the topic before," she said as they moved down the hallway together.

"Did you not want me there?" Harry asked, so mildly that Eliza was reminded that her first reaction ever to meeting him had been extreme annoyance. Perhaps she had been trying to protect herself from whatever this man unavoidably was to her.

"I'd like to be at a professional conference without feeling like a coworker is looking over my shoulder and checking up on me everywhere I go," Eliza said.

"Wait." Harry's eyes widened with something like realization. He touched her elbow lightly, barely a graze, but Eliza was helpless against his gentleness. He drew her into a little alcove by a massive potted fern. "Is that what you think I was doing?"

"You showed up at my panel! After we — well." Eliza felt herself flush, which did not speak well for her struggle for composure.

"And you thought I went to find grounds to criticize?" Harry looked hurt. "Why on earth would you think that?"

"Other men would," Eliza said.

Harry's hand slid from her elbow down her arm until his fingertips rested gently, almost innocuously, against her wrist. She realized she'd taken an unconscious step closer to him.

"I'm not Cody," Harry said gently. Earnestly. "I like to listen to you talk. Whether it's me you're talking to or the whole room. I'm sorry if it made you uncomfortable, and you're within your rights to object, because as you say, *professional*, but my interest was personal."

"Oh." She felt foolish. And mute. And neither were helping with Harry. Who just liked to hear her talk.

"Oh," he said, mocking ever so slightly. He brushed the back of her hand with his thumb. Then he said, "Tonight?" so softly that Eliza could barely hear him and lifted his eyes from their hands, to hers.

She realized with a jolt that he was nervous. Afraid that she'd say no. She nodded, not sure she was able to speak.

♦

When Eliza checked her phone after she got out of her meeting, she had a text from Harry.

Give me a ring when you're done?

"What's going on?" she asked when he picked up her call, torn between nervousness and excitement.

"Well." Harry sounded pleased. "Jonathan and Malik caught me on the way out of a panel and asked me to convey their regrets that they will not be at dinner."

"Indeed?"

"Yes. Some unspecified conflict between having any discretion at all and a king-size bed apparently."

Eliza laughed. "Did Jonathan tell you that or did you deduce that?"

"That's for me to know and you to find out," Harry said. "And not, actually, why I called."

There was something in his voice — that nervousness again — that made her ask, "So it's just us?"

"It would appear so," Harry said. "If you're up for it?"

"Harry, are you asking me on a date?" She couldn't keep the smile out of her voice.

"Do you want me to ask you on a date?"

"Yes," Eliza said firmly. "Do you want to ask me on a date?"

Harry cleared his throat. "Yes. Yes, I do."

"Good. Then that's settled."

"Excellent."

♦

After another conference session, a long shower, and a nap — Eliza wasn't sure, but she did hope, that she was going to be up late tonight — she regarded her mess of a suitcase. She was going to have to do some ironing.

She picked up her phone. *Where are we going?* she texted Harry.

I've not decided yet, came his reply.

Well, what should I wear?

I leave that entirely up to you.

Eliza groaned to herself as she tossed her phone onto her bed. That was no help at all. And his tone was impossible to read via text. But she couldn't help but hear his words in the warm, slow tone she'd only ever heard him use for her.

Eliza washed, dried, and curled her hair into its heavy waves, wriggled into a cocktail dress she'd brought in case of fancy dinner meetings, did her makeup, and fished her pearl earrings out of her jewelry case. As she blotted her lipstick, she caught sight of her bare left hand in the mirror.

Being free of Cody meant she was free of the need, emotional or social, to belong to someone else. Eliza didn't know how to belong to anyone, and Harry didn't know how to own anyone. She had no idea how that worked in the world beyond a business junket to Paris and for now, she couldn't let herself wonder. It was too much, too hard, too strange and far too uncertain.

Harry was waiting for her in the lobby when she came downstairs, lounging in one of the chairs beside the ridiculous gas fireplace. He stood up as soon as he saw her and, when she reached him, leaned in and kissed her cheek. The hair stood up on her arms.

"You look lovely," Harry murmured.

"So do you." Harry did look handsome. He wore a grey suit with just a bit of sheen to it and a white shirt unbuttoned at the collar. Eliza had seen him without a tie like that, rumpled on a weekend or at the end of a long day, but never sharply put together as he was now.

She took his arm as soon as they stepped outside of the hotel and made their way to the Marais. The bells of Notre Dame were ringing in the distance, the sound different somehow than the one that had awoken Eliza in the night. Despite all the reasons they had to be newly nervous with each other, she felt as if they had been doing this forever, as if they'd been lovers even when all she had ever done was curl up innocently in the armchair in Harry's office.

The restaurant was along a little alley in an old stone building with an angel carved into the lintel over the door.

"You're taking me to a restaurant named after an alchemist?" Eliza asked, only faintly incredulous.

"He only got that reputation after he died," Harry intoned. "He was actually a bookseller. And this is the longest continually operating restaurant in Paris. I very nearly had to commit alchemy to get the reservation."

"How did you?" She was curious now.

"I bribed someone."

As they were led to their table, Eliza had no idea if he was telling the truth

♦

Eating proved to be difficult — even with scallops and wine-braised lamb and the most perfect herbed potatoes Eliza had ever had — when they couldn't stop touching each other. Harry seemed to have a compulsive need to play with her fingers, and the room, already dark and hushed compared to restaurants in New York, seemed to fall away from them. They talked about the things they always did — books and coworkers and places they'd been — but without worrying about whether they should be quite so easy with each other.

They talked of the times they'd spent in Paris before this, Eliza for holidays with her parents and Harry for work and an apparently dubious European backpacking trip when he'd been in his early twenties.

Eliza couldn't hide her surprise. "Backpacking? You? Nooooo."

Harry grinned, his teeth white in the light from the little candle on the table. "A lot of things were different then."

"Have you got any pictures?"

"Oh, somewhere, I'm sure. In my house — I'll dig them out when we're back in New York."

Harry's words were the first time either of them had mentioned anything that might happen when they returned and should have been the perfect opportunity to discuss that issue further. But what was there to say? Trying to come to a better understanding would only complicate and constrain.

"I'll look forward to it," she said.

"One night — our first night here, in fact, I had flown in later than the others, and I was supposed to meet Dennis in the city."

"Dennis who?" Eliza interrupted.

"Oh! Dennis Chakraborty."

"Wait, what? Surely not…." She trailed off.

Harry nodded at her to go on.

"The one who has that late-late-late night show?" Eliza asked.

"*The Really Late Show*. Yes, that's him. We've known each other forever. He and Meryl and Steven and I went to college together."

"Steven, the…." Eliza trailed off again.

"Yes. The one who died." Harry looked startled, as if he'd forgotten the fact, for a moment or a day or a week. But rather than cloud over with grief, his face brightened as he went on. "So I was supposed to meet Dennis, but I got lost because that's what happened before smartphones —"

"I do remember life without smartphones." Eliza interrupted him, her voice dry.

Harry chuckled, and ran his thumb over her knuckles. "And I got lost, which was how I ended up sitting in some tiny backstreet café eating pastries and being told French fairy tales by — God, I need to put that proprietor in a book someday."

Eliza rested her chin on her free hand. "What fairytales?"

"Strange ones. At least strange to me, given that I was alone in an unfamiliar country and still wasn't positive I hadn't fallen off the edge of the map myself. She told me about Ys — you know the story?"

Eliza shook her head.

"It's like Atlantis. A perfect and drowned city under what is now Douarnenez Bay. In Brittany. Filled with art and pleasure. They say that when Paris sinks, Ys will rise out of the ocean, intact and filled with its people, as if it never left."

Eliza shivered. "Like Brigadoon?"

"If Brigadoon had vanished — and stayed vanished — when the devil opened the gates and let the sea in," Harry said.

"…Naturally."

"Well, what do you expect from a legend about an ancient king designed to cement France's turn from the pagan faiths to Christianity?"

"Real guy, fake island?" Eliza asked.

Harry nodded. "Real guy. Fake island. As far as anyone can tell."

Eliza laughed. "What's that supposed to mean?"

"Well, if something like that could happen, I'm fairly sure we wouldn't be able to solve it with science. When Paris sinks, we'll know."

"Then we'll probably never know," Eliza pointed out, charmed by the strange topic their flirtation had settled on.

Harry shrugged. "Don't discount global warming."

◆

They emerged from the restaurant to a world wreathed in white. Fog had rolled in off the river while they ate and shimmered now in the streetlamps and the lights of windows.

Eliza drew in a breath at the unexpected beauty of it. Beside her Harry made a humming sound of satisfaction. But then, in the distance, there was a low rumble of thunder.

"Perhaps we should hurry back?" He suggested.

Eliza knew they shouldn't dawdle. But the beauty of Paris silent, muffled, draped in banners of white and gold at midnight, was extraordinary. With Harry's hand warm in hers she couldn't help but be overjoyed at the chance to see such a sight.

A few blocks from their hotel there was another ominous roll of thunder. Then the skies opened. What Eliza thought at first was the patter of rain was in fact tiny balls of ice. They stung as they hit her, and they were getting bigger. Harry grabbed her wrist and tugged her across the cobbled street into a deeply recessed doorway. There was a crash and then a roar.

The air turned sharply cold. Hailstones an inch across were now setting off car alarms up and down the street and probably through all of Paris. If they'd been stuck in the open they'd have been lucky to get away with bruises.

Harry turned his back to the storm and wrapped his arms around her. Perhaps he was trying to shield her from any hail that found its way into their little shelter; perhaps he just wanted to hold her. Either way, Eliza was glad for the solid warmth of him in a night whose peace had been so suddenly shattered. She rested her chin on his shoulder to watch the ice crash down. Nearby a car windshield splintered into spiderweb cracks.

"Have you ever seen anything like this?" Harry asked.

She could feel his hair, curled with the humidity, damp against her cheek. "I know Europe gets hail more than we do, but I've never seen it larger than peas."

For more than a quarter of an hour they stood in the doorway watching the ice fall. Eventually, the hail tapered off and the clouds rolled away, leaving a velvet black sky in which a few stars, undaunted by light pollution, flickered faintly. People began to emerge onto the street to look at the sky and inspect the damage.

"We should get home," Harry said when Eliza made no move to disentangle herself from him. As frightening as the hail had been, she didn't want to leave the alcove. But Harry was right. They could hardly stay here.

Back at the hotel Eliza again went with Harry to his room. The door had barely closed behind them when they began peeling each other out of their clothes, and it was with luck Eliza didn't trip over her discarded dress or Harry's trousers on their way to the bed. There was still ice melting in Harry's hair, little chips and flakes of it. It made her overheated skin burn as Harry pressed her down onto the coverlet and then kissed his way down her body. He pressed his mouth to her when she opened her legs, and settled in, apparently determined to stay there for quite a while.

Harry lapped at her gently. Eliza drifted, only becoming aware of how badly the hail had frightened her as her breathing settled into pleasure. Harry must have noticed when she finally relaxed entirely, because it was then that he picked up the pace, pressing his tongue against her in small, hard circles. He grabbed her hips to yank her even closer. Then he snaked one of his hands up the center line of her, but instead of grabbing a breast he closed his fingers around the lace that held the key.

All of Eliza's muscles contracted at once and she gasped sharply, which only encouraged him. She pulled one of her legs up and braced it against his shoulder, finding the exact angle she wanted. She tugged at his hair, making him redouble his efforts, and pried his hand from the key to put it where it belonged.

When she came, she came loudly, and his mouth didn't stop until she finally wailed with exhaustion.

"Are you done?" Harry asked eventually, with a gentle kiss to her inner thigh.

Eliza lifted her head to stare at him in confusion. "I don't fake them. And if I did, they wouldn't sound like that." She wondered if she should be offended that he thought she might.

"Not what I mean," he said. "Can you come again?"

She frowned, still confused and out of breath. "I — why?"

Harry looked torn between concern and amusement. "Because I would like to get you off again."

"Oh." She levered herself up on her elbows to look at him. "Really?"

"Yes, really." Harry looked more concerned now. "Has no one ever done this for you before?"

That was not a question Eliza wanted to answer, now or possibly ever. She pulled Harry's hair again. She wanted him fully beside her; she wanted to kiss him. He didn't move except to let his eyes flutter closed.

"You like that?" she asked.

"Yes." He seemed as if he could barely speak.

Eliza chuckled. "Come up here," she said. "I need to kiss you."

He obeyed, but only briefly, and that was fine. As he slid back down her body, he traced his fingertips across her breasts and stomach, then lowered his head between her legs again.

Eliza frowned at him curiously. In her experience, whenever men told her something was about her pleasure, they made her do all the work. As ever, Harry was strange, and different, and exactly, everything right.

As first she squirmed with oversensitivity, but Harry's mouth was gentle and determined and soon she relaxed into a puddle of pleasure even more profound than before. It took her longer to come this time, clenching and spasming around two of Harry's fingers thrust inside her.

"Good?" Harry sounded unbearably smug as he worked his fingers as she came down.

Eliza reached behind her, grabbed a pillow, and threw it at him. Harry laughed and finally withdrew his fingers. His hair was an absolute wreck, his cheeks and chest red with exertion. He crawled up the bed to kiss her, his erection hard and flushed against his stomach. Eliza closed her hand around him and gave an experimental stroke, and was rewarded with a gasp as Harry's mouth fell open, warm and pliant, against her own.

⬥

Hours later Eliza was awoken by a thud, followed by a distinct squeak. Then there was a low moan. She blinked in the darkness as her sleep-fogged mind tried to make sense of what she was hearing. Her brain offered two options: Either a ghost of the hotel was being particularly restless, or….

The moan came again. Next to her, Harry squinted his eyes open.

"Is that…?" Eliza began, in horrified amusement, but couldn't finish the sentence. Jonathan's room was next to Harry's. And if things were going as well between him and Malik as they were between herself and Harry….

"I'm afraid it is." Harry sounded sleepily amused.

Again the squeak from next door, and a few more thuds that, now Eliza was listening for it, were definitely that of a headboard banging against a wall. She started to giggle. And then she gasped in alarm. She grabbed Harry's arm. "If we can hear them…."

"Betts." Harry shook his head and gave her a reassuring smile. "They're making too much noise to have heard us."

Eliza stared at him. And not because of anything Jonathan and Malik may or may not have heard. "Betts?!"

"Elizabeth. Betts."

"What's wrong with Eliza?" she asked with a vague sense of encroaching horror that had nothing to do with her amorous and too-loud colleagues next door. There were so many shortenings of her name that she loathed. And endearments…that was how people owned each other.

"Nothing," Harry said easily. He rolled onto his side to face her fully and ran a thumb down her cheek. "But it's too many syllables when we're quite so familiar."

"Betts?" she asked again, more quietly this time. She needed to test it out.

"Yes? No? Maybe?" Harry asked. His thumb brushed the lace of her necklace, just gently, and pulled away.

Eliza considered it. Harry waited, eyes on her face, ever patient and calm for her to reach a decision.

"Never Betty," she finally said. "*Never* Betsy. And never," she said pointing at the wall from which the sounds emanated, "in front of them."

"You have my word," Harry said solemnly. There was yet another thud and moan from next door and he smiled. "Not, I think, that they'd notice anything we did in front of them now."

Harry

When Harry's alarm went off the next morning it was so dark outside that he thought he'd set it wrong. A glance at the clock on the nightstand, however, said otherwise.

"What is it?" Eliza asked sleepily when Harry got up and pushed the curtains open.

Outside, the rain was coming down in torrents. Now that he was awake, he wasn't sure how he had slept through the sound of it against the window. Below, the water was pooling in the streets. As Harry watched a woman waded out of a building, umbrella held futilely over her head. The water was well past her ankles.

"I think Paris flooded overnight," he said.

The news, when Harry got the TV on, confirmed his suspicions. The ice from the sudden storm had all melted, and then record-breaking amounts of rain had fallen. Combined with a wetter than average month already, storm drains had backed up and the Seine had overflowed its banks.

"Does this mean we're not going to the book fair today?" Eliza asked, sitting up next to Harry on the bed, a blanket wrapped around her shoulders.

"I hope not." With Eliza in his bed, warm and soft and sleepy, Harry didn't know how he was possibly going to drag himself away from her for a day of bookselling. Even assuming they could make their way to the venue through the rain and still-rising water.

Eliza reached for her phone on the nightstand. While Harry tried to justify staying put all day to himself, she typed furiously and then paused, apparently waiting for a response. It came, seconds later.

"Jonathan says all events today are cancelled," she said, looking up.

"How does he know?"

"Bulletin just went out. He says he'll...oh," Eliza trailed off, color rising on her cheeks.

"What is it?" Harry asked, with some trepidation.

"He says he'll see us later...assuming we aren't already engaged for the rest of the day." Eliza still looked a little embarrassed, but she gave Harry a smirk.

Harry barked a laugh. "As if he and Malik aren't going to be *engaged* all day themselves. Now," he said, turning to face Eliza on the bed. "What would you like to do first, on this glorious day of unexpected freedom?"

The first thing they did was fuck, because now that they were both awake and had no demands on their time it was impossible not to touch other, and once they began it was impossible to not want to be as close as humanly possible. Closer.

After kissing for what seemed — and very well might have been — hours, Eliza pushed Harry back gently on the covers and rode him. Exquisitely, painfully, perfectly slowly, until Harry was out of his mind for her and Eliza was hardly more composed. Her hair was a mess, her lips were bitten red, sweat trailed a line between her breasts and her skin was flushed and pink.

She came like that, seated on Harry's cock, and once her tremors had subsided Harry gave into the temptation to flip her. He held her down against the bed with one hand in her hair and the other holding her wrist. Eliza kissed him, hot and wet and open-mouthed, and he came with Eliza's breath in his lungs and her name on his lips.

◆

"I've never fucked anyone the way I fuck you," Harry blurted some time later. They had fallen asleep and woken up to find it even darker outside even though it was near mid-day. Eventually, they would have to find sustenance. Hopefully room service would be available despite the storm. "I've never wanted to."

"Thank you?" Eliza cracked an eye open to look at him. They were tangled together on top of the sheets, and the rain still pounding against the window made the grey light shimmer ever so faintly over her skin. She looked like she was underwater.

"Possibly." Harry skimmed a hand down Eliza's side and watched as goosebumps broke out in its wake. "I know everyone says things like that when something is new and good and right."

"But this is different," Eliza said.

"This is different," Harry confirmed. "I'm glad you're here. I can't believe you ever weren't."

"Tell me about Steven," Eliza said.

Harry scoffed. Coming from anyone else, such a non sequitur might have felt terrible. But from Eliza, like everything else with her, it felt exactly right.

"You don't want to hear about my dead lover," he said.

"I do. And I didn't know that."

"I'm exaggerating. Mostly. But that's how it feels." Harry met Eliza's eyes. They were grey, sea-bright even in the dark of the room. She could ask for Harry's heart and he'd give it to her, on a platter but preferably, cradled in her cool white hands. She would, he knew, keep all of him safe. Even those parts of himself he had never known what to do with.

"Steven and I danced around each other the first year we were at college together. We were almost something, but then the summer before our sophomore year I started dating Meryl and we just never happened. Except then the four of us — Meryl, Steven, Dennis, and I — we took that backpacking trip across Europe."

"This is when you wound up lost in Paris waiting for Dennis?"

"Yes, exactly. Meryl dumped me the week before we left, but of course we still all went together. I spent the first month drunk and with random people hopping in and out of my bed. I couldn't understand why the rest of them cared so much about that, or why they thought it was something to talk about. And then finally…Steven and I. He thought I was beautiful. I wanted to make out and wake up with him next to me. It was not a good match. We never talked about why."

"Mmm." Eliza touched Harry's hand, as if to make sure he knew she was listening to everything he said. Harry squeezed her fingers in return.

"By the time we got home," he said, "it was like it had never happened. We both kept assuming it would make sense eventually. He really only ever dated women. And

Mallory — his wife — they were the right match. Absolutely. And then he died."

"Thirty years later."

"More or less, yes."

"So what happened in the meantime?"

Harry lifted one shoulder. "Nothing happened. But the relationship with Meryl and then the affair with Steven made me realize — I don't know always how to be with other people the way they want to be with me. I crave familiarity. The family of friends. I don't see strangers and want to devour them, but occasionally, I seem to see people I want to know forever."

"Like me."

"Like you. You're so familiar to me. I still don't know why. It's been like that with others too, but they're people I've known for years, so it's different. That's about being comfortable and not having to think and, frankly, being submissive. It's easier, sometimes, to give people things, but with you I *want*."

"I'm fairly sure," Eliza said, tugging on a lock of Harry's hair, "that being a little submissive is a form of wanting things."

Harry shrugged. "Sure. Generally not things that involve fucking the other person into a wall though."

"I certainly don't mind," Eliza said with a little laugh.

"I've noticed," Harry said, playing again with the key around her neck.

"Does that frighten you?" she asked.

Harry shook his head. "I feel like I should say yes. But no. Also," he said, because this seemed very important to add. "I still like men and women. It hasn't been like...my male ex-lover had to die so I could be with a woman."

"Why would I think that?"

"I don't know. Some people are strange."

"You're strange. And not because of who you do or don't take to bed."

"Quite." Harry smiled at her.

"I want to tell you about my key," Eliza blurted.

"You don't have to," Harry said. "You didn't seem to want to talk about it." The truth was, the key hanging around Eliza's neck unnerved him. He was a rational man of the twenty-first century who believed in science and logic, and yet...and yet. He'd already tied the story of meeting her into the myth of Ys and Dahut, the woman who unlocked a gate and flooded a city. And now Paris was a little bit under water and Eliza was here, a key around her neck.

"I know I don't have to," Eliza said. "But that's why I want to."

"All right." For all his fears, Harry couldn't refuse to listen to her story. Not after she had listened to his.

"It's odd. In a lot of ways. But then, you're the kind of person who understands strange things, I think." Eliza settled herself more comfortably on the pillows.

Harry didn't find that particularly reassuring, but he nodded at her to go on.

"It's the key to my hope chest. The one filled with all the things I was going to need for my marriage to whoever suitable I was going to marry. It's been missing for years, but I found it in my room the last time I was home. The one where I went wedding dress shopping -- and where I decided not to marry Cody."

"I always wondered what happened that weekend," Harry said softly, already a little ashamed of his fears. What right did he have to weave the life of this woman into a narrative of his own imaginings? She had her own dreams and goals and struggles and needed no one to add to her burdens.

"I know you did. Well, that's what happened. I went wedding dress shopping, and realized...well, but that's a longer story," Eliza said, her cheeks coloring slightly. Harry was deeply intrigued by that, but didn't interrupt her to ask. "Anyway, I realized I couldn't marry Cody. And then that night I found the key and.... Something in me broke. Or was fixed, perhaps. It felt like the key to my own freedom. That as long as I had it, no one could control my fate except me. I kept the key, as a talisman, I guess. Of everything I still needed to guard myself against. The life I was raised to want and now, hopefully, will never have."

Harry stared at her. If he had wanted to invent a narrative for Eliza's key he couldn't have come up with one that fit his own Ys obsession so well. He was horror-struck, and he was elated. And he felt, as he had never felt anything so strongly before, that he and Eliza were meant to be together.

♦

They spent the rest of the day lying twined on the bed, talking and reading and getting up eventually only to confirm that yes, room service was still operating, and then to eat.

They sat at the little table in the corner of the room, Harry wrapped in his robe brought from home and Eliza in one of his cardigans, sharing bread and cheese and wine. It was as enjoyable as the rest of the day had been, but the darker it got outside the more Harry felt a growing sense of dread. Which perhaps was natural enough, regret at a perfect day winding to a close. But he couldn't shake the sense that it was something more.

Eventually the rain outside slackened. Eliza pushed herself up from her chair and went to the window, the navy cashmere of his sweater just covering the swell of her ass.

"Do you think it will stop by morning?" she asked.

"I don't know. Probably."

"Then I suppose it's back to the book fair."

"Yes," Harry said. He wondered if Eliza felt as melancholy and uneasy as he did.

"And then New York."

"Also yes."

"Should we talk about that?" Eliza asked.

Harry wished she would turn around. He wanted to see her face. "Would it change anything?" he asked carefully. Talking was probably good. But he'd never made an art of it, not with Meryl and certainly not with Steven. There seemed to be more to lose in the exercise than gained.

Eliza did turn her head then, a little, a smile pressed into her shoulder. "I don't think much could change what we are."

◆

He woke the next day to Eliza sitting up in bed next to him, scrolling through her phone, a slight crease between her eyebrows.

"What is it?" Harry asked muzzily.

Eliza tossed the phone aside and slid under the covers next to him again. "Cody won his election, as Twitter has just informed me. And one of my meetings from yesterday is apparently important enough to have been rescheduled. So I'm staying for an extra day, maybe two. Waiting for final word from on high from your boss who I still have never seen."

"Are you?" Harry asked, feeling at least six emotions in rapid succession, beginning with disappointment that he wouldn't be able to fly back with Eliza and ending with the glorious hope of even one more day with her here in Paris. As far as her ex-fiancé's electoral victory went, Harry had no idea what to say, so he said nothing.

"Mhmm." Eliza rested her head on his shoulder. He wrapped an arm around her.

"I could stay too," he said, trying to keep his voice level and not sound as excited as he really was.

Eliza's laugh reverberated through his body. "You can try. But Harry, one of us at least should try to get some work done after yesterday. You're lovely, and if you can convince Charley I won't be sorry to have you here, but I can survive without the distraction."

Charley, who Harry emailed while Eliza dried her hair after their joint shower, apparently felt the same as Eliza. Her reply came quickly and was not propitious.

We already let you 'work from home' for a week while you were in Vienna, and we both know how much 'work' you got done. Come back to New York and don't be one more person we have to change flights and schedules for.

Which, Harry had to admit, was fair. Especially when Eliza emerged from the bathroom bundled back into her clothes from the night of their date and the hail. He'd spent that week in Vienna writing a book he never should have about her, and she still had no idea. After the last few days, he more than owed her a confession.

Just…not now, he thought, as Eliza leaned over to brush a kiss against his mouth.

13

♦

At the End of All Things

Harry

Sun broke through the clouds as the plane lifted off the tarmac, leaving Paris and its still-wet streets behind. For the first half of the flight Harry managed to doze in between pleasant daydreams about Eliza — walking with her through the city, eating together, sleeping together. He tried to keep his thoughts of the latter to a minimum. Jonathan, seated next to him, couldn't read his mind, but Harry felt it was more decorous to save such musings 'til he was truly alone.

He was jolted out of his reveries by a sharp bump of turbulence somewhere over the North Atlantic. While he'd flown too often to be particularly bothered by the routine shudderings of a plane, he wasn't able to settle back into his own head again. At least, not so pleasantly.

Next to him, Jonathan had a movie playing while he typed away on his laptop. He was already reviewing Harry's schedule for the upcoming week at work, the beginning of which Eliza wouldn't be there for. Harry was going to miss her, but once she was back....

Then what? Harry was brought up short. Once Eliza was back, how was that going to go? They wouldn't be in

France any longer. They wouldn't have the twenty-four seven atmosphere of the conference as an excuse. They would go back to their separate, ordinary lives. Even if Harry knew how to date — and he wasn't sure that he did — the magic of their time together in Paris wouldn't follow them back to the everyday grind. Travel was separate. Special. Non-replicable. Like holidays. That was, after all, why his relationship with Meryl had the shape it did.

"Jonathan," Harry said.

"Mmm?"

"May I talk to you about something that is completely outside your role as my assistant?"

"Uh." Jonathan looked vaguely alarmed. He usually did when Harry asked such a question. "Sure?"

"Stop me if you want. Whenever you want."

"You're not making me any less nervous, Harry. What is it?"

"It's, well." Harry tried to pull his thoughts together and organize them in a way that would make sense to Jonathan while having to provide the least amount of context. "I'm confronting the likelihood that something very lovely has come to an end. I don't necessarily want it to end, but I have no idea how it could ever continue."

"Eliza?" Jonathan said, as if Harry were very stupid for trying to be discreet about the matter.

So much for not providing context. "Yes."

"If it makes you feel any better, I've been thinking the same thing about Malik."

"It does, a little," Harry admitted. "If only because then I feel less alone in my inability to carry on relationships the way I see other people do them."

"You mean, between two people in the same place for an extended period of time?" Jonathan's tone was slightly sharp.

"More or less."

"In my case," Jonathan said thoughtfully, closing his laptop, "it's less of an inability to date locally than the reality that being in a relationship with the person I want to date creates a situation where I'd need a visa to be able to be in the same place as him for any extended period of time. Which makes things harder, obviously. But in some ways it makes them easier."

"How's that?"

"I don't have to overthink my next steps. The world, not me, is the failure here. We both knew going in what the distance issue was, and I don't have to spend time worrying about what's going to happen tomorrow. Don't get me wrong, it still sucks," Jonathan said with a half smile. "But it saves me some regrets. You, on the other hand, have gone and done a very messy thing."

"It's going to get worse, isn't it?" Harry asked, dismayed.

Jonathan quirked his lips. "With you, it usually does."

Eliza

Alone in her hotel room, Eliza let out a giddy, confused, and frustrated scream as she flopped down on the bed. The only good thing about Harry being on a plane headed back to New York while she was left behind in Paris, is that she had time to think about…everything.

While falling into bed with Harry — *Hooking up? Getting together with? Are we dating now? Is he my lover? What should I call it? Or him?* — had seemed inevitable and lovely, now that she had time to consider it, the choices they had both made struck her as reckless and bizarre. Wonderful, yes. But what on earth had either of them been thinking?

Nothing. Nothing but that we fit.

Eliza didn't know how she had gone from being someone so dutiful to this, but she wasn't sure she cared. This, whatever it was, was right. She tugged at the key hung around her neck. Maybe she knew exactly what she'd done.

The larger problem, perhaps, was what to do next. She desperately wanted someone to talk to about her strange life and lucky heart, to gossip with about Harry's body and everything that they'd done. But she didn't have any friends like that who weren't Harry himself. Not yet anyway. Which left her with a choice between her sister (still confused by her breaking off her engagement) and Jonathan (a wildly inappropriate choice, and also currently on a plane).

"I knew right away how this was going to go," she said to the empty room. It wasn't as good as gossiping, but hearing her own voice did somehow make the heady memories of the last few days feel more real. "I wouldn't let myself believe it. Who hooks up with their much-older colleague in a catastrophic hail storm that floods Paris, anyway?"

With no one there to answer her, she picked up her laptop. *I am not going to email Harry*, she admonished herself. Not because she wanted to play games or make him chase her, but because she had no idea what to say.

Checking her email, however, meant dealing with everything she had let slide while they'd been wrapped up in each other. She deleted a brief, snide message from her sister about Cody winning his election without bothering to reply. She responded to a long, rambling email from Philippe with a quick note to let him know she had stayed behind in Paris all for him. Then she opened a note from one of her colleagues from her work in Wales.

Don't know what you're up to these days, beyond the notes I see in the trades. But I'm jumping ship for next year's Berlin Book Festival. *Please tell me you're looking for a job?*

Eliza took a moment to enjoy the implicit compliment before considering her life. Her current position wasn't forever and she owed nothing to anyone. Harry was Harry…and whatever it was they were doing could surely encompass even more of the world than it already had.

I'm not yet, she wrote. *But tell me more.*

Harry

After a profoundly uneventful first day back at the office Harry returned to his apartment. He was exhausted but couldn't sleep even after taking a long shower and making himself a pot of tea. In each case the hot water and steam reminded him too much of Eliza for ease or comfort.

In an effort to think of something — anything — else, he pulled out Steven's diary from where he'd left it on top of a bookshelf. Setting his mug of tea on the end table, he pulled the belt of his bathrobe tighter around his waist and settled into his armchair.

He frowned as he began to read the final entry.

Harry, the message began. Which was a jolt in and of itself. It had been evident since the beginning that this diary had been meant for him. But Steven had never directly addressed him, and Harry had been able to stay in determined denial of Steven's motivations and intentions.

I'm a fool for taking so long to get to the point. Our mistake always was thinking we had all the time in the world.

I've always been a man of science and logic. And yet neither science nor logic can give me an explanation as to why I've felt compelled to keep this diary for you. I could just send you email. Or wait until the next time we see each other, to gripe about all the small troubles life brings. But I've known for months that we're going to run out of time, very soon now. Since long before science and the doctors could have told me so. And now you have this diary in your hands, a love letter to the ordinary life we all leave behind — and to you. For the life we never had together, though I think we could have. If we'd known how to talk about it. That fault isn't yours alone, although I spent a few bitter years in my twenties thinking it was. That was a long time ago, and the life

I've had instead has been brilliant. It's been decades since I blamed you for anything. More than I blamed myself for anything, at least. We were both so stupid and so young.

We neither of us are young anymore, though I'm not sure we've grown much wiser either. Certainly if age or disease or impending death could have imparted wisdom I could have told you all of this much more plainly. But instead, here you are, in your study or your office or wherever you are, and here I am, dust returned to dust.

There's not much time left. By the time you get this, there will be none left at all. I'm sorry for that, my very old and very dear friend. But maybe panic and the fear of slipping unheard into the unknown will motivate me to do what I never had the courage for.

Speak your truth, Harry. We were both afraid of ourselves and our words for so long. No more.

And finally: know that I loved you and if there's any sort of soul or anything that survives the body, I always will.

— Steven

"Well what the fuck am I supposed to do with that?" Harry said aloud. His first impulse was to throw the diary across the room in anger. How dare Steven get all wise and holier-than-thou about how to live life in the face of fear and loss? "Was that supposed to be encouraging?"

Because it wasn't. However Steven had meant it, all Harry could feel was rage burning beneath his soul-deep grief. Nothing could help that, certainly not kind words from a man who didn't have to live to see the hole his own death had left in the world; not regrets over what they had or hadn't done decades ago; not comforting thoughts that their fellow Miscreants were suffering the same loss as he was.

Harry made himself set the diary down gently on the end table and covered his face with his hands. Knowing that anger was part of grief and experiencing it were two very different things.

◆

The next night you have off, Harry emailed Dennis, *can you meet me for a drink?*

Only if you promise not to have any more terrible news to break to me, Dennis replied immediately. Five minutes later came another email. *That was a joke. Possibly in poor taste. I'm off tomorrow. But please don't have any terrible news.*

Knowing that Dennis had been as traumatized by Steven's death as himself wasn't comforting, but it did make Harry feel less alone.

◆

He met Dennis at their regular bar, to the extent they had a regular bar. They might have lived in the same city, but they didn't spend much time together. An inevitable outcome of being adults with complex schedules, perhaps. But in the wake of the conversation with Jonathan about relationships, Harry wondered why he found keeping people in his day-to-day life so hard.

As always, Dennis was a few minutes late. When he appeared at the corner of the bar Harry had staked out he pulled Harry off his stool and into a brief, but fierce, hug.

"What's going on?" he asked, once they were seated and Harry had ordered drinks for them both.

"Steven sent me his diary; I had an affair with Eliza, who I also wrote a book about, in Paris; I think we flooded the city; and I'm possibly on the verge of a breakdown of some sort." Harry paused. "No terminal diagnoses, though."

The laugh that pealed out of Dennis was, Harry knew, a testament to how terrible both of them were as human beings — and also the tension that existed in their lives that such a statement was greeted with almost giddy relief.

"Okay, but seriously, what the fuck?"

Harry pulled the diary out of his bag and pushed it across the bar towards Dennis, who looked at it as if it were a live grenade. "Steven's diary."

Dennis poked it gingerly with a fingertip. "Only the first of many *what the fucks*. He sent this to you? When?"

"It was waiting for me when I got back from the funeral. Mallory put it in the mail. Same way she hit send on the 'Sorry, I died' emails."

Dennis nodded; they'd not spoken of them, but Harry was certain he'd gotten one too.

"So that's messing with my head," he said. There was, in the midst of his angst about Eliza and the rest of his life, a comfort in speaking about this with someone who'd known him as well.

"I would think." Dennis was still looking at the diary as warily as Harry had regarded it the first time he saw it.

"And then in Paris…. Actually." Harry stopped himself. "Let's start with Brittany. You recall when I was doing the Brittany book?"

"You mean the only book you've been more annoying about than the Vienna book? Yes."

"Remember when we were there?"

"And in Paris and Marseilles. Yes, of course. It was thirty years ago and we were drunk the entire time."

"You almost got run over by a horse that didn't exist."

Dennis laughed. "Oh shit, I actually had forgotten about that. We were *really* drunk."

"It was foggy, you heard hooves, I heard hooves, Steven heard hooves, and then you screamed and jumped out of the way and there was absolutely nothing there."

"And?"

"I went to Brittany four times because of that book. And no matter where I went, or what I was trying to research, or how much I wanted to be alone and stare at that ocean, people told me ghost stories. So many ghost stories, that my editor called me four days before it was supposed to go to production to ask me if we could kill one of them out of the supposedly final manuscript."

"Why?"

"Because exile and despair is not sexy and does not travel books sell."

"Your point, other than angst and this stroll down memory lane?"

"Eliza is a quarter of a century younger than me and that's nothing compared to the fact that a lot of evidence is piling up to indicate we're living in a ghost story."

Dennis stared at him unkindly. "You have *got* to be kidding."

"I really wish I were."

"All right." Dennis got himself situated more comfortably on his bar stool and clasped his hands together. Harry could see him transition into his mode for interviewing a somewhat dotty guest on his show. "I'll bite. Why do you think you're living in a ghost story?"

"Not just any ghost story. The myth of Ys. The one where the woman falls in love with the devil and opens the city gates to him, and it all floods. And drowns. And disappears beneath the waves. Waiting."

"Variation number three hundred and forty-seven on the classic story of 'Don't piss off gods because floods aren't fun?'"

"Yes," Harry said somewhat irritably. "The thing is — well, one of the things is — she wears a key around her neck."

"The girl in the myth?"

"No. Eliza."

"Like, a Tiffany key?"

"No. A key-key. To her hope chest. The one she's not going to need anymore because she broke off her engagement. She wears it like a necklace."

"That's...different."

"We all need talismans of our own agency," Harry said. "I asked her about it, when we slept together, and she told me. When we woke up the next morning we found out that the city had flooded."

"It made the news here," Dennis noted. "So, you think her wearing her hope chest key while you had magic sex made the sky open up? Come on Harry, I know you're a man and a writer, but even you're not that terrible."

Harry shook his head. "No, I know. But I wrote a book about her while I was in Vienna. About Eliza. That my agent can't possibly find a home for because it's six types of odd and too short, but it's the best thing I've ever written. I need to publish *something* to keep my career going, but all I have is that and my broken Vienna book."

"That's easy," Dennis said. "Self-publish the one you wrote about Eliza."

"What?" Nothing about that solution seemed easy. Or even appealing. "Jonathan mentioned something about self-publishing as an option once, but...." Harry trailed off.

"But you're a publishing industry professional and can't stand the thought of abandoning tradition and convention?"

That was exactly what Harry thought, but to hear it put so baldly was somewhat embarrassing. "It sounds bad when you put it that way," he muttered.

"It *is* bad. But you are who you are, with the structural privileges that you have, and we all cling to the things that give us power and a sense of stability. Also, you've worked in publishing your whole adult life. But I think that means you should break the mold. Anyone can be a publisher. What do you think we do on *The Really Late Show* every time we come up with another absurd idea for a book mocking the rich and powerful? We get it done and out the door and on the bestseller list and all that money to charity so fast because we do it our damn selves."

Harry had to admit Dennis had a point. Several of them, actually. But the question of what to do with the book was only half of the issue.

"All right," he said. "So that's one problem. But the other problem is the hook, the thing I framed it around, was

Ys. And then…this all happened. I know this is my brain recognizing patterns that probably aren't there, but it's odd and it's reminding me that there are consequences to what I did — what I'm doing — with Eliza, and that they aren't okay. For me or for her or for the flood insurance underwriters of Paris."

"And what you're doing with Eliza is…?" Dennis left it hanging.

"I don't even know. She's still in Paris. She had a meeting that got postponed."

"Because of the floods?"

"Because of the floods."

"Good. Sounds like you could use some distance."

The fact that Dennis's calm assessment of the situation aligned with Harry's own more rational instincts should have been helpful, but all it did was make him feel depressed.

"Plus," Dennis went on. "Even if you *did* cause Paris to flood by having sex with her, at least now the flood thus caused is giving you some time apart to sort yourself out."

"I guess?"

"Look, Harry, if you're going to be irrational about probably random events, at least go all in." Dennis paused. "Have you talked to Meryl about any of this?"

"Ah. No." Harry traced the grain of the wood on the bar. "Meryl and I are…figuring some things out."

"You seemed fine together in Italy," Dennis said, but a faint crease appeared between his eyes. Sweet of him to worry about a relationship that both didn't exist and had been continuing in one form or another for almost thirty years.

"We're always fine in Italy. But she's moving to New York, and it's throwing off our, well," Harry swallowed. "Our everything."

"Because you excel at keeping people at a distance," Dennis said.

"Yes. Apparently. Which Steven felt the need to scold me for from beyond the grave which is why I'm now here talking to you."

Dennis looked at him reproachfully. "Because you thought I'd have more wisdom than a dead man?"

"Death didn't make Steven any wiser. Or funnier," Harry said.

"So what do you want from me?" Dennis asked.

"I can actually argue with you."

Dennis shook his head. "You don't want to argue, you want someone to tell you what to do with your book and this woman and your entire mess of a life."

"My life has always been a mess."

"That's less true than you think. But anyway. I'm not going to tell you what to do. I'm merely going to point out that if you publish a book about Eliza I'm not sure how likely she's going to be to want to date you. Also you turn fifty in, what, like a month? So you need decide between your career and a woman who is too young for you."

"Thanks," Harry said bitterly.

Dennis took a sip of his drink, 'til then left untouched on the bar. "Anytime."

◆

Back at home in his study, lit by the glow of a solitary green-shaded lamp, Harry sat with his hands folded in his lap and stared at his computer screen. He definitely needed to sell books, and he probably needed not to pursue a relationship with Eliza. Both of those things were as true now as they had been last week, before Harry spent a glorious few days in Paris pretending the dilemmas before him were entirely different. But reality always caught up in the end. If nothing else, Steven's death had taught him that.

So he made himself reach for the keyboard and Google *how to self-publish a book.*

Harry was not a newbie when it came to computers or the internet, and he was well aware of the gains in indie titles from his own professional life. But he was still surprised at how easy this was going to be. Within an hour he'd set up an account on a major ebook distribution site and made a list of what he was going to need. Which boiled down to a cover and a copyedited manuscript. Harry worked in publishing. He knew where to look for cover designers and copyeditors.

He almost wished it were harder. Anything to delay the inevitable would have been welcome. Because he shouldn't publish this book. That much was certain. He hadn't even needed to discuss it with Dennis. Not really. This book was about Eliza, and he had never told her it existed let alone asked her consent to publish it. Once it was out in the world, Harry would never have to worry about what the future held for them collectively. It would be a monument to what they could not have.

He would tell her, once he worked up the courage. It was the right thing to do.

One right thing, he thought, staring at the release date he'd created on the screen. He already felt awash in shame and guilt. But all his other choices were worse in this great deep sea of wrong.

●

Two days later Harry had just arrived in his office and was hanging up his coat when someone called his name. He whipped his head around to see Eliza standing in his doorway, returned from her extended Paris sojourn. She looked awake and refreshed as only the young could after a transatlantic flight, a laptop cradled against her chest and a mug of tea in her hand. Her face, as she looked at Harry, was very soft.

"Elizabeth." Harry wondered if her name on his lips sounded like a cry of pain to her, too, or just himself.

"Hi," she said, leaning against his door jamb, her expression somewhere between teasing and concerned. "Is everything all right?"

"Close the door," he told her.

Eliza gave him a puzzled look and then swung it shut with her foot since her hands were full.

"Do you want to put that down?" Harry asked, gesturing at his own desk.

Eliza looked confused; she'd long ago commandeered the window sill by her chair as her place of work in Harry's office. But she set the mug and the computer down and then folded her arms over her chest. Defensively, Harry thought. Uncertain. And not a little afraid.

"What is it?" she asked.

Harry had to swallow to be able to begin. "I think we should talk."

"We talk a lot," Eliza said. Her voice was cheerful, but an uneasy calm came over her face.

"About Paris."

"Harry —"

"I don't think we should do this."

For several long moments, Eliza stared at him. Then she said, very calmly, "Why?"

Harry had rehearsed this. Because he couldn't very well say because *being with you feels like living in a story and not one that has a happy ending*. "Because we work together. And I'm twice your age."

Eliza's face rapidly shifted from calm, to confusion, to anger. "You're telling me this at *work*?"

"This is where we spend most of our time."

"Except for seventy-two hours in Paris where I spent every possible moment in your bed."

"Betts —"

"No." Eliza was wroth. "You don't get to call me that. And don't do me, or yourself, the disservice of acting like this was a stupid business trip fling. We've been doing this for months and you know it. If you don't want to keep seeing each other, that's fine." She spoke with a chill calm that made Harry shiver in his seat and remember streets full of ice in Paris. "But at least have the decency not to treat me like the secretary you shouldn't have fucked. I would have expected that from other men. But not from you."

With that, she picked up her laptop and her mug again. Her hands must have been shaking; tea sloshed over the rim of the mug and landed in dark spatters across the polished surface of the desk and the papers scattered on it.

Long after Eliza had shut the door behind her, Harry was left staring at the little, dark, reflective spots of tea. With an effort, he grabbed some tissues from the box on his desk and scrubbed them up.

Eliza

Eliza spent ten minutes at her own desk trying to come down from the pitch of fury with which she'd stormed out of Harry's office. She didn't have longer because she had to go to the weekly staff meeting. Where Harry would also be. The universe had a cruel sense of humor.

She had to pull herself together and put her game face on. She'd had plenty of practice. With Cody, with her parents, with the very world she lived in. But she wasn't sure she'd ever been this angry before. Or so hurt.

I thought you were better than this, was the refrain that ran uselessly through her mind as if Harry could hear her. Maybe he could. They were strange like that.

Either way, she wouldn't give him the satisfaction of being late or looking at all concerned. So she blew her nose, touched up her makeup, and gulped the last of her tea.

Harry was already in the conference room when she arrived. He glanced up briefly when she walked in, but that was likely only a reflexive response to someone coming through the door. He didn't acknowledge her in any other way.

The meeting itself was torture. Eliza did her best to act normal, while not engaging in any of the little glances and email exchanges she and Harry usually entertained themselves with. Which meant that neither of them were acting anything like normal. Harry, in fact, sat stone-faced. Jonathan, seated next to him, also tried to act normally, but Eliza saw him glance occasionally at Harry and herself, his eyebrows furrowed with concern.

Her attention was only called to the business at hand when she heard her name.

"Eliza and Jonathan," Ioanna was saying. "Are our two lucky winners. They're going to be representing us at BEA in Chicago next month."

Eliza's first thought was to wonder if travel assignments always got handed out at meetings like candy. Then she wondered why Jonathan and not Harry was going. A quick glance at the younger man, who looked positively startled, suggested that he was wondering the same.

To hell with this game of trying to out-poker face him. Under the guise of taking notes on her laptop about the BEA trip — which Ioanna was still talking about — Eliza shot Harry an email.

Any reason your assistant and not you is getting the business trip to Chicago?

Eliza bit her lip as she pretended to listen to Ioanna while really watching Harry out of the corner of his eye. He took an irritatingly long time to see the message on his own computer, and an even longer time to respond.

He's perfectly capable of travelling by himself.

That wasn't what I meant, Eliza typed before deleting the message. She wasn't going to argue with Harry. Not now. Not in email.

When the meeting finally came to a close Harry was out of the room before Eliza had even gathered her things. She walked back to her office slowly, acutely aware of the sharp press of metal against her skin that was her hope chest key. She didn't have Cody — *thank God*. And she didn't have Harry — *who can go right to hell*. But at least she had herself, even if she was adrift.

♦

Over the course of the next week Eliza barely saw Harry at all. She missed him, more than she would ever have thought possible. Certainly more than she had ever missed Cody when they were on separate continents for weeks at a time. She could force herself to imagine a world where she wasn't romantically involved with Harry, but she couldn't imagine a world where she wasn't involved with him at all.

It was with that in mind that, one evening, she ventured to Harry's office and rapped on the door. Harry's familiar call to come in floated through the wood. She missed, violently and not for the first time, their easy intimacy before Paris.

"Oh." Harry looked up from his desk and blinked. He looked surprised to see her there. "It's you." He collected himself, or at least seemed to try to. "Can I help you?"

"I'm about to put in an order for Chinese food," Eliza said. "Do you want me to get you anything?"

Harry shook his head and dropped his eyes to his laptop. "No, thank you."

"Are you sure? It wouldn't be —"

"I told you, this isn't a good idea," Harry all but snapped.

"I just asked if you wanted —" Eliza began, but Harry cut her off.

"You should go."

"*Harold*." Eliza was both hurt and taken aback. "What is wrong with you?"

"Nothing's wrong with me," Harry said, not looking up from his computer. "I simply think it would be best if you left right now."

For all the fights Eliza had ever had with Cody, she had never been quite so angry as she was right now. The edges of her vision blurred, and she felt like she was looking at Harry through a deep pool of water.

With effort she kept her voice steady. "And I think you need to understand the very large difference between 'I don't think we should continue this affair' and 'you are now my mortal enemy.'"

"I have said no such thing," Harry said tartly.

"But you're acting like it."

"What I am acting like is a professional."

Eliza scoffed, which did not do the depth of her scorn justice. "Barely. I miss my friend. I miss my colleague, and good heavens, you don't even have to eat with me! Now do you want anything or not?"

"I said no the first time, Eliza."

How dare he. Eliza stepped all the way inside the office and slammed the door behind her. "You can be angry with me. You can not want to be with me. You can be cold. You can be rude, but how dare you imply I pushed you into anything!"

"I implied no such thing."

"Would you listen to yourself!" She was nearly shouting. "Bad enough you've decided to be an asshole but I will not tolerate you gaslighting me on top of that."

"I'm not —"

Eliza shook her head furiously and took another step toward him. "You not understanding the choices you made is not my fault. You spending days in bed together with me is not my fault! I blame you for plenty of things right now, but none of that. You could do me the same courtesy."

"Then stop pestering me and I will."

Her hands were trembling. "Stop speaking to me like a child and I'll consider it."

"YOU ARE A CHILD!"

Eliza drew herself up to her full height, let out a long breath, and then said, very quietly. "I think we both know that's not true. You can order your own food." She handed him the menu. When he refused to take it, she let it fall onto his desk. "I've another in my office."

14

♦

A Book but Not a Refuge

Harry

Spring was a special sort of hell. The days were warming, the flowers were blooming, and Eliza wasn't speaking to him. Harry was wise enough not to waste time telling himself he was glad of it; he wasn't wise enough not to miss her desperately.

Meryl moved to New York at the end of April. Harry didn't spend as much time worrying about her arrival as he had expected to. But then, the relationship he wasn't having with Eliza was taking up most of his emotional bandwidth. He hardly even had enough energy to fret about his fiftieth birthday, which he passed quietly at home, alone, with a book.

He met Meryl for dinner a week after her relocation was complete. She recommended a French restaurant near her apartment. Harry agreed, and didn't realize his mistake until he walked in the door and was instantly transported back to Paris — and Eliza — by the scent of the place.

The Miscreants hadn't teased him about Eliza since Steven had died. Perhaps they, collectively, hadn't had the heart. Or maybe they were just less keen to pounce on what might be bringing one of their number any joy. But, seated across from him at a corner table, Meryl waited patiently while the waiter poured their wine. Once the waiter left, she said, "So tell me about the girl."

"You don't want to know." Harry shook his head.

"If I didn't want to know, I wouldn't have asked. Besides, you're not my only confidant in New York."

"Dennis?"

"What you don't tell me he will. And don't think he won't. Or that I won't ask."

For a moment, Harry considered. He would be relieved to confess everything: Not just Paris, the book he had written about her, and his own lesser-of-two-evils decision to publish it. But also the end of their relationship and his own subsequent misery. Meryl was right that Dennis would tell her everything he knew, if and when she asked.

But he'd already put enough of his longing and desire out into the world. He shook his head. "Maybe eventually. But right now I'll spare you an hour of listening to me pine for things I know I shouldn't have."

"Considerate of you." Meryl looked amused.

"Besides," he said, "right now I'd much rather hear about what you're getting up to."

"You mean aside from unpacking and cursing my decision to bring quite so many CDs with me when I can stream any music I want?" Meryl asked.

"Even that would be a pleasant break from my own brain."

"Oh, Harry." Meryl patted his hand. "You're lucky you're handsome. I would distract you with my own adventures…but a lady doesn't kiss and tell."

She looked so pleased with herself that Harry couldn't help but take the bait. But try as he might, Meryl would tell him nothing. He knew that this was not payback for his own reticence, though. She simply held her cards closer than he did, and always waited for the right time to play them.

♦

Harry needed to tell Eliza about the book. But how? In the mornings at work he would catch a glimpse of her at the end of a hallway or around a corner, dressed meticulously, her hair perfect, and his courage vanished. She would hate him for what he was doing. And he would deserve it.

As the release date approached, he felt more and more wretched about it. Especially because, shortly after the book's release, Eliza would be at BEA in Chicago. With Jonathan. Harry's assistant didn't know precisely what Harry was doing with the book, but he knew he'd written it. He'd been the one to suggest self-publishing in the first place.

The day the book released, at midnight, Harry sat in his dressing gown at his kitchen table and kept hitting refresh on the sales dashboard. But no matter how long he sat there and willed the counter to go up, it never did.

Harry finally went to bed at two a.m., tired and discouraged and yet, strangely relieved. No one was ever going to find, or buy, or read, a random too-short navel-gazing angst fest he'd published independently. With any sort of luck, Eliza would never need to know about it at all.

Eliza

Chicago in May was nothing like Paris in March. From the moment Eliza stepped off the plane with Jonathan it was hot and unseasonably humid, and even her fondness for the city couldn't make the weather any more bearable. The hotel, in turn, was air conditioned past any level of comfort.

BEA was a special sort of hell, especially since the ban on roller bags had been reinstated. At least she wouldn't have to worry about hunting anything down for Harry now. She grimaced at the thought and at having to spend ten hours a day in the cavernous convention hall. But there was nothing else for it. At the end of the first day she was happy to take Jonathan up on his suggestion of drinks at the hotel bar.

"I'm sorry my boss is being such a dick to you," Jonathan said as soon as they got a table near the window. He looked as tired as she felt.

Eliza took a deep breath and then realized she probably looked angry, or terrified, as Jonathan started to stammer his apologies.

"No," she said, putting out a hand to calm him. "It's fine. I mean, nothing about it is fine, but that's not your fault."

"I know that," Jonathan said with a half smile. "But still. I'm sorry you have to put up with it."

"I hope he's not taking it out on you."

Jonathan shrugged.

"Well," Eliza said. "I hope your Paris affair has proven to be less of a disaster than mine."

Jonathan gave another half smile. "Less of a disaster, but also far less proximate. London's a hell of a long way away from New York."

"It's only a six-hour flight."

"Six hours and many hundreds of dollars," Jonathan pointed out.

Eliza was reminded, with a stab of guilt, that she and Jonathan were nearly the same age and had, to date, very different career trajectories. Jonathan was working his way up the ladder slowly, and surely wasn't making that much. Eliza, on the other hand, had essentially bought her way into her current position with a very expensive degree.

"But something you'd do if you could?" she asked.

"Absolutely," Jonathan said with a certainty she envied.

She rested her chin on her hand and listened to him talk about Malik. She was still enraged at Harry, but she found herself charmed by Jonathan's enthusiasm about his relationship and the optimism with which he viewed their future together. To her own surprise she asked questions, not to be polite, but because she was genuinely interested in the details of a friend's life. The experience was somewhat of a new one, and she found herself pleased — not just on Jonathan's behalf, but on her own.

Eventually Jonathan ran out of words to describe how well he and Malik fit. "All right, forgive me for asking," he said. But what *did* happen between you and Harry?"

Eliza lowered her arm and looked at her hands on the table. "He's your boss — I don't want to make life complicated for you."

"I've known him for years and this is hardly the most complicated he's made my life." Jonathan paused, evidently considering. "All right. So this might be the most complicated he's made it. And you don't have to tell me anything you don't want to. Obviously. But this is me asking as a friend, not a colleague. I mean, who the hell else can I talk to about Malik? It's not like I have a lot of friends to gossip with."

Maybe I'm not so alone as I thought, Eliza thought. "Neither do I. I mean people…what are they for?"

Jonathan gave her a look of sly understanding. "Right? I mean, they're fine, but, *ugh*."

Eliza laughed. "Though friends might be better than my sister. When I went home for my engagement party, she told me I should have an affair."

Jonathan hesitated a moment, then asked, "Can I ask you what happened to your fiancé?"

"You can. But you might have to get more specific."

"You had a ring. And then you didn't. And then there was Harry. Or had been all along. I don't know. Like I said, he hasn't told me anything. I only see what's been undone, but I don't know what any of it was."

"Harry had nothing to do with the end of my engagement," Eliza said primly. It was perfectly true. And also a complete lie.

◆

Staffing their publisher's booth at BEA would have been far worse had Jonathan not been there. He was organized, diligent, funny, and kind. That he worked for Harry didn't matter at all. Eliza liked his company, and he was doing a good deal to keep her sane through simple competence alone.

When there were quieter spells — floor traffic seemed to come in waves they could never quite predict — they took turns fetching each other coffee and grabbing what ARCs they could get their hands on. Making the same, repetitive small talk with each and every visitor to their booth was harder, but Eliza couldn't complain about being on autopilot. Having a chance to turn her brain off was exactly what she needed, even if twelve-hour days in a windowless concrete bunker of a trade show hall was draining.

"Do you think if I stop making eye contact, people will go away for five minutes?" she asked Jonathan.

"I wish," he said flatly. A pair of people, a white man with greying hair and a woman with her black hair pulled back in an artfully messy bun approached the booth.

Jonathan's eyes widened. "Oh God, hide me."

"What?" Eliza didn't have a chance to do anything of the sort before the pair reached the table. The man stuck his hand out in greeting. Jonathan shook it, without matching the man's enthusiasm. The man then turned to Eliza and offered his hand to her as well.

"Hello, Mr. —?" Eliza asked.

The man leaned back, in a pantomime of laughter, as if she was telling a very clever joke.

"It is me, Philippe, your star author. Surely you recognize me. I know you work with Harry!"

"Oh my God," Eliza muttered to herself.

The woman who Philippe had detached himself from in order to make this little scene approached her, not with an outstretched hand, but with an eye roll.

"Sorry, he's like this," she said. "He tends to think of these things as his big moment."

"No publisher ever complained about an enthusiastic author," Eliza said diplomatically even as she prayed this woman would save her from an unexpected face-to-face with Philippe. She knew she should be a professional about it, but at the moment all she could feel was relief that she'd never done a video call with Philippe which meant that there was little reason for him to recognize or identify her now.

"I'm sure that's not true," the woman said. "Hi, I'm Gina. And that's 'Philippe.' But I guess you figured that out."

"Are you his...?" Eliza trailed off. There were too many opportunities for insult here.

"Fiancée, not assistant. His assistant isn't allowed to use the air quotes on the name." Gina laughed a little obnoxiously. Eliza considered the possibility that she was slightly in love with this woman.

"Well, we never use air quotes at the publisher either." She leaned forward to whisper conspiratorially, "although, sometimes we want to."

Gina clapped her hands together. "Oh, I like you! Let's be friends. In fact, let's take a walk. No one becomes friends at work. Not really."

You don't know how right you are, Eliza thought. And then she said yes.

Eliza let Gina lead her back towards the café at the edge of the exhibit hall. It would be her third visit there today already, but she didn't care. Someone had offered her friendship, and she had said yes.

"Cute key," Gina said as they walked.

"I always worry it's strange," Eliza blurted. She had to fight the urge to tuck it back inside her blouse. She normally kept it under her clothes, but she'd been bending over to pull books out of boxes for the table and it must have slipped out.

"It's a little Nineties, but we all need a quirk. It works for you."

"Thanks," she said, uncertain how enthused she should be about the compliment.

"Now, what I really wanted to talk to you about is Philippe's editor's book."

"What?" Eliza was confused. "Which?" She didn't remember Harry having had a book come out.

"The one about the girl!"

"Which was one is that?"

"Oh my God," Gina exclaimed. "You are being worked too hard if you haven't had time to lay your hands on that. It's just come out. Self-published. And so so sexy. And thoughtful. Is that weird? Sexy and thoughtful? Anyway, I want to know everything about Harry Sargent now, but 'Philippe'" — she paused to properly render the air quotes — "is far too heterosexual to tell me anything interesting. So I'm relying on you."

Eliza had no idea what Gina was talking about, but panic was welling up in her soul nonetheless. She didn't want to talk to anyone about Harry. She needed to find out more about this book, and she knew that was a bit of research she was inevitably going to regret.

◆

By the time she and Gina returned from coffee, during which Eliza told her that Harry dressed well, had a lovely sense of humor, and seemed like a terrible person to be in a relationship with, Philippe was nowhere to be found. Jonathan was instead speaking with a distinguished-looking gentleman with combed-back white hair and a well-tailored suit, who was also asking after Harry.

Eliza set her coffee down. Whatever hope she had that 'the book about the girl' had nothing to do with her was fading fast. When the inevitable final blow came and she fainted — or felt the urge to throw something — she didn't want her coffee to be a casualty of it.

"Do you need any help, Jonathan?"

Jonathan turned to look at her, opened his mouth and then snapped it shut. His cheeks were red and his eyes were wide. Gina looked between the two of them, her brow creased in curiosity and concern.

Oh, this is bad, Eliza thought. *This is very, very bad.*

The visitor to their booth turned to her. "It's about the book Mr. Sargent has self-published. *The Girl with the Key*?"

"Ah...yes?" Eliza asked.

"My publisher wants to offer him a contract for that title and similar. We think with a proper marketing campaign and distribution. Well.... Let's just say Mr. Sargent can start fantasizing about six-figure print runs along with this girl. Can one of you please make sure he or his agent gets in touch with me with some urgency?"

Eliza took a deep breath. She wished desperately that she had hidden the key again when Gina asked about it. Stuffing it away now would be far too conspicuous. But more than anything right now she needed this man to go away.

"Yes, we can get you his agent's contact information," she said as pleasantly as she could. She felt like she was suffocating. Beside her, Jonathan sprang into action and scribbled down a name and number on the back of one of the many business cards they had out on the table.

"It's really quite an extraordinary book," the man said as he took the card from Jonathan with a nod of thanks. "Have you not read it?"

"I'm afraid I haven't had the chance, no." Her voice strangled as she spoke.

"Oh, it's well worth your while, I assure you. Sargent has always been a marvelous travel writer, but he's outdone himself. Seventy-two hours in Vienna, but it's all framed within this remarkable love affair he's having — or, I should say, not having, with a young woman he's quite fallen for...."

Eliza didn't hear the rest except in snippets. Something about a sense of exile, about the way cultures melded in

Vienna like lovers. And something about how the book had picked up all sorts of attention online and in the trades and was starting to make bestseller lists. She wanted to murder Harry. Beside her, Jonathan, bless him, once again took over the conversation as she managed to lower herself into a chair with what she hoped was some grace.

"Oh my God," Gina said as the man went on. "You're the girl!"

♦

"Did you know?" Jonathan asked, when both Gina and the acquisitions editor had walked away.

Eliza shook her head even as she reached for her tablet and Googled *Harry Sargent* and *The Girl with the Key*. She was going to kill him.

Buying it and getting it on her Kindle was the work of a moment. *To B.*, the frontispiece read. Until that moment, Eliza had clung to the hope that Gina had been mistaken. But no. She covered her mouth with her hand.

"'B'?" Jonathan asked. His cheeks were white in what Eliza interpreted as sympathetic rage.

"For Betts. It's what he calls me. Called me. In — Paris," Eliza said. She wondered about that now. Had Harry thought of her that way for months, or added the dedication sometime between Paris and when he'd dumped her?

Jonathan nodded, looking as horror-struck as Eliza felt.

She spent the rest of the day on the convention floor in a daze. She didn't trust herself to pick up the book and read it right there, and she couldn't leave her post and abandon Jonathan. As soon as the floor closed, though, the two of them packed up and left.

Of the many non-glamorous realities of what was supposed to be Eliza's glamorous life, sitting in a hotel room with her ex-lover's assistant, eating takeout and reading an erotic love affair travelogue about herself was the one she had least anticipated.

15

♦

America's Newest Heartthrob

Harry

The day after Eliza and Jonathan were slated to fly back from BEA, Harry got a video call from Anika. About *The Girl with the Key.* And a publisher who was offering him a traditional contract for it. Harry could hardly believe his ears. The book had barely been out for two weeks and he hadn't been able to make himself look at sales numbers since the day it had released. He was entirely unprepared for this development.

Harry stumbled through some routine questions about the contract being offered. Anika had answers ready, but Harry couldn't focus enough to take notes. For one thing, he'd assumed that no one was reading the book. For another, the more attention the book received, the higher the likelihood that Eliza would learn of it before he had the chance to tell her.

"Harry."

Harry looked up from his computer. As if his thoughts and fears had summoned her, Eliza stood in the doorway, her right hand on her hip and her left holding an e-reader.

She wore a pale green dress cinched at the waist with a thin belt in a darker shade of the same color. The palette set off her dark hair, which hung loose in waves like a stormy sea or, worse, some sort of peculiar fire. She was beautiful, because she was always beautiful, but Harry had a very bad feeling about this.

"Do you have a moment?" Eliza asked.

"I'm afraid I'm in the middle of a call —"

"*Do. You. Have. A. Moment,*" she repeated.

Harry quailed at her tone. He was in trouble. And it was personal. *Please don't be about the book*, his brain supplied. Then, less helpfully, *Of course it's about the book, you absolute tool.*

"I'm going to have to call you back," he said to his screen where Anika was mid-sentence. Without waiting for a response, Harry snapped his laptop closed.

He looked at Eliza. "Yes?"

"Were you planning to tell me?"

"Tell you what?" Harry knew playing innocent wasn't going to make this better, but buying himself time, however foolishly, seemed life or death. Eliza had any number of legitimate reasons to be angry with him and maybe it wouldn't be as bad as he feared.

"Harry, I have never been so fucking furious in my life, do not make me more angry, I swear to God —"

He held up his hands in protest, even as he wondered if his palms had the word *guilty* written on them. "I have no idea what you're talking about —"

"You wrote a book about how much you wanted to fuck me and you didn't tell me!" Eliza stepped fully into his office but didn't close the door behind her.

"It's not about how much I —"

"I read it! The whole thing! Yes, it is!" Eliza brandished the e-reader which Harry could only imagine contained the book he'd written. Most definitely about her.

"I —"

Eliza threw the device. Not at him, but close enough. The thing clattered against the bookshelf behind him and hit the floor.

"What the hell makes you think you can do something like this, Harry?" Eliza demanded. "You fucked me, and then you dumped me, and then you wrote a book about me!"

"Technically." Harry got out of his chair and circled around her to close the door to his office. "*Technically*, I wrote a book about you, and then fucked you, and then dumped you."

Harry knew he deserved every bit of the scorn and disbelief Eliza's eyes sent at him.

"So, what?" she demanded. "Did it not live up to your expectations or did you just need to get it out of your system?"

"Betts, you know that's not —"

"Don't you dare call me that."

"Eliza."

"Did you dump me so you wouldn't have to tell me you wrote this monstrosity?" she demanded.

"No." That was true. Mostly. He'd dumped her because the whole affair was destined to end in tears. Also he needed to publish a book, and it seemed easier if...*I've made an entirely terrible calculation.*

"Then when were you going to tell me?"

"I don't know. It didn't feel like it mattered when we were together." Truth be told, Harry had barely even thought about it while they were in Paris. He'd barely thought about anything in the midst of the storm and all the time they'd spent in bed. The melancholy period of wanting Eliza had been so different from the magical period of having her that the experiences might have belonged to two different men.

Not that Eliza would accept that as an explanation. Nor should she.

"Didn't matter? *Didn't matter?!*" Eliza stared at him.

Harry wanted to retreat behind his desk again, to put some physical buffer between him and the woman he'd wounded so badly. But he couldn't seem to move. Eliza's rage pinned him to the spot.

"What is wrong with you?" Eliza demanded when he was silent. "There's already an article in *Publisher's Weekly* about this book speculating who it's about. It seems everyone has a theory, and most of them are right! I keep getting calls for comment from publications I'd *wanted* to submit my own work too, except now I'm *the girl in the book with the goddamn key!*" She pulled viciously at the key, which still hung around her neck. "What possible conditions would make this less egregious? Was there some non-disaster scenario you were able to envision?"

"It's the best thing I've ever written," Harry said helplessly.

"Then it should have been a gift." Eliza's voice was soft and solemn.

"What do you want me to say?"

"I don't want you to say anything. I don't need anything from you. I've been yelling at you because you deserve to be yelled at, and I have the right to do it. I'm certainly not here to make you feel better about any of this." Eliza paused.

They stared at each other, breathing harshly in the terrible silence. In sync, even now, in Harry's failure and her fury.

"I loved you," she said, more calmly, but he would have given anything to have her take those words back and return to yelling at him. "I loved you, and you called me a child, and then you published a book about the great love affair it turns out you didn't actually want to have with me. Well congratulations," she said, reaching for the handle of his door. "I guess you got what you wanted."

"Eliza —" Harry had no idea what he was going to say. He was miserable and sorry and, he suspected, only beginning to realize how truly and spectacularly he had fucked up.

"*What!?*"

He wondered, for a split second, whether it was even in his power to fix this. He could fantasize about falling on his knees and begging forgiveness. But Eliza wasn't going to take him back. She had broken off an engagement with a fiancé because he had treated her like a prize, not a living, breathing person who was his peer, his equal, and, very probably, his better. Had Harry done the same? The thought was a paralytic, and he was too horrified, it seemed, to speak.

In any case, Eliza was done. Without saying anything more she left, slamming the door behind her.

Whatever suffering Harry now faced, he most certainly faced it alone.

◆

Harry's first call that evening when he was back in his apartment was to Meryl. She finally answered after letting her phone ring what Harry thought was an excessive number of times.

"I did something horrendously stupid and need your advice," Harry said. "Can I come over?"

"Right now?" Harry could hear her eyebrows hitting her hairline.

"Right now would be preferable, yes."

There was a pause on the other end of the line, and then muffled speech as though Meryl had covered the receiver with her hand while talking to someone else. Finally, she came back.

"Unfortunately, Harry, I have company." Something about her tone, not to mention the whispering, told Harry she didn't mean a dinner party. If it had been a dinner party, Harry was sure he would have been invited.

"I thought you didn't fuck people in your apartment?" he blurted.

"I don't fuck *you* in my apartment," Meryl clarified with exactly as much iciness as he deserved. Harry could only imagine what her company thought of her end of the conversation. "Are you all right?" she asked.

Given that unearned scrap of graciousness, Harry could hardly tell her anything but the truth. "Yes. Just pathetic."

"All right, well, let's schedule another time to talk. And then you can be as pathetic as you'd like. Are you free on Thursday?"

A date for drinks and moping scheduled, Harry hung up.

●

Harry had a phone meeting with Anika the next morning to talk more about the publisher's offer for *The Girl with the Key*. He spent the rest of the day wishing he dared turn it down.

He was willing to recognize the irony; he'd been reluctant to self-publish the book, and, now that an actual publisher was interested, he was terrified. The book was already getting more attention than he'd ever expected. Placing it with a publisher might only increase its visibility, not to mention Eliza's ultimate fury with him for publishing it at all. She had already thrown her e-reader in her rage after saying some very pointed, very true things that Harry could not get out of his head.

The most gentlemanlike thing to do would be to decline the contract — and pull the book out of its current sales channels. Certainly that might go some small way toward making amends to Eliza. But it would also mean letting the best thing he'd ever written about a woman who now, very fairly, hated him, languish as an odd abandoned e-reader file of creative genius. It would be easy to argue that the damage had already been done. Signing a new contract could hardly make things worse.

●

Late that afternoon he arrived at her office door with a paper cup of tea prepared the way she liked and what he hoped was a penitent expression. The door was slightly ajar, and he took a moment to look at the sliver of Eliza he could see through it. Today she wore a grey pencil skirt and a pale blue cardigan that looked so soft that Harry longed to see how it felt under his hands. It was nearing the end of the day, but her dark hair was still perfectly swept back in an elaborate French braid, every strand in place. She was working on something on her laptop, Harry couldn't tell what, and her chin was leaning on her hand.

Before Harry got carried too far away in mingled fantasy and self-recrimination, he knocked softly at the door frame. Eliza sat up straight and looked at him. Her eyes narrowed.

"Can I help you?" she asked coolly.

"May I come in?" Harry asked. "There's something I'd like to talk to you about."

Whatever Eliza's emotions were or what subject she thought he was going to bring up, her face was a mask, terrifyingly placid. "Yes. Of course."

"I brought you tea." Harry held out the cup to her.

Eliza looked at him, the faintest note of despair moving across her features before she schooled them again. "I wish you hadn't."

She took the cup, but it didn't feel like the acceptance of an olive branch that Harry had hoped it might be. She also didn't drink from it.

"May I sit down?" he asked.

"You know," Eliza said. "We could have avoided a lot of grief if you'd decided to be this polite earlier." She didn't tell him he could sit, and so he didn't.

"Yes, I could have," Harry admitted. "That's why I'm coming to you now."

"Oh?" She raised an eyebrow.

"There's a publisher that wants to offer me a contract for *The Girl with the Key.*"

"I'm well aware."

"You are?"

"Yes. In case you didn't know, they approached me at BEA in hopes of finding you. Five minutes later the entire North American publishing industry knew I was the 'the girl.'"

Harry actually hadn't known that was the chain of events that had led to her discovering the book. His shame, if possible, deepened. "Oh."

"Yes," Eliza all but snapped.

Harry steeled himself to plow ahead. "Before I sign anything I wanted to talk to you."

"You want my permission to sign a deal for a book you wrote about me — and already published — without telling me."

"I know. I'm trying to make amends."

"By asking me to be okay with a bad situation getting worse. You don't want my permission, you're trying to assuage your guilt. This — this book, this choice. It's your life. It's your words. Don't put this on me."

"I'm not —" Harry started to say, but Eliza interrupted him.

"I have a collection of essays. I was putting together the submission materials when we got back from Paris, before I went to Chicago. And now I have no idea how to submit that work or anything else I do anywhere. Not to agents or publishers or literary magazines. Your book is the only thing anyone in publishing is talking about, it's going to get bigger, and everyone knows it's about me."

Harry said nothing. There was nothing he could say, really. Eliza looked down at her desk, straightened a fountain pen on top of a notepad, and went on. "I was raised to spend my life in the shadow of important men, until that became the one thing I never wanted. Whether I do or not, apparently isn't within my control. But how I respond is. I'm not going to give you permission, and I'm not going to tell you no. Do what you need to do. But please understand, I will also do what I need to do. Whether that's saying what I need to say or pretending you never existed, I haven't decided yet."

●

Back in his office, Harry signed the contract. On his way home that night he opted to walk rather than take the train. The last few days had been stressful in a way he never could, and had never wanted, to imagine.

He'd had the career breakthrough of his — and many other writers' — dreams. A big five press had picked up his self-published book. Anika, exasperated at his refusal to look at his Amazon sales dashboard, had sent him screenshots of the book's rankings. He'd never had a new release that even came remotely close. He didn't even have to worry about the book being unavailable for a time while the publisher took over — they were apparently dealing with all that.

But at what cost? Eliza was furious with him. She had every right to be. He'd behaved horribly. And while he'd never intended to continue a relationship with her, he'd never wanted to be cruel.

As he was lost in these dark musings, his cell phone rang. It took Harry a moment to fish it out of his pocket, and once he did it was from a number he didn't recognize. Given that he'd just signed a contract with a major publishing house, the best thing seemed to be to answer it.

"Harry Sargent?" a crisp female voice asked.

"This is he." Harry wondered what could possibly have gone wrong so quickly.

"I'm the producer on *The Really Late Show*. I've been told you're friends with Dennis."

"Yes?" Harry said. He vaguely wondered if Dennis had had a heart attack on set and somehow he was the man's emergency contact. It was the sort of thing Dennis would do to him out of spite.

"I'm afraid we're short a guest for the show tonight. Would you be available to come in for the taping? I see you have a book that's just come out."

"I — what?" Harry struggled to shift gears out of potential emergency-response mindset.

"A guest cancelled last minute and our backup guest has come down with food poisoning. In his dressing room. Taping needs to start in an hour and Dennis said I should call you."

Harry sighed. "When do you need me there?"

"Within the hour. Do you need directions?"

"No, I know where to go." Harry stood and reached for his jacket. "Tell him I'm on my way, and that he owes me."

◆

The studio was freezing, Dennis was too busy to talk to him, the sound of the live audience was mildly terrifying, and Harry couldn't decide if he was absolutely, positively supposed to call Eliza about this or keep making his own choices. Clearly, she was sick of hearing about the whole thing, perhaps most especially from him. And she was right — it wasn't her job to absolve him or give him permission.

He turned his phone off and left it in his pocket while he submitted to the mild indignity of having his hair done and makeup put on for the camera. He'd occasionally hung out backstage waiting for Dennis to be done with work so they could get up to some form of mischief together. All he had done then was watch the action and try to stay out of the way. He'd never been here to actually *talk*.

He heard Dennis's introduction with a rising sense of stage fright mingled with a good dose of straight-up panic. He didn't actually know how to do this. A P.A. had to nudge Harry in the ribs to get him to stop lurking in the wings and step out onstage. The lights were blinding, which was the best thing that could be said for the situation. It meant Harry could hear the audience and their middlingly enthusiastic applause, but he couldn't see them.

Dennis rose from his chair to give Harry the sort of back-slapping hug they never exchanged in real life. He wore a sharp grey suit with coordinating tie and pocket square in dark green and gold, and his wavy hair was styled to perfection. He looked almost intimidatingly put together. Harry was well-dressed too, of course, but Dennis was in his element and it showed.

Harry paged through his memory trying to think of some immensely embarrassing anecdote he could tell about Dennis to level the playing field a little. At least, one that wouldn't also indict himself. There weren't many.

Dennis was skilled at what he did, but Harry didn't know if he could pull off a good interview with such an old, close friend. He also worried about his own ability to be at all appealing on camera. But to his relief Dennis led him through a conversation that was well-paced, funny, and sprinkled with bits of interesting information about Harry's life and work. If Harry had the chance to do this another dozen times or so, he might actually get used to it. Not that that was ever going to happen.

"So you've written a book," Dennis finally said.

"I have."

"And you self-published it?"

"Would you like me to say something erudite about the democratization of publishing or be inappropriately judgmental of millions of authors who have done the same, with varying levels of success?"

"But I understand it's been picked up by a publisher," Dennis said, his voice leading. Harry supposed that was his job.

"I'm pleased to say, yes. It was always a bit of a problem child of a book. Less than a hundred pages. So I'm grateful someone wants to kill trees for such a thin volume."

"You realize no one here cares about publishing. What's the book about, Harry?"

"Well, apparently it's currently a digital best-selling not-quite-memoir about a love affair that never happened," Harry said. He forced himself to smile. 'Hadn't happened yet' would be the more honest thing to say, but he wasn't going to talk about *that* on national television.

Dennis turned to the audience. "I'm sorry, I think we're going to have to pry more out of him. Harry here has spent thirty years pretending to be the dignified party in our friendship. I can assure you, that's not the case. I have seen things."

"I've seen things too," Harry snapped, smiling in spite of himself.

Dennis looked delighted. The audience sounded delighted. "Harry, there are network standards even at this appalling hour. So tell us about the book. And the girl. And the book and the girl."

"I wrote the book during seventy-two hours in Vienna while I was supposed to be writing something else entirely. But I couldn't get her out of my head. And Vienna's a city of exile — I couldn't be there without thinking of all the things I wasn't supposed to be or have in my life. My agent told me it was the best thing I'd ever written and that she couldn't sell it. Yet, here we are. It's all been a little overwhelming."

Dennis waved a hand as if to bat away the insignificant details. "But the girl, Harry. Has she read it?"

"Unfortunately, yes."

"Why unfortunately?"

"Because I didn't tell her I wrote it, and when she found out she threw her e-reader at — well, not at me. But in my general direction."

The look of pure enjoyment on Dennis's face was not just for the benefit of the cameras. The audience roared with laughter…and a few boos, for Harry and his bad behavior.

Harry turned his head to find a camera; it wasn't hard, the damned things were everywhere. "Eliza," he said to it, as if there were the remotest chance she were watching. "I'm so sorry."

Eliza

At one in the morning Eliza lay awake, staring at the ceiling while the sounds of the city rumbled beneath her. When her phone rang she fumbled to answer it. Phone calls at this hour could not possibly be good.

It was Jonathan, which didn't reassure her at all. He might have pocket dialed her, or there might be something dreadfully wrong.

"Did I wake you?" he asked.

"No, I was up."

"Good. I mean, not good, but —"

"Jonathan, what's wrong?" Eliza sat up. Random colleagues, even those who might be becoming friends, didn't call in the middle of the night unless something was very wrong or someone was very dead. Her heart lurched. *Harry.*

"You should turn on your TV or computer or whatever and watch *The Really Late Show*."

"Why?" Eliza asked groggily.

"Because Harry's doing something *monstrously* ill-advised."

Worse than what he's done already? Eliza wasn't sure she wanted to see him clear that bar. But she leaned over the edge of her bed to grope for the laptop she'd left on the floor.

"I emailed you the link to where it's streaming," Jonathan said as she woke her computer up.

"Why are you so perfect?" Eliza asked.

Jonathan laughed but the sound was hushed and nervous.

In only moments she had a browser window open and the show playing. Harry, curse him, looked lovely. The camera softened his wry edges and brought out the sadness that lurked in the corners of his mouth. That sadness had drawn Eliza in since she had first met Harry; now, it was drawing in everyone who was watching.

Irrationally, the notion that Harry should be so available to the world made her flare with anger. She tried to push those feelings down. Her reaction would have been unkind and inappropriate even if she and Harry were together. For now, it was useless.

"I wish they'd stop referring to me as 'the girl,'" she said when she remembered she was still on the phone with Jonathan.

"Better than your name," he pointed out.

"Better to be an adult person than a child object." Eliza kept her voice low, not wanting to miss a word of this rather unlikely event.

"He's very good at this," Jonathan murmured.

Eliza wished Jonathan was wrong, but he wasn't. She had no idea if Harry's irritable but slightly flirtatious banter with Dennis was an act or not. Similarly, she had no idea of the sincerity of his chagrin regarding the book and her rage. But whatever he was doing, it played very well. If Harry hadn't been talking about her she might have fallen a little in love with him.

Then Harry turned and looked directly into the camera.

"You're not supposed to do that," Jonathan said.

Eliza would have laughed at his very firm opinions on talk show rules, but Harry was looking right at her. Harry was, in fact, talking directly to her, even if this had been recorded hours ago.

"Eliza, I'm so sorry," tiny TV-on-a-laptop Harry said.

"How," Eliza asked Jonathan as the audience cooed and laughed, "can this possibly be happening to me?"

Outside there was a flash and a crack of thunder. Wind pushed rain furiously against the windows. The hair on the back of Eliza's neck stood up. Whenever she thought of Harry, the world seemed to flood.

♦

Eliza got to work early, in part because she couldn't sleep any more, and in part because whatever Harry's plan for the day was, she wanted to arrive first.

The office was mostly empty when she got there, but as she walked down the hallway to her office Jonathan appeared holding a muffin and a cup of coffee. He put both of them down on top of a copy machine and pulled her into a brief, but tight, hug.

Eliza clung to him, startled both by the kindness of the gesture and how strongly it was affecting her. Until this moment she hadn't realized that going through life without friends also meant, to some extent, going through life without allies. Having someone on her side meant more than she knew how to express.

So when Jonathan gave her one last squeeze and let her go, she blinked hard — was she about to cry? At work? Again? *Oh please no* — and grabbed Jonathan's hand.

"Thank you." Her voice was a whispery croak.

Jonathan, apparently completely unbothered by the breakdown she was on the verge of having, handed her the coffee cup and the muffin.

"You're going to need some fuel for the day," he said. And then, with one last supportive smile, he disappeared down the hall and behind the barricade of his cubicle.

♦

Eliza had been at her desk about an hour when there was a knock on the door. It wasn't Harry's familiar one — or Jonathan's, for that matter.

"Come in?"

A young woman, about Eliza's age, opened the door. "Elizabeth Abgral?"

"That's me."

"I'm Jackie Park, from HR. Do you have a few minutes?"

"What for?" If she was about to get fired for Harry's appalling stunt, she…well. She wasn't sure what she would do. Maybe write a book.

"Just to ask you some questions. You're not in trouble," Jackie added hastily. "But after Mr. Sargent's appearance on *The Really Late Show* we want to make sure you're okay."

Eliza scowled. Harry's book — and him talking about it on TV — may have been unwanted, but it was a very public manifestation of a very private situation. She didn't want to talk about it with anyone else, and certainly not with human resources.

"Do you mind coming with me?" Jackie asked.

Eliza sighed and stood up. It was hardly a request she would be allowed to turn down.

She ended up in the HR office on a floor of the building she hadn't even known the publisher had offices on. Seated in the room with her was a kindly looking woman in her sixties who introduced herself as Cate Sanchez, the head of HR, and Jackie, who sat with a notepad on her knee. For the next half an hour, Eliza answered the same questions, asked over and over, from different angles and all with the same degree of caution and sympathy.

What was the nature of her relationship with Harry Sargent? Had he ever suggested, implied or stated that reciprocating his interest was a condition of employment? Had he used his position to harass or stalk her? Had he ever harassed or stalked her outside of his position? Was any of the attention he paid her unwelcome, unwanted, and did it make her uncomfortable in any way? Did she feel safe?

It was evident that this entire mess had only been brought to their attention by Harry's appearance on that damn show last night. Eliza thought, rather darkly, that if she ever had needed HR's intervention, they were a little late on the uptake.

"Look, I appreciate what you're doing here," she finally said. "I especially appreciate that you're taking the safety of women seriously. But really, I'm fine. We were in a consensual relationship and now we're not. We've both behaved poorly." Which was ninety percent Harry's fault, but then, she had thrown an e-reader. "But that's between us as adults, and it's fine. Though I promise," she added, because she could tell Cate was about to object, "that if I ever do feel harassed or uncomfortable or whatever by Harry, I will come tell you right away."

Cate and Jackie exchanged looks. Jackie nodded, which was evidently a signal, because Cate turned back to Eliza and asked, "Now, if that's settled, do you mind if we ask Mr. Sargent to join us?"

Eliza deeply regretted not staying home in bed today. "Not at all."

Cate left the room and returned less than a minute later with Harry. Eliza wondered how long they'd kept him waiting outside. In spite of herself she gave him a weak smile. If nothing else, they could commiserate on this.

Harry tried to smile in return, but mostly he looked deeply alarmed.

In all, Eliza decided she preferred the questions about whether Harry was abusing his position relative to her to the grilling about whether their personal relationship overstepped the bounds of professional propriety. Especially since the only honest answer she could give to all questions in that regard was *no*, they most definitely were not. Not anymore.

Harry joined with her in roundly denying any current relationship. Ironically, it was the most united they'd been on anything since Harry had left Paris.

◆

When they were finally released on their own recognizance, she and Harry stood awkwardly by the elevator bank waiting for a car to arrive.

"I'm sorry about that," Harry said, his hands tucked in his pockets.

Eliza shrugged. "The HR part of this mess was probably on both of us. But for the rest of it, thank you." An apology was the least he owed her, but she would take it.

"Can we talk?" Harry asked.

Eliza thought about snapping at him. No conversation could solve *accidental bestseller* or *national TV*. But it wasn't worth the effort. "I have a ton of work to do, and I lost two hours dealing with your need to talk about the book you wrote about me on national TV."

Harry said nothing.

While she wanted to be angry with him for not walking away, she was also keenly aware she hadn't gone anywhere either. Why were they still drawn to each other, even in the middle of this giant mess? She sighed in irritation with herself, with Harry, and with the universe. "Fine. Later?" she asked.

Harry closed his eyes for a moment, as if in relief. "Yes. Thank you."

◆

At seven that evening Harry knocked quietly on Eliza's open door. "Hi," he said, almost sheepishly. "I didn't want to presume and order food, but...?"

She was hungry, but uncertain. And exhausted. She wanted to come to terms about this massively untenable position Harry had put them both in. But she didn't have the energy for another fight, and she really didn't want to have one over a meal. Even if it was just out of takeout containers.

"I don't know yet," she said. "Did you want to come in?" Harry was still hovering in the doorway.

He nodded with evident caution.

"Sit down," she told him, not brusquely.

"Why the change of heart?" he asked as he slid into one of the chairs at her desk.

Eliza looked at him with something approaching disbelief. "That is presumptuous," she said.

"I'm sorry." Harry looked contrite, but Eliza wasn't in the mood to be affected. "I just wanted to get everything out in the open."

"You mean like you did before you wrote a book about me, published it, and then went and talked about it on a TV segment that's now gone viral?" she said sharply.

"I know I can't fix that," Harry said. "But I was a coward for a long time, and the least I can do is make myself available for whatever you want to say to me."

"And if I don't want to say anything to you?" she asked.

"You did ask me to come in," Harry pointed out.

Eliza had to concede that. "It's not a change of heart," she said. "I'm still furious with you. But I'm also tired of this." She waved a hand to encompass the tension between them and the mess that was rippling outwards from them to the world beyond.

"Were you really in love with me?" Harry asked.

From the offer of a meal to this. If it had been anyone else, Eliza would have ordered him right back out of her office. But it was Harry, and Harry had never been like anyone else. Until he had been awful.

"I still am," she said. "I just hate you too."

A complicated expression that might have been hope or relief fluttered across Harry's face. "Can we fix this?" he asked.

Eliza felt lost. "In what capacity? I don't even know if there's anything to fix."

"You've read the book — and again, I am so sorry —"

Eliza held up a hand. Further apologies would do nothing.

"You read the book," Harry repeated, quiet but insistent. "You can hardly think your feelings aren't returned."

"I most certainly can. I don't even understand what happened. Both the good part and this..." she fished for a word. "Disaster."

"I got scared."

"So? People are scared all the time." Harry looked distressed, but he didn't say anything. Eliza pressed on. "Are you still a child? Do you still think I'm one?"

"I'm twenty years older than you. An incredibly close friend of mine died in January. I don't do relationships —"

"You never told me you were a cad," Eliza interrupted scornfully.

"— because they don't interest me. Didn't. And then there was you."

"What do you mean relationships don't interest you?" Eliza asked. "You've told me so much about people who have mattered to you tremendously."

"But the way other people do them," Harry said. "What are they for?" He sounded so bewildered that Eliza was taken aback. She'd asked herself the same question as a teen, but answers were so easily forthcoming from everyone around her. They were for status and security. They were for barter, cooperation, and trust. None of that was awful or unreasonable, but it had all always seemed so bloodless to Eliza, and she'd never really known if that was about her or about everyone else.

"They're for talking to people about books when you're not at the office," she said.

"I have friends for that," Harry replied.

"None of this explains why you wrote a book about me. While you, let's not forget, completely disregarded any and all respect I, and my work, deserve. Not to mention my autonomy. Or my ambition." Eliza fidgeted with the key she still wore around her neck.

Harry looked down at his hands and then back up to her. "Because the only time I don't feel as if I am in exile is when I'm with you."

◆

The next day Eliza did her best to bury herself in work. Gina, Philippe's fiancée, sent her an email — she had evidently seen Harry's TV performance — that was both sympathetic and kind. Eliza was touched by her thoughtfulness, and even made herself exert the effort to reply and say she was fine, just furious with Harry.

And confused about him, she admitted. The confession to a near-stranger felt less awkward than she had expected, and she felt better once she'd made it. Perhaps this was why people gossiped to casual acquaintances at work — or talked to therapists.

Eliza worked late that night, and it was with great relief she watched Harry slink home shortly before seven. After he was gone she slipped out of her office and headed for the test kitchen.

Once she reached the door she closed her eyes, trying to remember the code Harry had punched in the first time he'd brought her here. In her mind's eye she could see his fingers deftly pressing buttons; she tried the same pattern and was relieved when the lock gave way with a heavy click.

The kitchen was blessedly empty and she stood in the door taking a moment to collect herself. It was hard to be here without Harry in his shirtsleeves, making them food and being so charming.

But that was absolutely the point. She closed the door firmly behind herself and crossed the kitchen quickly. She opened cabinets and storage drawers, looking for the sturdiest pan she could find and pulling out every fire-related tool she could lay her hands on.

When she was satisfied with a dented five-quart sauce pan and a small kitchen torch, she pulled the key from around her neck and dangled it over the pot. She didn't actually know what it was made out of, or if the stove or a little torch meant for crème brûlée would get hot enough to melt it, but she was determined to find out. The only way to be truly free — from Cody, from Harry, from any man that would impinge on her freedom — wasn't to possess this talisman, but to make sure it didn't exist at all.

The process did not go as intended. With the small torch, she burned the ribbon before she managed to melt the metal, and the key clattered into the bottom of the pot. She turned a burner on to high, and hoped it would be enough. And also that she was not about to poison herself with toxic fumes.

She was holding the handle of the pot with a trout-shaped oven mitt and stabbing at the half-melted key when the door to the kitchen opened.

Eliza jumped, but it was Jonathan.

"What are you doing here?" she asked.

"I am one hundred percent certain I should be asking you that," he said drily.

"I'm melting a key."

"Ummmm…"

"The one I wear around my neck. The one in the book. The one I have because I didn't want my wretched ex-fiancé to have it."

"The honorable representative from the state of Massachusetts," Jonathan intoned.

"That one. Yes." Eliza stared down at the key, and stabbed it with the fork again. Then she looked up at Jonathan. "I think I ruined your pot."

16

♦

The Evil Eye

Harry

Working with an Eliza who did not hate him was an improvement. But that lack of animosity held little promise beyond peace. They were not co-conspirators, and they were not friends. They did not spend meetings emailing each other, and Eliza did not spend her evenings sipping tea and dozing in his office. Instead, spring turned to summer, and she went out with the women in marketing or grabbed coffee with Jonathan. She had friends, and Harry felt relief.

As the days passed and grew sultry as only June in New York City could, things between Eliza and Harry began to warm too. Not back to where they had been. But they started, once again, to chat in the halls when they passed each other and exchange covert glances over the most egregious presentations at meetings. Sometimes one or the other of them lingered in an office doorway for a moment, and they traded stories there was no need to trade.

Eliza had stopped wearing her key.

Harry noticed right away but didn't dare ask about it. Not when the origin of that particular fashion choice was so personal, and not when she had been naked except for it when she'd first explained.

At first he thought she might be tucking it into her tops, but she wore her hair up often enough that he'd have been able to see the lace at the back of her neck. Then, he considered that she might have secreted the thing somewhere else on her person or simply been lugging it around in her purse.

Eventually, however, he succumbed to his curiosity about the matter. He cornered Jonathan in his cubicle to ask if he knew what had happened to it.

"You mean the one that's the star of your book?"

Harry took a deep breath. Titling the book after Eliza's key had not been his gravest mistake. But that he hadn't fully considered the narrative behind the object when he had inserted it into his tale, must have only served to make everything worse. "Yes."

Jonathan's eyes widened in a look of mingled judgement — about Harry, he was sure — and excitement. "You're going to love this."

"I am one hundred percent sure I am not."

"She destroyed it."

"What do you mean she destroyed it?" Harry asked with something approaching alarm.

"I mean she melted it down in a pot in the test kitchen using the stove and a crème brûlée torch," Jonathan said, stunned disbelief all over his face.

Harry smiled. "Did she really?"

"Oh yes."

"She is —"

Jonathan held his hands up. "Yes. I know. Just because you have bad judgement, doesn't mean you have bad taste. But you both seem halfway all right now. Don't...don't make a thing of this. It wasn't about you. And I only know because I caught her at it."

"Is that why the blossoming friendship?"

Jonathan shook his head. "No. We're friends, Harry, because we're friends. That's how it works."

♦

The more he thought about it, the more relieved Harry was that Eliza had destroyed the key. She must have felt safer — from her past, from Cody, from Harry himself — to let that charm go. And while Harry would have never admitted it aloud, he felt safer too. Without that damn key, Eliza was slightly less the girl in the Ys story. Meaning, in turn, that he was slightly less a devil.

Life moved on for all of them. Harry went through the editorial notes for the traditionally published edition of *The Girl with the Key*, and marketing plans and galleys came and went. As June melted into July the trades handed out starred reviews, and only a few industry newsletters wrote a second article on who they felt so very sure the girl must be.

Harry, Eliza, and the whole office kept their heads down that day, but eventually, he felt duty bound to at least check on her again, if it was welcome or would mean anything at all.

"It's fine, and I don't want to talk about," she said when he knocked on her door at the end of the day.

"I can't imagine it is."

"It's not your fault. Not this part of it. And I can't keep retreading this with you every time someone falls in love with your prose. Or with me."

"But what are you going to do?" Harry asked.

"Everything I've been doing all along. My job. My words. My life. I already have my next gig lined up." She leaned forward over her desk. "You're powerful, Harry, but not enough to stop me."

He laughed at that, and she echoed him. He missed her every day. And yet, somehow, this was also, almost enough. "What's your next stop then?" he asked, jovially.

She smiled. "Berlin."

The world fell out from under him.

♦

The world, however, continued to turn. The advance for the traditionally published version of *The Girl with the Key* arrived in his mailbox the same day Amazon sent him an email about how much he could expect from them for its brief self-published availability. The numbers were not insignificant. Certainly, they were more than most authors could hope for, not due to the quality of their work, but because the business was cruel and unfair at every turn to the people who produced the raw product. Harry had gotten lucky.

And the money…well, the money felt tainted.

So he set out to spend it. Immediately. Where maybe it could do a little more good or at least be a little more kind.

♦

"Harry," Meryl said with a heavy sigh. She was at Harry's house for coffee on a Sunday afternoon, a cautious attempt towards finding their new normal together. So far, having her here felt about the same as it did when she had visited the city for brief periods before. *Maybe we're making too much fuss out of nothing.*

"You are my favorite," Meryl went on. "But since when do you make expensive plans you want me to participate in without asking me first?"

Harry looked from side to side, as if his sitting room could provide the answer. But the Eames armchair and the midcentury prints on his walls stayed silent. Buying tickets to a charity ball designed to raise funds for literacy and arts education with some of the initial royalties from *The Girl with the Key* had been a lovely idea. Assuming that Meryl would be on call to go with him, less so. And he probably should have just donated the money directly to the cause.

"It seemed like a blameless way to express my affection for you, and my appreciation for the lack of drama between us, despite our fears?"

"Your fears, Harry. I knew everything was going to be fine."

Harry wasn't convinced of that, but now was also not the time to press the point. "If you say so."

Meryl twisted the head of her cane around. "Your thoughtfulness, as far as it went, is noted," she said dryly.

"So…is that a yes or a no?" Harry asked.

"It's an 'I'd love to go, darling, but I have plans that evening,'" Meryl said, uncrossing and re-crossing her ankles.

"Ah." The noise was awkward. "Plans with who?" *A lady doesn't kiss and tell* and the voice Harry had heard in the background of his previous phone call to Meryl stuck in his mind. He knew little of Meryl's relationships that didn't involve himself or the rest of the Miscreants. Up until this moment that had always been a feature, not a bug. But now it left him feeling — unfairly — left out and cut off.

"If you want to ask if I'm seeing someone, just ask," Meryl said.

"I thought I had. But. Very well. Meryl, are you seeing someone?"

"I am."

felt himself go cold at the confirmation of his suspicions. He never cared what Meryl did with anyone, but there was something in the mischief of her grin that made him terrified of being displaced. She'd had serious relationships here and there that had precluded their vague affair from time to time, but Harry had never thought much of it. Even with things between him and Eliza a hopefully redeemable mess, Harry felt uneasy. And Meryl, of course, saw it.

"Oh, Harry," she said.

"I am happy for you, and I want to hear all about him —"

"Her."

Harry raised his eyebrows. "Really?"

"Don't look so excited."

"I wasn't. I wasn't!" Harry held his hands up. "I just feel untethered." Steven was dead, Dennis's show had helped change the course of his career, and Meryl had slipped out of his bed.

She leaned forward in her chair, her perfectly made-up eyes ready to drive some point home. "Maybe that's because it was time for you to be untethered." She sat back again. "And that is why I'm not available on this particular occasion for your not-terrible impulse of generosity. But I think I know someone else you owe something to, and might not despise the gesture."

"Eliza?" Harry guessed, even as he trembled at the idea. No — not the idea. The fear that if he asked, she might say no. But if he owed her anything — and he owed her a lot — offering her a chance to reject him was the least he could do.

Eliza

Eliza did the best she could to tune out the noise of the publishing industry speculating about her relationship with Harry. Instead she focused on her work, her own writing and, increasingly, the friends she was making at work.

"You're still here."

Eliza looked up to find, as she increasingly did these days, Harry in her doorway. "Trying not to be."

Mostly at this point his presence pleased her, but that pleasure always coexisted with what had been lost, and sometimes it was more than she cared for. Especially since it was all his fault.

"Do you have a moment?" he asked.

"Yes…no. I mean, I'm trapped here at my desk, Harry. I have a moment whether I want to give you one or not."

"I'm sorry, I didn't mean."

Eliza sighed and closed her laptop. "Neither did I, believe it or not. It's not your fault that I always have time for you. Mostly."

"Am I allowed to laugh at that?" Harry asked.

"Yes. Please do in fact."

Harry finally stepped into her office and gestured to the door. "All right?" he asked. She nodded, and he shut the door.

"Worried about HR?" she teased, although she regretted it almost immediately.

"I don't think so. I hope not anyway."

It wasn't like Harry to stumble over his words. Eliza folded her hands in front of her. "All right. What is it?"

"Well," Harry said again. He reached into the breast pocket of his jacket and pulled out a long, slim box that he turned over and over in his hands. "I got the first part of my advance for the book. And seen how much I'm getting for its short-lived self-published life. Which was far more than I expected or have ever gotten for first quarter sales before. So, I got you something, because it made me think of you. I hope you don't find it too strange or extravagant or inappropriate, although if you do, no harm, and we can pretend I've never done this."

"Harry," Eliza smiled up at him, confused but also terribly fond. Harry could be so bad at things sometimes. Maybe it would be too much, and they'd have to argue about it. That would be unfortunate.

"Yes?"

She wondered what he would look like, in the universe where he would ever get married, if he tried to propose. All his polished urbanity would go out the window if he couldn't even try to give a simple gift without awkwardness.

"What are you so afraid of?" she asked.

Harry made a sound that might have been dismay or might have been him clearing his throat, Eliza didn't know.

Without further explanation, he pressed the box into her hands.

She opened it efficiently as if that she could, somehow, assure both of them this would cause no further explosions. Tucked inside a fold of tissue paper was a delicate gold necklace with a pendant of sapphires and the tiniest of diamonds in the shape of an eye.

"It's lovely," she said. "And it's staring at me."

"To replace your key."

Why do you always have to keep talking in a way that makes things worse? "Jonathan told you."

"Yes."

"It wasn't about you," Eliza said. "Not really. Or, not entirely. But, I got rid of it, because I didn't need it anymore, and I was safer without it. All your stories about Ys…it didn't make me feel better."

"I know. And I'm sorry for making you a girl that never was. But…we almost drowned Paris. Who doesn't need a talisman?"

Eliza laughed wetly and put a hand over her mouth. *Don't cry, don't cry, don't cry. Don't spill any more water for this man.* "That we did." Then she smiled, because Paris, like so many of the things that had happened between them, deserved that always. Even if things hadn't turned out the way she wanted.

"No one, I don't think," she answered his question.

Harry gave a relieved but still self-conscious grin. "Exactly. It's an evil eye. To protect you from bad things."

"Like you?"

"Like the expectations the world tries to put on you," Harry said. "Or on your journey to Berlin or wherever life takes you. But yes. The bad parts of me, at least. Or the myth between us. Consider it an apology to you, and a reminder to me of what an asshole I've been."

Eliza held the box back out to him. "Help me put it on?"

Harry walked around the desk toward her. She turned in her chair so that her back was facing him. She held whatever wisps of hair had come down throughout the day up off her neck with one hand and soon she could feel cool metal at her throat, and the soft, warm brush of Harry's fingertips at the nape of her neck. She shivered. Harry chuckled softly behind her.

"Here, let's see," he said.

Eliza turned to face him again. The eye rested as the hollow of her throat, too high for her to see.

"It looks lovely on you," Harry said. "Regal. As it should be. Queen of a lost city."

She reached up to touch it, aware that after everything they were suspended in one of the deeply strange and lovely moments that had always existed between them. "Thank you. I'll pull out a compact to look at it as soon as you're out of my hair."

"I should let you get back to things," Harry said. "But I have one more question. And it's a slightly more awkward one."

"Now I'm terrified," she said like she wasn't. *Is he going to ask me out?*

"I have an extra ticket to a charity event. A ball, really. Benefitting a literary and arts education group."

"Extra?" Eliza asked. People didn't just have extra charity ball tickets.

"Meryl turned me down."

"What did you do?"

"I did nothing, I'll have you know. And she suggested I take you. So, my strange colleague in literary adventures, would you like to go? Not as a date — but as friends?"

◆

Eliza only managed the first three blocks of her walk home from the office before she texted Jonathan. *Your boss asked me to go to a charity ball with him.*

Jonathan responded almost immediately. *Oh God. Is that good or bad?*

Yes, Eliza replied.

Okay. And at literally any other moment I would love to explore that in depth with you, but I'm about to start a phone interview with the London branch. Can we catch up later?

London branch because Malik? Eliza asked.

Uhhuh.

Tell me more later?

Only if you'll do the same, Jonathan replied.

All of which was utterly fair, and Eliza felt an added burst of excitement that Jonathan's life — professional and romantic — was moving in the direction that he wanted it to. But right now, she *really* needed someone to talk to. But who? She hadn't spoken to her sister in months. Her work friends, while lovely, were work friends, and she didn't want to gossip with them about a mutual colleague, especially after the HR incident. Who else was there?

No one wise, her brain traitorously supplied. But wisdom was already so far out of the picture. And Philippe's fiancee, Gina, had been there when Eliza had discovered Harry's damn book, and had offered her friendship even before Eliza's world had turned completely upside down.

They'd exchanged a few emails, giddy and gossipy, since BEA, and Eliza scrolled through her phone to start a new text thread with her.

Hi, I know this is out of the blue, but I need someone to kickyfeet at and because our lives are odd, I suspect you're the best choice for it.

Eliza slipped her phone into her bag, knowing it could be hours or even days before she might expect a reply, but the device chirped with an incoming message instantly.

WHAT DID HARRY DOOOOOOOOOOO??? Gina had written.

Eliza couldn't help laughing. *How do you know it was him?* she texted back.

Please, Gina replied. *I'm not a writer, but I know how to thread a story together. Tell. Me. EVERYTHING.*

Grinning to herself, her thumbs flying over the keyboard, Eliza did.

Harry

Harry went to meet Dennis for what was supposed to be dinner and drinks late on a Thursday with the intention of demonstrating how much he had pulled his life together since they had last met. But the restaurant was crowded, Dennis greeted him with "Heyyyy, heartthrob!" and everything went rapidly downhill from there.

"Can you stop?" Harry snapped, lifting his head from his hands eight minutes into a monologue from Dennis about all the tail Harry was surely getting now that he was a famous author. He wanted to tell Dennis that Eliza had said yes to going to the ball with him. He wanted to ask Dennis what he knew of whoever Meryl was seeing. He did not want to get needled about the worst and most embarrassing choices he had made all year.

"I don't see why I should." Dennis said innocently.

Harry huffed. "Look, it would be nice to spend an evening as someone other than the man who wrote a book about a girl."

"It would be," Dennis acknowledged. "But I suspect that Eliza would like to spend an evening as someone other than the girl about whom a man wrote a book."

"She and I are all right now. Don't act disappointed. And don't forget you're the one who suggested I publish it. So taking her theoretical side against me is uncalled for." Harry was annoyed at Dennis and wanted to dig in.

"Just about everyone is on her side. Even the people buying up your book in droves and wishing they could be in her incredibly unenviable position."

Harry wasn't sure if Dennis meant her position sucked because she had been the unconsenting subject of a memoir about an affair that hadn't, at that point, happened, or because she was the object of Harry's affections at all.

"I'm not going to deny that I deserve any number of lectures on that point." Harry's irritation was growing. "But since you asked me on your show and helped make my book the whatever-number bestseller it currently is, you're not innocent in all this either."

"Maybe," Dennis said with a shrug. "But I don't know this girl of yours and have no obligations to her. And you're still the one who wrote the thing. And published the thing. And now you're the one everyone is drooling over."

"You think I don't know that? I didn't write the damn book to seduce Eliza, much less anyone else. I've started making amends with her, and it's still incredibly complicated."

"That lack of intention was a mistake," his friend pointed out unhelpfully. Before Harry could say anything else or beg again for a topic change, Dennis posed a question. "But has it worked?"

"Has what worked?"

"The book. Seducing the fair Eliza."

"I broke up with her because of your advice, and she threw a Kindle at my head." *She melted her key*, Harry thought. "There has been no seduction since my series of bad choices. Nor should there be."

Then why did you invite her to the charity ball? his mind asked traitorously. "If she wants something from me, she'll tell me. I don't need you lecturing me. She can yell at me all she wants, but you can go to hell."

Harry pushed himself away from the table. He was well aware that his anger at Dennis was merely residual displaced anger towards himself, but that wasn't enough for him to quell it or direct it appropriately. Right now he wanted some air and some distance from his friend.

Dennis, who too much loved a good adventure, followed him out of the restaurant and onto the sidewalk.

Thankfully the bar did have Harry's credit card for the tab; he didn't need to add dining-and-dashing to his list of sins.

"You know," Dennis said, folding his arms and looking up at the sky as if he were commenting on the weather. "You can storm off in a huff all you want, but nothing's going to change the fact that this predicament is entirely your fault."

"I am more than aware of that," Harry said as a woman with a white poodle scurried by. "Meanwhile, haven't you been helpful enough?"

"You didn't ask me to be helpful. You asked to go to dinner so you could whine about the mess you'd made of things with this woman. Now you're back for another round and so am I. I'm a willing audience to the theater of human folly, to be sure, but this is getting ridiculous."

"I have no idea why I listen to you. You've never had a relationship that lasted more than six months in your life."

"And you have?" Dennis sounded delighted, the way he had on his show a few short weeks ago. "You had a beautiful young woman ready to eat out of the palm of your hand. And instead of treating her like a queen, which any sane man would have done, you wrote a book about your intimate fantasies about her. Emotional and physical. And then you moaned and moaned about how it was the best thing you'd ever written, so I told you to put your career first and somehow you were surprised when she was furious. Let me tell you, that makes exactly one of us."

"Good of you to say something, before you *invited me on your talk show.*"

"I didn't know how much of a jerk you'd been until you confessed it yourself on camera. Besides. I was desperate."

Harry had never hated him more. "Would you stop?"

"Why?" Dennis asked. "You've been terrible about this from start to finish. And I don't just mean an emotionally stunted failure the way you so often are. I mean you had something perfect going and you managed to screw it up. And instead of trying to fix it you moped around feeling sorry for yourself and made it all worse. You've shown up to tell me everything's just fine, but none of your choices make sense and I don't know why I don't get to have an opinion. I know Steven dying fucked you up," Dennis said. "It fucked all of us up. But you're the only one who has systematically and deliberately made a mess of his own life *and* other people's because of it."

The swing Harry took at Dennis was halfway decent. He was proud of both the satisfying thud that resonated up his arm when he hit Dennis's jaw and the wide-eyed look of surprise on Dennis's face when he did.

Dennis's return punch, however, landed squarely on his nose, and any righteous anger Harry felt was submerged in a flare of pain and blood. He doubled over, eyes screwed shut while he cursed.

"Holy shit," Dennis said. Instantly he was at Harry's side. He pulled a handkerchief out of his suit pocket and pressed it into Harry's palm with one hand and with the other, pushed gently down on the back of Harry's neck.

"The hell," Harry spluttered, trying instinctively to shake him off.

"Keep your head down. *Shit.*" Dennis swore again and steered Harry to a crouch by the door to the restaurant, out of the way of foot traffic. "That's a lot of blood."

Harry grunted, but kept his head between his knees. "I'm fine," he said stuffily.

"Do you want me to get you home? Or to a doctor? I didn't break it did I? I mean I can't put you in a cab like that. You look like hell."

"Thanks to you."

"Hence my concern."

"I'm fine," Harry repeated. "It's not broken." *At least, I hope.* "But I need to get mopped up before I horrify any more passersby."

There wasn't much he could do other than wait it out and complete the ruination of Dennis's handkerchief. Once the blood stopped flowing, Dennis helped pull him to his feet and steadied him with a hand on each shoulder when he staggered slightly.

"I'm not going back in there looking like this," Harry said firmly.

"You're going to walk all the way home looking like that?" Dennis stared at him.

"I go back in there, and if someone recognizes me because *they saw me on TV*, my life and Eliza's both get so much worse than they already are. She's speaking to me again. I want that to continue. And I want to be able to show my face again in public, ever. The office is two blocks away, I can make it that far."

"Let me walk with you, at least."

Harry considered the offer. It was sincere. And kind. And he'd probably attract less attention with a companion, but he really, truly just needed some damn space. "If it's all the same, I'd rather lick my wounds in private."

"All right," Dennis said doubtfully. "But call me if you need anything." He looked worried when Harry turned and, still holding Dennis's handkerchief over his nose and mouth, headed up the street towards his office building.

It was late and nearly the weekend, so Harry didn't expect to run into anyone when the elevator clanged open on his floor and he made his pathetic way toward the bathroom. Which was a mistake of the deepest kind, because he was only halfway down the hall when an office door creaked open and Eliza poked her head out.

Her eyes went wide at the sight of him. "Oh my God, Harry."

He grunted something incoherent and wished for the floor to swallow him whole. It did not oblige.

Eliza emerged into the hallway and grabbed Harry's upper arms. "Are you okay? What happened to you?" She squinted to take in the damage.

"I'm fine," Harry said, for what felt like the millionth time. "I got into a fight with my best friend."

"Oh my God."

"Dennis. You remember? Of course you do." Harry tried to cover his bloody nose from view, well aware it wasn't working and was vastly too late. "We're fine, now. Just...this."

"I'm cleaning you up."

Before Harry could protest further, Eliza dragged him off toward the bathroom. She pulled him through the door of the women's restroom and pushed him down on one of the over-upholstered settees in the outer powder room.

"Stay there," she ordered before banging out of the bathroom again, returning a moment later with the first aid kit from the reception desk. She pulled a wad of paper towels out of the dispenser, turned on the hot water, and crouched down in front of him.

"Do you want to tell me what happened?" she asked while she sponged blood off Harry's upper lip.

"Dennis said some things that were true, and I was an ass."

"Do I want to know who took the first swing?"

Harry sighed. "It doesn't matter to Dennis and I."

"All right, then I won't ask." Eliza used Harry's knee to lever herself up to stand and threw away the pink-stained paper towels.

"If it matters to you — it was me," he confessed.

"Did he deserve it?"

"No."

"You are an absolute disaster of a human being." Eliza ran a fresh paper towel under the water.

"I know."

"And I'm dangerously close to changing my mind about this charity ball nonsense," she added.

"I know that too."

As she turned away from the sink and toward Harry the light caught on something at her throat. He squinted and then had to work very hard not to smile too broadly. Among other things, it made his face hurt.

"You're wearing the necklace," he said.

Eliza's expression was, in a word, smug. "I know."

"You like it then?"

"Shut up, Harry." She knelt in front of him again to wipe away the last smears of blood.

17

◆

Through the Stones and Behind the Gate

Eliza

Despite the fight Harry had gotten into with his friend, Eliza spent the day of the charity ball in slightly giddy anticipation. Perhaps she was a fool for being willing to patch things up with him when that damn book of his was still making headlines…and best sellers' lists. But they were who they were to each other, and now, strangely, the world.

Including their officemates. Jonathan knocked on the frame of her open door shortly before noon.

"Hey, do you want to grab lunch later — Oh. Is that for the ball tonight?" he asked, pointing at the garment bag hanging from the coat hook beside the door.

"Yes," Eliza answered, unable to keep a rather self-satisfied smile off her face.

"So you're going straight there after work?"

"Yes."

"Together?"

"That's the plan."

"Harry brought his stuff, too. Can we get pictures of you two together before you leave?"

"Who's we?" Eliza asked, trying to bite down a laugh. Her cheeks were growing warm, but she had to admit Jonathan's interest was gratifying.

"Me and everybody else who was to deal with you two crazy kids getting your shit together."

"Our shit is not together and it's not prom," Eliza noted, even if she was, possibly, lying. "Now out!" she waved a hand at the door.

"Seriously, let me know before you leave," Jonathan said. "It would be such a great piece for the company newsletter."

"We don't do a company newsletter."

"But we should!"

"Out!" Eliza was laughing now.

"Lunch, though?" Jonathan asked, backing out of her office with a grin.

"Grab me when you're on your way."

With that kind of a lead-up, Eliza really expected to spend the lunch hour getting questioned and teased about her not-date with Harry that night. Not just by Jonathan, but by the women she'd been making friends with. But to her surprise, no one else joined them at their usual lunch place.

"I have something I want to tell you," Jonathan said, knitting his fingers together as they sat down on a bench to eat. "And you can't tell Harry. Or anyone. But, fair is fair, and you ran away from everything you were supposed to do."

"I had to," Eliza said. "But I wouldn't recommend it. I mean, unless you have to too. What's going on?" she asked, not without trepidation. Jonathan always seemed extraordinarily level-headed, but there was a gleam of excitement in his eyes that potentially suggested something very ill-advised.

Or something wonderful.

Jonathan took a deep breath. "Malik and I are talking about me moving. To London. Or, rather, I'm trying to make that happen. Even though we've never lived in the same place and even though my whole life, no matter how tiny, is here."

"Oh my God, Jonathan." Eliza clasped her hands together. "This is *wonderful!* I'm so happy for you." And it really was. Jonathan was so brilliant and such a kind friend — he deserved every shot at happiness.

Jonathan, though, was shaking his head. "Don't be too happy for me yet. There's job stuff and immigration stuff to deal with, and I don't want Harry to know. Not yet. He'll be happy for me but —"

"He'll be devastated and intolerable, you mean," Eliza said.

"Yes, that too. And, I can't doubt myself right now. He makes it so easy sometimes, in the most nonsensical ways, to just want to stay here forever."

"Because he needs you," Eliza supplied.

"Yes, and I like to be needed. But my life is changing. Because I say so. If I need a reference for anything, can I list you?"

"Of course you can!" Eliza said, in lieu of adding her own commentary about the ways Harry complicated people's lives. "I promise I'll say good things that don't have anything to do with the absurdity we've been through together. And you have to promise that you'll invite me to any wedding."

Jonathan's cheeks colored, but he looked pleased. Eliza didn't know how she felt about weddings anymore, not after cancelling her own, not after seeing happiness — with or without someone else — in freedom. But she knew, no matter what, she wanted to see the next part of Jonathan's story, no matter how far it might turn out to be from her own.

●

As she got dressed and touched up her makeup in her office that evening, Eliza was glad that no one in publishing — other than her and Harry it seemed — made a habit of working late. Her chances of being able to get from her office to the elevator and outside without getting waylaid by Jonathan or teased by anyone else were decent.

She had just finished putting her earrings in when there was a tap at her door. *If that's Jonathan, I'm going to kill him.* But when she called "Come in!" there was Harry, immaculate in a somewhat retro shawl-collared tux. He looked as shyly embarrassed as she felt.

"You look lovely," he said, at the same time she blurted, "I'm not ready yet." She nodded for him to come in.

"I should have thought to bring some of Philippe's latest food truck adventures for us to discuss," he said as he stepped inside and let the door close behind him.

Eliza scoffed. "Please. If we're going to have a fun night out, no work talk."

"Is that an order?" Harry leaned against her desk, his eyes sweeping up and down her body before landing on her face. Eliza knew she looked good, but she couldn't help a bit of self-satisfaction at the open admiration in his expression.

"If you like." Eliza slipped on her shoes — strappy black ones to coordinate with her clingy grey golden-age-of-Hollywood gown — and grabbed her clutch and her wrap off her desk.

"Ready?"

"I am if you are." Harry straightened up and offered her his arm.

To Eliza's relief they encountered no one on their way out of the building. Also to her relief, the walk from work to the venue was not a long one. Her shoes were comfortable enough for being on her feet all night — she'd worn them to many functions with Cody — but not built for extensive walking, especially not over subway grates and uneven pavement.

She didn't let go of Harry's arm. She liked how the warmth of his body and the wool of his tuxedo jacket felt against her skin. They talked about little things: The weather (predictably hot and sticky for New York in July), the nonsense they'd both dealt with at work, the novel Eliza was reading for a lunchtime book club with her work friends. There was nothing particularly remarkable about the topics, but it was lovely to hear Harry's voice and feel his presence next to her. She had missed this. The sound of Harry's voice. The sense of his presence. Their easy conversation. Their even easier silences.

Eliza was almost sad when they reached their destination. She caught Harry's eye as he held the door for her, and thought she saw a similar regret written on his face. But then he smiled and his whole being seemed to brighten.

"What is it?" Eliza asked. "You look like you've remembered it's Christmas."

"I've remembered this is a ball," Harry said, still alight. "Which means there will be dancing."

◆

Before dancing, however, there was dinner and the sort of small talk Eliza and Harry were both way too practiced at. They made friends, such as it was, with the other people at their table, and when the meal was over, set about dividing and conquering. There was no real plan to it, but a lifetime of training resulted in unavoidable habits.

Harry had gone to the bar for a scotch and Eliza was in the midst of talking to a friend of a friend of one of their tablemates about children's publishing, which was not where her own expertise lay. Across the room she saw what looked like a familiar head of hair. It couldn't possibly be — Cody had absolutely no reason to be at this event.

Eliza tried hard to ignore the shade of her past, come to haunt her now that she and Harry were possibly starting to make some sort of sense. She was wearing her evil eye. Whatever ghosts lurked, surely it would send them off? Harry had promised as much after all.

But the social swirl of the room only brought the too-familiar figure closer. Eliza glanced around for Harry. But in the sea of people and the chaos of the event, she couldn't find him.

"Eliza?" Fingers — not her date's — touched her back. She shrugged them off immediately and turned to see Cody, handsome as ever, and with an extra shine to him, now that he was some sort of celebrity congressman. But it was all gloss. Not real, and not for her. And not just because she had dumped him. But because Alice Wolcott, a woman Eliza had known for years, was on his arm.

"Cody," Eliza said, somewhere between shocked and dismayed.

"What are you doing here?" he asked.

Eliza blinked. He couldn't possibly be serious. "What am I doing here? I live in New York, I work in publishing, and this is a literacy benefit. What are *you* doing here?"

Cody scratched awkwardly at the back of his neck and emitted several syllables which didn't quite come together as words.

Alice stepped in on his behalf. "Well, all the big donors are here in New York. Cody has to think about his next steps. Of course."

"Of course," Eliza echoed, a little sarcastically. The unkindness wasn't for Alice. Eliza didn't dislike her and, moreover, she was only doing what she was trained to do. It wasn't Alice's fault if it actually made her happy. Cody, on the other hand, was an absurd human being who wanted to be a Kennedy when he grew up.

Before Eliza could offer further commentary on the situation in her outloud voice, Harry appeared at her side and snaked the hand that wasn't holding a drink around her waist.

You perfect, ridiculous person, you, Eliza thought.

"New friends?" he asked with a casual, and completely duplicitous, shrug.

Eliza beamed at him. "You remember Cody," she said.

Harry acknowledged that he did only by taking a sip of his drink.

"And this is Alice Wolcott," Eliza continued. "We were debutantes together."

"How delightful." Harry's tone suggested he'd rather be dissecting lizards.

Eliza couldn't help herself. She had to ask. "How long have you two been…" She trailed off; she didn't know what Cody and Alice were to each other.

Cody coughed. "Engaged," he managed, still coughing.

Harry offered him his scotch, which he actually took.

"How lovely!" Eliza said, before looking at Alice's hand, which featured a very familiar ring. *Oh, Cody.* "A bold choice," she continued. "It suits you." She turned to Harry. "I'd like to dance," she said. "Right now." If she didn't get out of this situation immediately she was going to start laughing uncontrollably.

"As you wish." Harry winked at Cody before whisking Eliza away to the dance floor.

It was so easy to follow him to the parquet and be spun into his arms, and Eliza was too grateful. Harry's hand was warm and so was his shoulder, the heat bleeding through the fabric of his shirt and jacket.

"Are you all right?" he asked her.

"Yes. My God. Any emotion I'm evincing is entirely in response to the comedy of…of that!" She choked back a wild giggle.

Harry looked like he was on the verge of laughter himself. "Is Alice a close friend?"

"She's not even a friend, Harry. She's just someone I know. I never knew how to have friends 'til I came here, because it was always like that."

"Like how?" he asked.

Eliza sighed as she looked for the metaphor. "Like we were all crabs, climbing over each other in a bucket in hopes no one would reach a prize none of us even wanted." Eliza huffed softly and stared off into the distance over Harry's shoulder for a moment. "I feel bad for her, you know. For him too. They're going to be so bored."

"Not everyone cares for excitement," Harry said. There was the faint sheen at his temples from the too-warm ballroom and the exertion of dancing in so many layers. For a moment, Eliza had the completely unhelpful memory of Harry in bed, sweaty and sated. She felt her cheeks grow warm, and from the way Harry's eyes went soft, it was clear he noticed.

"You have no idea how to navigate any of this, do you?" she asked. They had reached some sort of juncture, and while she knew which path she wanted to follow, she did not know if Harry were truly up to the wilds of those woods.

"Not in the least." They danced in silence for a few moments. Their breath fell into a synchronized rhythm as easily as their feet did. Finally, Harry spoke again. "Do you have any advice?"

"For dealing with the ghosts of Boston past?" Eliza teased.

"No," Harry said. "Not with them."

Eliza shook her head. "No. I don't have any guidance to give," she said. "As angry as I've been with you, if our positions were reversed, I might well have done the same."

"I really am sorry. Not only about the book. About everything. Everything I said to you. It was horrid of me."

"Yes, it was." Eliza firmly agreed.

"I didn't mean it," Harry said. "I just knew it would work."

"Has it worked though? Because I am right here in your arms. I have a hard time believing that's happened just because you wanted to help me out of an awkward social situation."

"Do you remember the hail? In Paris."

"Of course I do." Eliza remembered everything about Paris. Everything it had cost her. And everything it had given her.

"You're going to think I'm utterly mad. And you may not be wrong. At the very least I'm letting superstition make a fool of me."

"I already think you're mad for all sorts of reasons. What are you talking about?"

"One more question first. Do you remember the night we heard Jonathan and Malik? And you kept complaining about the bells?"

"Yes?"

"There weren't any bells."

"So you think I'm going mad, too."

"No." Harry said. "I don't. I think you did hear bells. But I think they were from the drowned churches of Ys."

Eliza wanted to laugh, but when she thought of letting the noise bubble up through her body, it was tinged with panic. Her arms broke out in goosebumps.

"You know that's not rational," she said as much to herself as to Harry.

"I do."

"But I did hear bells."

"I'm sure you did. Paris was flooding." He spun her around.

"So Ys was rising, you're saying? Is this why nothing you do makes sense? Why you don't want to be with me? Or rather, why you told me you didn't want to be with me, gave me this —" she touched the necklace at her throat "— and asked me to come here with you tonight?"

Harry shook his head. "It isn't that."

"Then what is it?"

"Whether you heard bells or not, whether anything I've said tonight makes sense — you and I are deadly serious, without room for error, and filled with dire consequence. I think of everything that's happened since I met you — in the water no less —"

"That's not true," Eliza said. "We met in a hallway."

"And then in a swimming pool."

"We chatted."

"You kicked water at me."

"You were in love with me even then," Eliza challenged. This conversation had become too peculiar for her to have anything to lose, and in Harry's arms, she didn't feel like she could.

"Steven died. You left your fiancé. A hailstorm cost Paris millions of euros. And I've become some sort of odd celebrity. Because our fingers brushed while we shared a meal, because I will never stop thinking I've met you somewhere before. And because I am convinced that, you with your key, you're Dahut. The girl in the story who lets the waters in."

"And that frightens you?" Eliza asked.

Harry shook his head. "No. It delights me. And *that* frightens me."

Harry

Frightened or not, there was nothing for them to do after that conversation but flee together. Eliza was laughing as Harry led her out onto the humid sidewalk.

"We should get a cab," he said, tugging her towards the most likely spot.

Eliza locked her knees and looked up at the sky. "I think it's about to rain."

She wasn't wrong. Harry could already feel the thick drops of drizzle that presaged New York's deluges. He looked down the avenue. The traffic was thin and there wasn't a cab in sight; peak hours for Midtown had ended long ago. The wind picked up, and Eliza folded herself into his side.

"It's going to pour," he said.

"Of course it is." Eliza's smile was unsettling. If she had once been Dahut, she was surely her again now. She bent over to slip off her shoes there in the street.

"Eliza," Harry's voice was warning, but he didn't know from what.

She straightened up, her shoes slung over her fingers. "We're going to have to make a run for it," she said, as the sky split open.

Harry looked at her, soaked already and feral in the street lights, and then they ran west.

"Are your feet all right?" Harry asked her over the roar of the storm. The rough concrete and debris of their city wouldn't be kind to them.

Eliza ignored him and leapt into the road, the hand that wasn't held tight in his shooting into the air, shoes dangling wildly. A cab, finally. With relief, Harry let Eliza pull him into the backseat.

It was still pouring when they pulled up to the curb in the middle of a block in the West Village.

"I live in a mews," Harry told Eliza, as he handed the driver the fare and an exorbitant but perfectly deserved tip.

"I don't understand," Eliza said as she gathered her dress in her hands to step out again into the downpour. The front that had brought the rain had also brought cold, and in the lights from the street Harry could see goosebumps on her pale, streaming arms.

Harry fumbled for his keys. "Behind an iron gate. It's famous, one of New York's secret places. I always thought — maybe in another life — if things were different — you'd let me show you sometime."

"Well, I'm here now."

Harry smiled. "Yes, you are." He handed her his keys.

For a moment the weather ebbed but then redoubled as Eliza finally found the right one and managed the lock. She held the gate open for him before turning back to the mews and marching right up to the house that was Harry's.

"Why do I know this?" she asked.

Harry smiled. "Because you know me. Because you always have."

◆

They stripped in the foyer, letting their clothes pool on the floor. The garments would need more care after being so inundated than could be provided in this moment anyway.

"My bedroom's upstairs," Harry said, taking Eliza's hand. Her hair trailed water behind them as they went. He tried not to comment, or fret that her heavy locks contained all the water of Douarnenez Bay.

"I should hope," she said. "The storm is amazing, but I want to be in your bed, not fuck on the roof."

Harry laughed at that and exhaled in relief. She was just mortal and strange.

Inside his room, Eliza walked around to the far side of the bed closer to the windows, like it had always been hers. *It has; it has.* She sat with her back to him and swept her hair forward over one shoulder before reaching behind her to undo the necklace he'd given her. Once she got it off, she set it on the little night table and looked over her shoulder at him.

"I don't want to be safe from you," she said. "I don't want you to be safe from me either."

Harry felt all the air leave his lungs in a rush of relief. "We're on the same page then."

Eliza

Having sex with Harry somewhere they would remain felt strange. In that hotel in Paris all trace of their presence had surely been washed away as soon as they had left. But she was glad to leave her mark on Harry's house with her still-wet hair and the scent of her perfume, and on Harry's body with her desperate nails and eager mouth.

The storm went on through the night while she tasted him and rode him and told him everything he could do for her. He did all of it, with duty and joy and laughter, with reverence and relief.

If they slept, they slept fitfully in brief patches because nothing they wanted from each other was enough. Sometimes Harry woke her with a touch or a kiss. Sometimes Eliza woke him with reminders of the world beyond the storm.

"The offer I've accepted in Berlin," she whispered up at the ceiling, remembering the way the timing of the opportunity had seemed to save her. Even now, with Harry beside her, she didn't regret it.

"There are planes," he replied, against her skin.

"There are." She took a deep breath. "I hope you like them."

"I hate them," Harry said. "A thousand times, I hate them. And if I have to fly in them a thousand times to be with you, I will."

Eliza smiled into the dark.

18

♦

Every Day for the Rest of Forever

Harry

In the morning, Harry finally had to let Eliza go. She insisted — and Harry, reluctantly, agreed — that the way to avoid further gossip was *not* to show up at the office together.

"Also," she said, as she stood in Harry's foyer in her damp evening gown and slid her shoes back on. "I need to change. We really did not plan this well."

"Now we know for next time?" Harry said, trying to keep his voice casual and not sound as hopeful as he was.

He knew he had failed, though, when Eliza glanced up and gave him a broad if exasperated smile. "Yes. Yes, we do. Starting with always carrying umbrellas."

♦

The next few weeks were some of the happiest Harry had ever known, even if it rained and rained so that steam poured off the hot streets of the city every time it stopped. He and Eliza, it seemed, were an honest-to-God ecological disaster. And in the rain that he was sure they caused, all his secrets were stripped away and all his sins confessed and forgiven.

At work, they were exceptionally discreet. Many of their colleagues, especially those that knew they'd gone to the ball together, asked if they were seeing each other — or assumed as much without asking. If pressed, Harry always denied that there was any relationship whatsoever, but no one ever believed him, which was sort of the point.

"It's not like we're lying," Harry insisted one sultry Saturday afternoon in August. Eliza was spread across his sheets, wonderfully naked. There were goosebumps on her bare skin from the overcranked air conditioning unit and Harry tried to warm them away with his mouth. "Whatever this is, isn't 'dating.'"

"I'm pretty sure dating is whatever the people doing it says it is," Eliza replied lazily. "But I really don't give a shit about lying to them. Do you?"

"Not in the least."

♦

His relationship with Eliza quickly became the kind of easy domestic relationship he had never been interested in before. They slept in each other's beds — usually Harry's. Eliza's apartment, not to mention her bed, simply wasn't big enough for two people at a time, especially not when one of those people was as tall as Harry. As they discovered after a night of blanket-stealing and not particularly conscious turf battles over pillows.

They spent a long weekend together at the beach, Eliza reveling in the water and Harry reveling in watching her. Storms rolled in, but the lightning only came after dark. They went to brunch together on Sundays and cooked dinner for each other at Harry's house or in the office's test kitchen during the week. At least, Harry cooked for Eliza.

It was all so intimate and comfortable, in a way that Harry had only felt trapped by before. But when it was Eliza sitting across from him at his kitchen table, or lying in bed beside him, he only felt liberated.

Eliza wasn't the only one who needed her freedom to be able to love someone. She'd just been so much more self-aware about it.

"Everyone is more self-aware than you," Meryl said when Harry tried to articulate the entire situation to her one evening over drinks at what was rapidly becoming their regular bar.

"At least I'm working on it?" Harry asked with his most winsome smile.

Meryl rolled her eyes and took a sip of her drink. "If you say so."

Harry fidgeted with his napkin. "I wonder what it would be like," he said, "If I weren't counting down the days before she leaves for Berlin."

"Everyone's counting down the days to something," Meryl said. "Be grateful that, for now at least, you know how many days you have left."

♦

As much as Eliza's impending departure for Berlin loomed over both of them, they didn't talk about it much. Probably because they knew there was nothing to be done. Eliza was going to be gone for a year and no amount of planning could determine how their relationship would develop or survive over the course of that year; they could only try. There would be the bright spot of October, when Harry would be in Germany for the Frankfurt book fair, but other than that…neither of them were certain.

At least, Harry imagined, it would finally stop raining. New York would be glad for the reprieve.

♦

In the last week of August, a stack of mail landed on Harry's desk. He looked up, ready to chide whichever intern thought that an appropriate place to put it, but it was Eliza standing over him. She held a small white envelope and looked somewhere between distraught and amused.

"This isn't the mail room," Harry admonished. They were often still cranky with each other. It wasn't real upset, just a way to amuse themselves and channel the sexual tension between them into something marginally appropriate for the workplace.

"I know that. Look at this." She shook the envelope. "What do you think this is?"

Harry squinted at it and wondered why he was supposed to be psychic about anything that didn't relate to water, Ys, or Eliza. "I don't know?"

"It's addressed to me. From Gina and Philippe."

"Philippe and who?"

"Gina. His fiancée. Wait. You knew he was engaged, right?"

Harry's face must have betrayed his confusion on several fronts.

"I'll take that as a no." Eliza's smile was smug. "Which reminds me, next time you need to hear how horrible you are, there's an entire episode of the debacle around your book I still haven't told you."

"Joy," Harry said glumly, despite genuine amusement.

"Anyway, they've mailed it to me here, because Philippe doesn't have my home address, thank goodness."

"Maybe it's a note of appreciation for all your hard work?"

She flipped the envelope over and showed him the back flap. "There are doves. Embossed. In gold. Holding food trucks aloft."

Harry started laughing. Eliza grabbed the letter opener off Harry's desk, slit the envelope, and shook out the contents: A card, embossed in more golden doves — also holding food trucks — and a reply card with same. Eliza picked up the larger of the two with the tips of her fingertips. "As I thought. Wedding invitation."

"Maybe you'll be in Berlin by then?" He was trying to normalize it by mentioning it as often as possible. Sometimes it worked.

Eliza shook her head. "It's next month. No dice."

Harry started laughing and couldn't stop.

Eliza joined him. "I've done something to deserve this punishment, Harry, and it wasn't you."

Harry tried not to react further, but he couldn't help it. Eliza was living their collective worst nightmare and her predicament was, for the moment, hilarious to him.

Then she said, "There's a plus one and you're coming with me."

Harry's heart sank as the situation became abruptly less hilarious. "No. Oh no. Absolutely not," he protested.

"You assigned him to me," Eliza said, all outrage.

"Because you asked for an author to be a test case!" Oh, how Harry loved bickering with her.

"And you gave me *him* because you were annoyed at me, and because you are a perpetually difficult person!"

Harry could not, in all fairness, deny that accusation. "It's part of my charm."

"It's really not. At all." Eliza smiled at Harry, and he returned it. "But now, Harry, I am asking you on a date. To Gina and Philippe's absurdly expensive and ridiculous wedding. Which is coming from *me* and you know what my and Cody's wedding was supposed to be like."

"You are cruel. And manipulative. And I despise you right now." Harry gave a sigh of long suffering. "Of course I'll go with you."

Eliza clapped her hands together before snatching up the invitation and reply card. "Excellent!"

The event was going to be absolutely dreadful. But Eliza was so damn delightful Harry could hardly care.

♦

Harry was at his desk trying to get his unread email count down to zero for once. There were several messages from Anika, updating him on the edits and publishing schedule for his revised Vienna book. Finally, that albatross of a book was going to be out in the world, and Harry couldn't wait. Then, in a burst of organizational energy, he started an email to Dennis and Meryl about this year's Christmas trip with the Miscreants.

As he typed in their email addresses, his email client asked if he wanted to include Steven's address as well.

Oh, do I. Do I, Harry thought. Grief was never easy, but modern life made it a particularly peculiar experience. He had to take a moment to stare out the window and collect himself before he could continue with the message. The sky was a bright, clear blue, and the few trees visible down the avenue below were just starting to turn color with the longer nights.

Finally, Harry turned back to his email.

Since our fearless organizational leader has left us, he typed, *I guess it's up to us to make this year's holiday go. Burning issues, not necessarily in order of importance: 1) Do we invite Mallory? 2) I want to invite Eliza. How bad of an idea is that? 3) Meryl, are you bringing anyone?*

The resulting thread thoroughly distracted him from his initial task of clearing his inbox. Dennis and Meryl were both cautiously enthusiastic about the idea of inviting Eliza. Dennis offered to take the lead in finding the house. Meryl did indeed want to bring her girlfriend.

But if we don't get a place with enough bedrooms this year, she wrote, *I AM NOT GOING ANYWHERE AT ALL.*

Define 'enough' Dennis wrote back.

YOU KNOW EXACTLY WHAT I MEAN, Meryl immediately replied.

Harry was chuckling over that — and nodding along with her sentiment — when there was a tap on his open door. He looked up from his desk to where Jonathan stood, shifting his weight slightly from side to side, in his doorway.

"Hey, boss," Jonathan said. "Do you have a moment?"

The term of address was as atypical as the nervousness, and while Harry hoped nothing was truly awry, he did in some way relish a chance to help. He was terribly fond of Jonathan. The idea that he could, for a change, be the competent one in their professional dyad was wildly appealing.

"For you? Always," Harry said. "What is it?"

Jonathan shut the office door and took a seat in the chair across from Harry's desk. "I've worked here for a few years now, and I've loved every moment of it."

"Liar," Harry said, even as his heart sank. This was a leaving speech, there was no doubt about it.

"Okay, well, almost every minute. Which is what makes this so hard. But — I've accepted an offer elsewhere in our company."

"That's wonderful," Harry said and meant it. Jonathan had long outgrown his own position here. Harry would miss him desperately, but he deserved a step up in the world. Several of them. "Who do I have to be jealous of?"

"Not a who," Jonathan said, now looking shifty. "A where. London."

"You're moving to the UK!" Harry's heart plummeted. Jonathan nodded.

"Tell me you'll be more than some other poor disorganized slob's assistant?" Harry didn't think he'd be able to bear parting with Jonathan otherwise.

"I'll be getting into the editorial chain properly, yes."

"This is something you richly deserve. Well done. But I have to ask, even if it's none of my business, does your move across the pond by chance have anything to do with Malik?"

Jonathan looked down at his hands, a small, awkward smile playing on his lips. "We're moving in together. Or, well, I'm moving in with him. But. Yeah."

Harry stood up, walked around his desk, and held out a hand to Jonathan, who, still sitting down, took it uncertainly.

Harry pulled him to his feet and into a hug. Everything happening for Jonathan was good and as it should be and yet Harry, fond fool that he was, felt like part of his heart was breaking. This was nearly as bad as Eliza moving to Berlin. Jonathan had been at his side every day for years, Harry adored him, and they would probably never work or have daily contact with each other ever again.

He had to clear his throat before he could speak again. "Congratulations. On everything. And certainly for having your life together more than I ever have."

Jonathan laughed. The sound was a little wet.

"This place is going to fall apart without you," Harry opined, pulling back again. "You *and* Eliza leaving. We'll be plunged back into the stone age."

"Well, in about a year, I think Eliza is going to need another job. She might come back."

"Can you imagine HR's reaction? No, I'll worry about that later. For now," Harry said, settling back behind his desk. "Tell me all about your plans for this next great adventure of yours."

◆

Harry's own next great adventure, that of Philippe's wedding, was far less interesting, but at least he had Eliza by his side, as they schlepped up to Port Authority and then out to the far reaches of Long Island via ancient commuter rail.

They were wearing their summer best for the occasion and trying not to wilt. Though surely Eliza was cooler in her floral A-line dress than Harry was in his wool suit.

"Maybe we should have rented a car," Harry suggested, as the delay for their train ticked over from ten minutes to twenty.

Eliza didn't respond except to link her arm with Harry's.

"You're being placating," he accused fondly.

"No," she said. "I'm silently enjoying that you care about our getting there in a timely and appropriate fashion despite your horror at the invitation."

"Golden doves carrying food trucks," Harry said by way of explanation. He really didn't want to attend this event, but he suspected he'd be dining out on the story of it for years.

Eventually their train materialized from wherever it had been dawdling and Harry did his best to usher Eliza through the throngs at the gate to the platform to board. She didn't need him to be protective of her; she was tall and fierce and could throw an elbow in a crowd as well as any New Yorker, but if he had her by his side he was going to enjoy it.

They managed to grab a bench for two. Seated so close to Eliza, Harry desperately wanted to kiss her but didn't know if they could manage such affection chastely enough not to mess up her makeup. He settled for briefly brushing a finger over the sparkling evil eye at her throat and was gratified when she smiled sideways at him.

"I have always enjoyed this ride," she said, as the train trundled from Queens to beyond the city's limits and the view changed from industrial landscapes to that of charming suburbanness, filled with water and trees.

Harry personally found nothing remarkable about the sight and was grateful to consider himself a permanent resident of the city, but he thought he might understand.

"It's quite the fantasy, isn't it?" he said as they passed houses with yards that led down to boat slips.

Eliza turned her head away from the window to look at him, beaming. "Beautiful and terrible," she said. Her voice was cheerful. She pressed closer to him, and Harry wondered why they ever had to do anything that involved other people at all.

That feeling only intensified when they arrived at their station near the end of the island. The wedding hall was a mere few blocks' walk from where they disembarked, but

Harry could feel the ocean calling. Maybe it was Ys, from so very far away.

"Are you sure we have to go in?" he whispered to Eliza when they arrived at their destination, which was gaudy and over-the-top with plenty of doves and not a food truck in sight.

She gave him a sidelong look of judgmentalness. "Yes."

"Ah." He hadn't really expected Eliza to consider cutting out of the wedding after having come all this way, but still. It was a beautiful day. The sky was blue and the sun was bright but the breeze was pleasantly cool. This was a day for strolling with Eliza, not sitting and watching other people's life events.

"Are you having performance anxiety?" Eliza asked as they climbed the steps, her heels clicking on the stone.

Considering he hadn't been sure he knew how to kiss her appropriately on the train, Harry knew he really shouldn't swat her ass. Especially not as they were walking into someone else's wedding. But it was tempting nonetheless. He settled for giving Eliza his most charming smile and holding out his arm for her to take. "I'm only interested in performing for you."

He had the satisfaction of seeing Eliza flush a most enchanting shade of pink. She gave him a coy, almost shy smile as a teenage boy in an ill-fitting suit directed them where to sit.

The ceremony itself was surprisingly pleasant. It wasn't too long, and Philippe and Gina did not commit — in Harry's eyes — the grievous sin of writing their own vows. Which meant he was subjected to neither bad writing nor the sharing of too much private emotion. As an additional bonus, no one promised to obey.

None of which meant that the service kept Harry's attention. His eyes kept drifting to Eliza who sat next to him with her hands folded neatly in her lap. Occasionally, he would catch her looking at him too, and they would share a private smile before attending to the proceedings again.

Harry had been to weddings before, with people he'd been dating or sleeping with. It had always been rather awkward, listening to other people's vows while wondering and worrying what the person next to him thought about marriage or wanted from him in that regard. Meryl had been an exception to that — they'd gone to Steven and Mallory's wedding together — and now, it seemed, Eliza was too, albeit in an entirely different way.

"In the former life you think we had," Eliza whispered as the music struck up for the recessional. "Were we ever married?"

"Does it matter?" Harry asked even though he knew the answer was yes. But could anyone ever really marry the devil? Or a queen?

"Considering what it took for us to get here, yes."

She didn't mean the Long Island Railroad. She meant Cody, her broken engagement, the melted key, and the desperate need for freedom they both harbored.

"I know I've been difficult, afraid, and strange," Harry murmured. "But the life with you I care about is the one I'm having with you right now. I will never trap you behind a gate."

Eliza gave him a wide-eyed look of near disbelief. But before he could wonder if he'd somehow misstepped, she leaned into his side and slid her hand into his.

Eliza

The reception was at a banquet hall within easy walking distance of the wedding venue. She and Harry were seated at a table with a collection of Gina's more distant relatives. Eliza was prepared for a certain level of absurdity, and they did not disappoint. But they were also people who were gathered to enjoy each other. Between that and the open bar Eliza found herself, after a while, enjoying herself too. That the groom was a chef also meant that the food was far better fare than most weddings, even if Philippe was the king of supermarket sauces.

She also found it lovely to watch Harry thoroughly charm the table with his attentiveness and his interest in other people's lives. For someone who was bad at intimate relationships on his own behalf, he certainly was good at talking to other people. His fond anecdotes about working with Philippe, which Eliza suspected had been invented for the occasion, also definitely won him points.

Eliza was *almost* certain no one had caught on to the fact that Harry had his hand on her knee, his fingers resting right where the hem of her skirt gave way to silk stockings, the entire time.

The toast, given by the best man — Philippe's brother — and then the maid of honor were slightly drunken and were the usual fare of embarrassing childhood stories and slightly inappropriate recountings about how the happy couple had met.

"It seems Philippe got all of the writing talent in his family." Harry leaned over to mutter in Eliza's ear.

She dug an elbow in his ribs. "I thought we were being nice."

"That was nice."

During the first dance, Harry shifted in his seat as the people at the tables craned their necks to try to get a good look of Philippe and Gina on the dancefloor.

Eliza leaned over to whisper in his ear. "You just want them to finish up so you can dance with me, don't you?" she asked.

"A reason to like weddings," Harry acknowledged.

"And you whined and complained about coming out here with me!"

"Doves. With food trucks. On the invitation," Harry reminded her.

Finally, the song ended and the floor was announced open. The band picked up the pace from Gina and Philippe's stately waltz into a swing dance. Harry was one of the first out of his seat, offering his hand to Eliza.

She took it and stood. "How do you know I'm any good?" she asked. They had danced before at the charity ball. But that had been only a waltz under fairly bizarre circumstances at that. Swing dancing was more challenging, more full of improvisation, and open to so many more mistakes.

"A few reasons. One," Harry said as he led her to the floor. "I've danced with you before. I know you can follow a lead. When you choose," he teased.

"Two?" she asked as his hand found her waist.

"Two," he said stepping off. "You wouldn't be wearing that retro dress if you couldn't at least fake this." He walked them in a quick circle as he said it, then pushed her out to spin her around and pull her back in. "Do you want to hear three?"

Another spin bought them some more room on the dance floor. As he pulled her back in, Eliza still turning on her toes, he grabbed her so they were back to front, Eliza in his arms as they had been — after a fashion — in Paris.

"I definitely want to hear three," she said, but wasn't sure if Harry could hear her. The music was loud, and while his mouth was at her ear, she could only talk to the air, bewildered and joyful at her perfect and strange life.

"Three. I've been to bed with you. I've fucked you," Harry continued now, brazen. "So many times in so many ways. You can dance. Probably in all sorts of ways I haven't even seen yet."

Eliza pushed back against his lead, just a little. She usually didn't, not with someone this good. It was rude and not worth it. But she wanted to be pressed against him and look at him as she was. She wanted all of him, in fact, right now, but they were in the middle of a dance floor. Harry took her signal, helped her turn a time and a half in his arms to make it look good, and then laughed with pleasure as she fell into him, perfect and teasing and artful. Eliza pouted, all play, as he had to push her away again to keep moving as the song demanded.

They only took a break to catch their breath and to talk to Gina and Philippe, who were making the rounds amongst the tables and at the edge of the dance floor.

"I'm so glad you could make it," Gina gushed when they congratulated the pair, and pulled Eliza into a hug.

"We wouldn't have missed it," Eliza said. "After all, you've both had your own cameo in whatever our story is."

"One that will not be winding up in a book," Harry added dutifully.

"He says that now," Gina joked, winking.

Eliza became aware, as they talked, that Harry had gone from keeping a casual arm around her to rubbing his thumb in small circles that were drifting lower and lower on her back and soon wouldn't be appropriate at all. It stopped just short of being untoward, and Eliza wasn't even sure it was a conscious gesture.

In light of that touch, she resented the effort it took her to focus on the rest of the conversation with Gina and Philippe. But when they both made her promise to stay in touch about her Berlin adventures, Eliza felt sure she would. Gina had been a friend found in the strangest circumstances, and corresponding with both her and Philippe seemed like a tonic against homesickness that might amuse them all.

Eliza glanced at Harry and smiled. She'd never been homesick before. About anywhere. Or anyone.

♦

She and Harry made it through another few dances together, the other occupants of the dance floor clearly torn between admiration of their skill together and annoyance at the space they took up.

"Do you want to take a break?" Harry asked a little breathlessly as the song changed, from swing to something romantic and slow.

"We just took one," Eliza pointed out. She wanted nothing more than to be wrapped up in Harry's arms again.

A glint in Harry's eyes, though, told her he had a plan. "Do you trust me?"

Despite the absurd number of missteps between them along the way, she always had. She always did. Otherwise she never would have spent countless hours curled in the chair in his office. Or broken up with Cody. Or let Paris happen. She wouldn't have accepted the necklace he gave her, or run through the rain-soaked city with him the night of the charity ball. He'd saved her from hailstorms and ghosts and her own loneliness. And maybe, in the moments she felt like believing in all of Harry's strange superstitions, from forgetfulness of who and what she'd once been. And in some way, that seemed most important of all.

Harry was staring at her, gazing into her eyes really, and she realized she hadn't answered yet, but that somehow he wasn't worried. "Of course," she finally managed. It really was that simple.

"Then come with me."

"Where are we going?" Eliza asked, as Harry took her hand and led her out of the ballroom and down a hall towards the hall's entranceway.

"We are going to go outside, and we are going to find a place where people aren't hanging out smoking, and I am going to kiss you. Because it would be rude to upstage a wedding. Even one as bizarre as to have a giant food truck-shaped wedding cake."

"What if I have a better idea?" Eliza asked.

Harry gave her a curious look.

Eliza grinned at him, and pointed to a door along the hall. A cloakroom, unmanned, because who needed to check a coat on a day this fair?

She pulled Harry after her as she tested whether the door was locked and then grinned back at him in victory, before opening it just enough to slip inside. Where racks for absent outerwear didn't line the walls, dark wood and a cheap sort of red velvet did. She tugged at the curtain that covered part of the door, and then turned the lock inside.

"Everyone's going to know what we're up to," Harry pointed out even as he crowded her up against the velvet-covered wall.

"I don't care," Eliza said, "as long as they don't know where we're up to it."

Harry laughed, but it was breathless and cut off in a gasp as Eliza started fumbling with his pants. She knew they were being absurd, and she knew they should stop, but there wasn't much time until she'd leave for Berlin. She wanted Harry every second she could have him, and she wasn't going to apologize for that.

She had to grab onto Harry's shoulder for balance as she popped open the garter clips on her stockings and worked her underwear off. He held her, hands wrapped low around her waist, until she was standing on two feet again, her underwear looped around her wrist.

"Oh my God," he breathed.

Eliza was tempted to laugh, the situation was so absurd, but they had both turned serious with it. And if she was trembling just a little bit, Harry was even more.

"Are you sure?" he asked.

"Are you?" Eliza asked.

"We're going to ruin their wedding," Harry said.

"We are not," Eliza scoffed. "No one will notice; no one will know."

"Unless we cause another massive rainstorm," Harry said, half laughing at himself as he did.

"And if we do, they still won't know it's us."

There was a convenient radiator cover that ran along the wall, that Harry helped her sit right on the edge of. Eliza was impatient now, though, and no sooner had Harry steadied her in place than she wrapped her hand around him and guided him inside her without preamble. She'd been wet since they had started dancing together. Waiting was now beyond her interest or ability.

The low breath that Harry let out was very nearly a moan, and Eliza hoped it wasn't audible outside of this private, hidden spot. She pressed her mouth to his shoulder, warm and damp with sweat, and breathed his name, hoping it would somehow steady him and keep them safe in this silent, magic, breathless place.

It was less rushed, less frantic than the circumstances might have suggested. Eliza wanted to cry with the need to be closer to him, even when they were as close as they could possibly get. She dug her fingernails into Harry's back while he gripped her thighs and pushed into her with little whimpered gasps.

When they had the angle just right and there was no risk of them falling apart, Harry moved a hand up to splay his fingers along her throat and jaw. He held her there in place and kissed her and kissed her and kissed her.

Eliza didn't understand how for all everyone always liked to talk about destiny, no one told her it felt like this; they came at the same time.

For a long while after, Harry stood with his head pressed against her chest while they breathed together. When they finally stopped shaking in each other's arms Harry straightened up and slid out of her. She whimpered and stood, her dress a mess, her panties still around her wrist, and clung close.

He kissed her gently.

"We should get cleaned up," she mumbled against his lips, although she didn't want to. She wanted to stay here forever.

"As soon as we leave here it's going to be entirely obvious what we were doing," Harry pointed out.

Eliza shrugged. "I'll go to the bathroom. Fix my makeup. Your hair's curling from all the dancing and the late-summer heat."

"Not believable."

"No one will say anything," she said. She unlooped her underwear from her wrist and made Harry give her just enough space to wriggle back into it.

He slipped to his knees as she finished, kissing each thigh tenderly before smoothing her stockings back up her legs and reclipping them to the garters.

"There," he said, but made no effort to move. Instead he pushed up her dress and mouthed for a moment at her panties.

Eliza had to cover her mouth not to make a very audible sound. She hauled Harry up by the collar of his shirt.

"We have the whole night." She combed her nails through Harry's hair as he stood. "And weeks before I go. But we have got to get out of here first."

As they exited their hideaway, as neat as they could get, Eliza watched as Harry immediately darted out of the building, and looked up at the sky, still bright and clear as the sun dipped toward the horizon.

"I'm so confused," he said, as Eliza came to stand beside him.

She took his hand and smiled at the day. "I'm not." She tuned to him. "We're not a tragedy this time, with nothing to destroy."

♦

On the train back to the city, they wedged themselves into another seat for two, although larger benches were available this time. Eliza pressed herself against the window again, and Harry curled around her. She tried not to doze, wanting to take in the scenery in the gloaming and appreciate every moment of Harry's breath, warm and sleepy against her. Eventually, as church bells chimed in whatever town they were passing through, she slipped under the ocean of comfort and safety that was his arm around her waist, to wake again only when they reached the island citadel of their here and now.

Eliza led Harry off the train silently, pleased with the feeling of him trailing after her, and even more pleased when he put his jacket over her bare shoulders in the cool dark of the evening as they waited for a taxi to return to Harry's home, where they spent too much of their time.

Once they reached the little mews house and made their way inside, upstairs, and into Harry's bedroom he turned down the bed and handed her into it, as if it were just one more conveyance on the way to somewhere called home. When he climbed in after her, he skimmed his lips down the center of her, from nose to throat to sternum, and then further, to where she was still damp from where he had come deep inside her at the wedding.

Then they slept.

When the sun was still hours away from rising, Eliza found herself awake and restless. In bed next to her, Harry stirred. Finally, he put a hand on her waist to still her incessant tossing and turning.

"What do you need?" he asked, his voice quiet and slurred in sleep.

"I don't know. I can't sleep."

"Come here." Before she could protest, Harry pulled her bodily toward him until her head rested on his chest and his arms were wrapped, low and snug, around her waist. Their skin was hot and sticky and covered in the salt of their sweat.

"What are you thinking of?" Harry was fully awake now, his voice alert and kind.

"How much I'll miss you." Having finally managed to form the words, Eliza felt nothing but devastated. She and Harry had both been working so hard to be sanguine about Berlin, but now the reality of it was hitting her in a way she hadn't anticipated.

"I'll miss you too," Harry said. "But that's not it."

"I can't wait to go," Eliza confessed, her voice almost a whisper.

"I know."

"You're not angry at me for that?"

"Whatever you encounter on your travels," Harry said, running a hand through her hair and pressing his fingers, gently but firmly, against her scalp and then down the knots of her spine. "Whatever you want to experience. I will never do anything but help you do that. Or achieve it."

"I know."

"So tell me what you're afraid of, Betts." The name was so sweet on Harry's lips that Eliza — that Betts — had to turn her face into his chest and hide, just for a moment, while his fingers combed through her hair and he hummed comfortingly at her.

"Losing you."

"You won't," he said. "You never could. You never have." He touched her cheek and turned her face up to look at him. "We may not be marching towards everyone else's logical conclusion, but whatever we do, we do together. I'd like to say, you're my partner, if you'll let me, because I think you are. I know I'm yours."

Eliza nodded fiercely. The word was such a small, precise thing, almost clinical. But also the stuff of dreams and freedom, a past she didn't understand, and a future she couldn't wait to see.

Harry's hand settled on the back of her neck, his fingers resting lightly over where her pulse fluttered in her throat. "Good," he said. "Then let me show you the truth of that," he said, "every day, for the rest of forever."

More by these Authors

Get more information about new releases and sign up for our newsletter at our website, www.Avian30.com. You can also become a patron and get access to drafts, deleted scenes, and other bonus content at our Patreon, https://www.patreon.com/avian30.

A Queen from the North

Library Journal's Best Indie Ebook 2017

Lady Amelia Brockett, known to her family as Meels, is having the Worst. Christmas. Ever. Dumped by her boyfriend and rejected from graduate school, her parents deem her the failure of the family.

But when her older brother tries to cheer her with a trip to the races, a chance meeting with Arthur, the widowed, playboy Prince of Wales, offers Amelia the opportunity to change her life -- and Britain's fortunes -- forever.

After the Gold

Love is the biggest prize of all.

Katie Nowacki has an Olympic gold medal in pairs figure skating, incendiary chemistry with her long-time skating partner Brendan Reid, and a tendency to have panic attacks which have left her pushing him away for years.

As they retire from competition and cross America on an exhibition tour with their fellow athletes, it's time for Katie to figure out what she really wants and whether she's brave enough to accept it from the man who has always been by her side.

The Art of Three

Family is what you make it.

24-year-old Jamie Conway has just moved to London, is starring in his first feature film, and hasn't yet figured out how to navigate fame, adulthood, or being bisexual in public.

When Jamie hooks up with his much older polyamorous costar Callum Griffith-Davies, he sets off a chain of delightful complications, including an unexpected affair with Callum's no-nonsense wife, Nerea.

This Rainbow Awards-winning romance features three countries, two men, one woman, and absolutely no love triangles in a lush coming-of-age story.

The Love in Los Angeles Series

Starling, Book 1
Doves, Book 2
Phoenix, Book 3
Cardinal, Book 4
More coming soon

When J. Alex Cook, a production assistant on The Fourth Estate (one of network TV's hottest shows), is accidentally catapulted to stardom, he finds himself struggling to navigate both fame and a relationship with Paul, one of Fourth's key writers. *Love in Los Angeles* is the story of Paul and Alex – and of their friends and family – as they navigate love, and life, both in and beyond Los Angeles.

The Love's Labours Series

Midsummer, Book 1
Twelfth Night, Book 2
Tempest, Book 3

42-year-old John Lyonel has never been attracted to men before, but falling for 25-year-old Michael Hilliard is actually the least screwed up thing that's happened to him in years. Even if sometimes he thinks Michael's a changeling.